'What are you going to do?' she asked.

Richard pushed himself up and away, and stood regarding her for a moment. He said, with a touch of bitterness, 'You surely don't really believe I'm about to join you in that bed and make love to you, do you?'

'You...you said we were man and w...wife,' she replied nervously.

'My dear girl, I don't regard myself as particularly squeamish, but it would take a stronger stomach than mine to make love to a wife who has just threatened to kill me. What do you think I'm made of?'

Lexi gazed at him somberly. 'I don't know,' she said eventually. 'I thought I did, but I was mistaken. For a while I longed for you to make love to me, I couldn't imagine anything I wanted more, but now I think I would kill myself if you even tried.'

Richard moved away abruptly and went to the window. He turned round. 'We have an agreement. Are you prepared to discuss it with me?'

'It appears I have no choice.'

* * *

The Bridegroom's Bargain
Harlequin® Historical #814—August 2006

The Bridegroom's Bargain

SYLVIA ANDREW

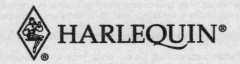

TORONTO • NEW YORK • LONDON
AMSTERDAM • PARIS • SYDNEY • HAMBURG
STOCKHOLM • ATHENS • TOKYO • MILAN • MADRID
PRAGUE • WARSAW • BUDAPEST • AUCKLAND

ISBN-13: 978-0-373-29414-5
ISBN-10:   0-373-29414-X

THE BRIDEGROOM'S BARGAIN

Copyright © 2005 by Sylvia Andrew

First North American publication 2006

This edition published by arrangement with Harlequin Books S.A.

® and TM are trademarks of the publisher. Trademarks indicated with ® are registered in the United States Patent and Trademark Office, the Canadian Trade Marks Office and in other countries.

www.eHarlequin.com

Printed in U.S.A.

Please address questions and book requests to:
Harlequin Reader Service
U.S.: 3010 Walden Ave., P.O. Box 1325, Buffalo, NY 14269
Canadian: P.O. Box 609, Fort Erie, Ont. L2A 5X3

Chapter One

October 1815

'*Dearly beloved, we are gathered together here in the sight of God, and in the face of this congregation...*'

A shaft of autumn sunshine shone low through St Wulfric's ancient stained glass and rested on Canon Harmond as he spoke these opening words of the marriage service. It coloured his surplice and halo of white hair with rich blues and greens, reds and golds. He could have just stepped down from the gathering of saints in the west window.

The sunshine rested on the bridegroom, too, but he certainly didn't look as if he belonged to any gathering of saints. Tall, standing as usual with an air of cool arrogance about him, Richard Deverell was very much a man of this world. In his black coat and close-fitting pantaloons, both obviously made by a master tailor, in his starched cravat, snowy linen and white silk waistcoat, he looked what he was, a member of one of the most exclusive and worldly societies in Europe—the English aristocracy.

But the strength in his broad shoulders and lithe, athletic figure owed more to four years spent fighting the French than to dancing the waltz in London's ballrooms. His tanned features and the small lines round his cool grey eyes were the result of long days spent in the saddle under the Spanish sun, and the scar on his cheek was a reminder of a very narrow escape at Waterloo. But then Richard Deverell was said to have the luck of the devil, and certainly his success at cards and other games of chance was legendary.

From her vantage point in the Deverell family pew the bridegroom's aunt, Lady Honoria Standish, viewed the congregation with a critical eye. Not a single member of the *ton* to be seen. She doubted any had been invited. With the bride's father barely in his grave it could hardly have been otherwise. Still, it was a pity. Richard's wedding ought to have been more impressive than this shabby affair.

'First, it was ordained for the procreation of children...'

That was more like it. It would be quite pleasant to have some children at Channings again. The place had been like a tomb for too long. It was high time Richard produced some heirs, too—the Deverell estates couldn't be allowed to go to some obscure cousin or other. She eyed her nephew and nodded. This marriage would put an end to any fears of that sort! Alexandra Rawdon came of good healthy stock and Richard was in his prime. Few women would find themselves able to resist him—it wasn't at all surprising that the Rawdon girl had been eager to marry him.

Lady Honoria frowned. But why had Richard chosen Lexi Rawdon of all people? She was attractive enough, but Lady Honoria knew of several real beauties—girls of elegance and wealth as well as breeding—who would have given their eyebrows to have become Lady Deverell. Any one of them would have made a more suitable chatelaine for an estate the size and importance of Channings than Alexandra Rawdon. The girl had always been an impulsive, high-spirited harum-scarum, more interested in roaming the countryside, keeping up with whatever her brother Johnny and Richard were doing, rather than sitting at home learning to be a lady.

As a boy, it was true, Richard had spent most of his time with the Rawdons. He and Johnny Rawdon had been the closest of friends, and Sir Jeremy and Lady Rawdon had always treated him as one of their own, giving him the love and affection he had never found in his own home. Was he marrying their daughter out of a sense of obligation to them? She was now quite alone in the world. She had lost her mother a few years ago, Johnny Rawdon had died tragically earlier in the year, and now Sir Jeremy was dead, too. Was this the reason Richard was marrying her?

Lady Honoria turned her attention to the bride. Alexandra Rawdon bore herself well enough—tall, slender, straight as a wand in her white silk dress, her mane of bright copper hair kept in check by her veil and hat. But surely Richard could have hoped for a more radiant bride. It was clear that the events of the past few months had taken their toll. The girl standing beside her nephew was as stiff as a board, and far too thin. Lady Honoria sighed. She had suggested that the wedding should be postponed, but Richard had been adamant—it could be as quiet as anyone chose, but it was to go ahead as planned. He was probably right. Rawdons had owned Rawdon Hall since the days of the Tudors, but Alexandra and her cousin, Mark Rawdon, were the last of them, and Mark, or *Sir* Mark as he was now, was still a comparative stranger.

Sir Mark must be relieved to have Lexi taken off his hands. Her old home had now passed into his possession, and, even though the cousins seemed to get on well, they could hardly have carried on living there together for very much longer with only an old nurse to chaperon them. He couldn't have married her himself, even if he had wanted to. Though it was hard to believe, rumour had it that the heir to Rawdon would have to marry a girl with a decent fortune if Rawdon Hall was to be saved.

She turned her attention to the young man standing on the other side of his cousin, ready to give her away. Sir Mark Rawdon. Now *there* was an open, good-natured fellow—nothing enigmatic about him. Lady Honoria had already experienced the charm of his frank smile and laughing eyes, and thoroughly approved of him. In his own way he was as handsome as Richard, and he was much better looking than his cousin Alexandra, if the truth were known. They both had the highly distinctive Rawdon looks, though Mark Rawdon's hair was a touch darker. He was very presentably dressed in a dark green coat and buff pantaloons, and his short chestnut locks, brushed into careless elegance, glowed in the shaft of sunlight.

'Richard Anthony, wilt thou have this woman to be thy wedded wife... Wilt thou love her, comfort her, honour and keep her in sickness and in health...'

Lady Honoria's wandering attention was caught as the couple started to make their vows. Those solemn promises in Richard's deep voice sounded as beautiful as she had ever heard them: *'To have and to hold...in sickness and in health...till death us do part...'*

She listened with a rare smile on her face as Richard finished the lovely old words and it was Alexandra's turn. Her voice was clear enough, but it sounded... forced. What was *wrong* with her? She ought to be beside herself with joy. After all, she was marrying the best catch in the county! In England!

'For better, for worse...for richer, for poorer...to love—' The voice broke off abruptly, then went on: *'To love, cherish, and to obey, till death—'* There was another abrupt halt, and this time the pause was longer. When she began again her voice was harsh as she repeated, *'Till death us do part...'*

Richard had heard the sounds of strain. He put his arm round her and pulled her gently towards him as he made his final promise. *'With this ring I thee wed, with my body I thee worship, and with all my worldly goods I thee endow...'*

Lady Honoria nodded. Richard had far more than his fair share of worldly goods—he was disgustingly rich. And though he might not wear his heart on his sleeve, as the saying went, he would look after his wife. All in all, Alexandra Rawdon was a very lucky girl.

When Canon Harmond began his homily she settled herself back against the cushions—the Deverells always made sure they were comfortable in church—and got ready to look as if she was listening. It was always the same speech, and usually quite short. In a minute or two they would all go into the vestry for a few signatures and the rest, and all would be done. Except for the lack of display, it had been a perfectly conventional wedding. And Richard would settle down at last to a peaceful family life at Channings. She closed her eyes...

* * *

Lady Honoria was not the only person present who was failing to give Canon Harmond the attention he deserved. The bride's nerves were as taut as a violin string as she waited for the end of the service. It wouldn't be long now. Soon they would go into the vestry for the last signatures, the delivery of the last documents and then...and then it would all be over.

Only dimly aware of Canon Harmond leading the way ahead of them, and Mark and Lady Honoria following behind, Alexandra felt Richard's hand on her elbow, escorting her out of the church and into the vestry. Once inside the little room she allowed herself be drawn to the table, where the lawyer sat with papers spread before him. She signed where he told her, then took a step back. Her head and her heart were pounding so hard she felt she might explode. She took off her hat and veil to relieve some of the pressure, and put them down on the table near the all-important document. Her wedding gift from Richard.

'Alexandra? What's wrong? Aren't you interested in the gift I promised you?' Richard was smiling at her.

Bile rose in her throat, but she forced it down and made herself smile in return. 'Of course!' she said. 'Is it ready?'

'I think so. Mr Underhill?'

The lawyer cleared his throat. His manner was disapproving, but he said clearly enough, 'I have here a deed drawn up in favour of Sir Mark Satterly Rawdon, of Rawdon Hall in the county of Somerset. Put briefly, it returns in full everything formerly belonging to the Rawdon Hall estate that was acquired during the past three months by Lord Deverell from Lady Deverell's father, the late Sir Jeremy Rawdon. The lands and monies are detailed below…' He looked up. 'The list is quite a long one.'

Ignoring the exclamations of wonder and surprise from Lady Honoria and the Canon, the lawyer took off his pince-nez. 'An extraordinary document. I can say with confidence that I have never known anything like it. Lord Deverell has been outstandingly generous! Do you wish me to read out the list, Lady Deverell?'

'No,' said Lexi tonelessly. 'I accept that it is as we planned.'

'Ah! We have inserted one clause, which I should perhaps point out to you,' said the lawyer.

Lexi was instantly alert. 'What is it?' she asked.

'That should Sir Mark predecease you or Lord Deverell without issue, the contents of this deed of gift will not form part of his estate, but will revert to your husband.'

A curious smile passed fleetingly over Lexi's face. 'I have no objection to that. By all means leave the clause in. May I have the deed?'

Richard took the bundle of papers from the lawyer before it reached Lexi's hand. 'Are you sure you want this, Alexandra? It's a strange sort of wedding present—there's nothing in it for you.'

'There is *everything* there for me! It makes Rawdon safe for the future. That was what my father would have wanted,' she said tightly. 'May I have it?'

'Don't you think I deserve a reward first?' he said with a smile. 'A kiss from my wife, perhaps?'

Lexi felt a surge of panic-stricken revulsion. 'No!' she exclaimed.

She looked round at the shocked silence that followed her cry. 'N…not yet,' she faltered. 'Let me give this to Mark first.'

Richard's eyes narrowed. 'Very well,' he said. 'But I think we can dispense with Mr Underhill. He has done his bit.' With a brief nod and a word of thanks he dismissed the lawyer. Then he raised Lexi's hand to his lips before putting the document into it.

Lexi had been waiting with every sign of impatience. Now she snatched her hand away and thrust the deed into her cousin's hands. 'Take it!' she said fiercely. 'And look after Rawdon. Our family has lived at the Hall for centuries. You're the last of them, and it's up to you to see that it carries on. It's all perfectly, legally, yours, and, now that its lands have been restored, it has the means to survive.'

'Lexi, I don't know what to say—'

'Don't say anything. Take it! And stand back!'

She turned to the shelves behind her, and when she faced the room again she was holding a pistol in her hand. 'All of you stand back!' The pistol was pointing at Richard. There was a moment of stunned astonishment.

Then Lady Honoria exclaimed, 'Alexandra! What do you think you're doing? Is this a joke? It's in extremely poor taste if it is. Put that thing down at once!'

'Oh, no! Not till I've done what I've sworn to do.' Her eye caught a movement. 'I warn you all. If anyone moves, I shall shoot Deverell straight away. And I won't miss.'

Richard spoke for the first time. He was slightly pale, but perfectly self-possessed, and his eyes never left his bride's face. 'I think I can vouch for that,' he said calmly. 'Alexandra is a first-class shot, I taught her myself. But I'd quite like to know why she thinks she wants to shoot me. Alexandra?'

'You need to ask? You're a coward! A villainous

coward! You killed my brother, and you ruined my father. Isn't that enough?'

A gasp went up at these words. Lady Honoria uttered a shocked protest, and Canon Harmond, looking bewildered, said,

'I don't understand. Why are you saying such terrible things, Alexandra? Lord Deverell has just made you his wife! Poor child, you don't know what you're doing. It has all been too much for you. Give that weapon to me.' He took a step forward.

Lexi's command stopped him. 'Stand back! I'm quite aware of what I'm doing. Stand back! I swear I will shoot Deverell before you can reach me.'

'Richard, this is disgraceful behaviour! I've never known anything like it! Stop her, why don't you?' said Lady Honoria, outraged.

Without taking his eyes off his wife, Richard said, 'There's nothing I'd like more, Aunt Honoria, but I'm not quite sure how.' He was now very pale, but remained cool. 'But I am sure that it's no joke. She means what she says.' His voice changed as he spoke. 'These are very serious accusations, Alexandra. Do you really believe them? They can't possibly be justified, you know.'

'Oh, indeed they can! I have all the evidence I need for that! And now Rawdon is safe, I intend to make you pay for what you've done.'

Lady Honoria turned to Mark Rawdon. 'Sir Mark!' she said forcefully. 'Haven't you any influence with her? Say something! Do something! I can't believe she seriously means to shoot anybody, but pointing a gun like that is dangerous. Tell her to stop acting like a fool, to put it down. Make her listen to you!'

'Don't do it, Lexi!' said her cousin. 'You've got what

you wanted—Rawdon will survive. Surely you don't need to do anything as mad as this? It's not necessary any more.'

'It is! It's more necessary than ever. He's my husband, Mark! Do you imagine I could *live* with such a villain?' She lifted the pistol, and the tension in the little room rose again.

'Wait, Alexandra! Wait!' Richard spoke urgently, but still without fear. 'Give me just one moment. As the condemned man I could surely be allowed one moment to put my case.'

'To plead your innocence, perhaps?' Lexi's lip curled.

'Yes, dammit! I *am* innocent!'

'You did not shoot my brother?'

'No, I did not!'

Lexi went on relentlessly, 'You did *not* play cards with my father? Gamble with him? You did *not* win everything he owned? Ruin him?'

Richard hesitated. 'He was ruined before I began the game, but, yes, I did play him for what...what was left. And I won.' Lexi gave a sob and her hand tightened round the pistol. Lady Honoria and the Canon both made a movement of protest.

'Keep still, all of you!' Richard spoke sharply. 'I absolutely forbid anyone to interfere! This is between Alexandra and myself.' He held Lexi's eye as he went on deliberately, 'I did what I had to about your father. I wanted to save him, not ruin him. If he had not died so suddenly, I would have proved it. To him, and, if necessary, to you.'

'Not very convincing! *I* made you return my father's lands to Mark. If I hadn't, they would now all be yours, swallowed up in the Channings estate. Rawdon wouldn't exist any more.' Her voice rose angrily. 'Good God, Deverell! What sort of man are you? Wasn't Channings big enough for you? Did you *have* to take Rawdon as well?'

With a touch of steel in his voice, Richard said, 'You didn't *make* me give anything back, Alexandra. It was all freely given as a wedding present to you. You chose to pass it on to your cousin.'

'Not so freely! I had to *marry* you to get it!'

'Are you saying you wouldn't have married me otherwise? I find that hard to believe. You seemed willing enough when I asked you.'

'That was before—' She stopped and swallowed. 'Before I found out what you'd done. After that, nothing but the thought of saving Rawdon could have reconciled me to it.'

If possible, Richard grew even paler. 'I…see…' Then, after a pause, he went on, 'But, as you have said, Rawdon is saved. Whatever I did or didn't do, surely it's been put right again?'

'Put right again? You drove my father to his *death*! And there's still my brother to be paid for!'

'I've told you,' Richard said steadily, 'Johnny's death was an accident.'

'Oh, I could believe that! But accidentally or not, *you* shot him, Deverell, though you told everyone he had shot himself. Why else would you have tried to cover it up afterwards? You are a liar and a coward, Richard Deverell. I know that, even if the world doesn't.'

Richard grew white about the lips, and Lexi held the gun up more threateningly as he took an involuntary step forward.

Lady Honoria shrieked, 'No! No! Please God, no!'

After a momentary pause her nephew was once again

cool as he said, 'If that was true, I would deserve everything you say of me. But it isn't. I wasn't even there when Johnny died. If I had been, it—' He stopped for a moment, showing for the first time a hint of strong emotion. His jaw tightened, then he went on, 'If I had been there it wouldn't have happened. I'd have saved him. But he was alone when he died.'

His voice carried conviction, and for the first time Lexi hesitated. But after a moment her confidence returned and she said flatly, 'I have proof. Very good proof.'

'Then show me! Come, Alexandra, where's your sense of justice? Tried, convicted and condemned, all in one breath? Is that to be my fate?'

The pistol did not waver, though Lexi's voice rose in despair. 'I loved you, Richard! My father loved you. Johnny was your friend. And you betrayed us all! You lied and cheated people who had trusted you all their lives! You don't *deserve* to live.'

Richard's voice was still measured, still calm. He said drily, 'My dear girl, try for once to think of the consequences before you act! At the moment you are convinced of my guilt. But what if you're wrong? Suppose, just suppose, you shot me now, and discovered later that I was innocent after all. How would you feel?'

Lady Honoria broke her silence. 'Of *course* you are innocent, Richard! How can you treat this so calmly? Look at her! She *does* mean what she says! The girl has gone mad!' Her elderly voice trembled as she pleaded, 'Alexandra, you can't do this! You mustn't shoot Richard, he's a good man. He's certainly been more than good to you! He wouldn't lie to you, nor anyone else. Your brother's death was an accident—we all know that. The army said so. And Richard says he wasn't even there when it happened, so how could he have had anything to do with it? As for your father—'

Lexi wasn't listening. She stood, her burning eyes fixed on Richard, holding the pistol in an unwavering hand. Richard intervened. Still not taking his eyes off his wife he said, 'Thank you, Aunt Honoria! I don't think you'll manage to convince my bride I'm not a villain. She's so certain of it that she won't even hear any arguments in my defence. But perhaps she'll listen to this.' Holding Lexi's eyes, he went on, 'Alexandra, I agree that there has been some villainy at work against the Rawdon family. When your father died I thought there would be an end to it. It seems I was wrong. Shooting me won't solve the problem, I assure you. I am not the man responsible. But, if you give me time, I'll find out who was.'

'There wasn't anyone else, Deverell!'

'I swear there was!' Richard's quiet insistence had some effect, and as Lexi still hesitated he went on, 'Look, I'll make you an offer. Show me what you have by way of proof. Tell me why you are so convinced that I betrayed my best friend and all his family—people—' He stopped, then went on, 'People who had meant so much to me. Then give me six months. Six months to prove you wrong about Johnny's accident. Six months to find out who or what ruined your father.'

'That at least was you! You've already confessed.'

'No, I did not. You weren't listening properly. I did my best to stop the damage and failed. Let me prove to you that I'm telling the truth. I'll make a bargain with you. Put your gun away. If, at the end of six months, I can't prove everything to your satisfaction—whatever it is—I'll save you the bother of shooting me. I'll do it for you, I swear.'

Canon Harmond and Lady Honoria spoke together. 'Lord Deverell, you must not make such a rash promise!'

'Richard!' Lady Honoria was scandalised. 'Have you gone mad, too?'

Neither interruption was heard as Lexi stared at Richard.

'I give you my word,' he repeated.

'The word of a liar and a coward?' she said scornfully. 'How could I possibly accept that?'

'More confidently than I can accept yours, apparently,' he replied. 'Haven't you just sworn to love, cherish and to obey me? Or was that somebody else standing beside me at the altar?'

'I swore to love you till death parted us, Richard.'

'Ah! Quite. I see. And that made it all right?' He pulled a face, then straightened up and gave her a coolly challenging look. 'So, what is it to be, Alexandra? A bullet now, or in six months' time?'

Canon Harmond cleared his throat. 'Lord Deverell, I refuse to stand by while such a dreadful bargain is made.'

'Harmond, can't you see she won't accept anything less?' Richard said impatiently. 'Don't make it impossible for her to compromise!'

Canon Harmond stopped short. After a moment he sighed, shook his head and turned to Lexi. 'Lady Deverell, I cannot approve of what your husband has promised, but if it prevents what would be an act of cold-blooded murder then I must ask you to accept it. My child, you are putting not only the lives of your husband and yourself in danger, but you run the risk of damaging your immortal soul. Give me the pistol, Lady Deverell!'

Lexi looked at them all, her eyes huge with anguish.

'I don't know what to do,' she said. 'I don't know! I don't want to kill anyone. I never thought I would have to... I never wanted this... But when I found out how he had lied to me...what he had done...I only knew I had to avenge my family somehow....' She gave Richard an agonised stare. 'You'll swear? Before everyone here? On your honour?'

'I swear on my honour.'

'Very well. I accept.' The pistol was lowered and an audible sigh of relief went through the room as she put it down on the table. As Canon Harmond picked it up she stared at it and gave a shuddering sigh. Her hair stood out like a flame against a face that was as white as her dress. She put her hands to her throat and started to sway... Richard caught her as she fell.

No one else moved for a moment, then Lady Honoria demanded, 'What are you going to do, Richard? What in God's name are you going to do with the girl? If you ask me, she'd be better off in the nearest madhouse. You'll have to send her back to Rawdon!'

Holding the unconscious Lexi in his arms, Richard raised his eyebrows at his aunt. 'Why should you even think of such a thing, Aunt Honoria? My wife will naturally come with me to Channings. Rawdon, would you be kind enough to find my groom? I want the carriage brought round to the side door immediately. Lady Deverell has been taken ill.' He cast a glance at the others. 'And that is *all* anyone outside this room needs to know.'

He held their eyes until they all signalled their agreement. Then he nodded to Sir Mark, who went out to find Lord Deverell's groom.

Chapter Two

Two days later Lexi opened her eyes and slowly turned her head. She was in bed, in a room that was quite strange to her, large, luxuriously furnished, with two windows on one side. A collection of bottles and powders was on the table beside the bed, together with a glass and a carafe of water. Beside them was a vase of roses. A bowl of autumn flowers and leaves stood on a handsome chest of drawers between the windows. Lady Honoria was sitting to one side of the window nearer the bed, but when she saw signs of movement she came over.

'So!' she said. 'You're awake at last.'

'Where am I?' Lexi's voice was a mere thread of sound.

'Have some water.' Lady Honoria held a glass to Lexi's lips. 'You're at Channings, of course.'

'Channings?' Lexi frowned. Then memory returned, and with a cry of dismay she turned the glass away and struggled to sit up. 'That's Richard's house! I shouldn't be here.'

Lady Honoria pushed her back. 'I couldn't agree with you more!' she said. 'But Richard insisted.'

'He shouldn't have brought me here. I can't live with *him*! It isn't possible!'

'You must keep calm. The surgeon says you need complete rest.'

'But I can't—' Lexi turned her head restlessly on the pillow. 'How long have I been here?'

'Nearly two days. Richard brought you here straight after the wedding. You collapsed in the vestry after that extraordinary scene, and you've been more or less unconscious ever since. Doctor Loudon has called several times.'

Lexi gazed round her again. 'Whose room is this?'

'It's yours.'

'Mine?' Lexi sounded nervous.

'Oh, you needn't think you're sharing it with my nephew,' said Lady Honoria acidly. 'He isn't completely mad. He has a room at the opposite end of the house from this one.'

Lexi closed her eyes and frowned again at a vague memory of Richard's voice, asking her to talk to him, and her own agitated refusal before seeking refuge in sleep again... She opened her eyes and looked at Lady Honoria. The old lady had sat down in the chair next to the bed, but her expression was not encouraging. Lexi said with a touch of defiance, 'I expect you hate me for wanting to shoot Richard.'

'Nothing so dramatic,' Richard's aunt replied. 'You were obviously out of your mind at the time! But I don't find it easy to forgive the fright you gave us. Richard is very dear to me, and I thought for a moment you *were* going to shoot.'

Lexi lay silent. 'I should have!' she said at last. 'I planned it so carefully. I promised myself I would. But when it came to the point... Why couldn't I?'

Lady Honoria got up. 'Stop this nonsense *at once*, Lexi! You are no murderess. Of course you couldn't kill Richard! Unless you stop talking such rubbish I shall get Murdie to come to sit with you. I'm not staying here to listen to any more of it.'

'No! Don't go! Please don't go!' Lexi grasped Lady Honoria's hand. 'I have to know. Is he...? Does he...? Are we really married?'

'You are certainly married. But it would surprise no one if Richard sent you away. I should imagine that a wife's threat to murder her husband would be unquestionable grounds for divorce. I for one wouldn't even blame Richard if he sent you to a madhouse.' Lady Honoria removed her hand from Lexi's grip. 'You certainly fooled me. I would have sworn you loved him.'

A tear rolled down Lexi's cheek. 'I...did...' she whispered sadly. 'It was all I ever wanted, to marry Richard. I loved him so much...'

Lady Honoria snorted scornfully. 'A fine way you have of showing it!' she said. 'And a fine mess you've created, too! If you hated Richard so much, why didn't you simply leave him alone, you stupid girl?' She gazed angrily at Lexi for a moment, then went on, 'There isn't an eligible female in the county who wouldn't have jumped at the chance of being Richard's wife. Why the devil did he have to settle on you?'

Lexi shook her head. 'I don't *know* any more why Richard wanted to marry me. I don't know *anything* any more!'

'Well, I'll tell you why *I* think he did!' said Lady Honoria, unmoved by Lexi's obvious distress. 'It's all of a piece with his present behaviour. Because he was *sorry* for you, that's why! He thought he owed it to your family to protect you. He even set Rawdon on its

feet again for your sake, and I dare swear that cost him
a pretty penny!' She ignored Lexi's cry of protest and
went on, 'And what did you do in return? Threaten to
shoot him! I don't know what maggot got into that head
of yours, Lexi Rawdon, but I hope you're satisfied. You
may not have managed to kill Richard, but you've certainly ruined his life—' She stopped short, then went
on, 'To think that just two days ago we were all at his
wedding, all so happy for him—safely home from the
army, about to settle at last with his wife at Channings...' She made a gesture of impatience. 'Richard
has asked me not to be unkind to you, but even if *he's*
a saint, *I'*m not! I can't stay here—if I do, I'll only say
even more than I should...'

Lexi's eyes were huge pools of darkness. 'I'm sorry
you're so angry,' she said, 'but I didn't want Richard's
pity. He'd have done better to save it for my father.
You don't understand.'

'No, and I don't suppose I ever will. Why this should
happen to Richard of all people... How could you?
How *could* you, Lexi?' She stared at the girl in the bed
for a moment, then shook her head and said, 'It's no
use. Murdie will have to sit with you. I can't.'

She went out and the door shut behind her. Lexi
closed her eyes. She was trembling again. The feelings
of panic and loss, which had plagued her ever since her
world had turned upside down, returned in full force.
Why *had* Richard asked her to marry him? At the time
she had thought that he loved her as deeply as she had
loved him....

She remembered the occasion with painful clarity.
How foolish she had been! When Richard had come
into the library at Rawdon, she was standing at the desk
where she had found her father the day before, slumped

over his papers. The papers still lay there in an untidy heap. She had been making an effort to gather them together, to put them into some sort of order, but tears had made her progress slow...

'My poor girl! You shouldn't be here alone.'

At the sound of Richard's voice Lexi turned to him blindly, and he took her into his arms, holding her close, her head pressed against his chest. She felt safe, as if she had reached some kind of refuge. In the confusion and distress of the day before she had been aware of Richard's presence, taking charge, issuing orders. He had made sure she was being looked after, but there had been no opportunity for them to talk.

He held her now, giving her time to recover a little, then led her to the fire. 'You're cold. When did you last have anything to eat?'

'I don't know. Does it matter?'

'Of course it matters! Let me send for something.'

Richard waited till she had eaten a little of the food he ordered and drunk some wine. 'Isn't that better?' he said. She nodded and he smiled, the special smile he seemed to keep for her alone, warm and affectionate. It worked its usual magic, and for a moment she forgot her heartache in its glow. He took her hands in his and held them in his own, gently warming them.

'What were you doing when I came in?' he asked after a moment.

'I was...I was trying to sort out some of Papa's papers.'

'That was foolish,' he said. 'They would be better dealt with by your father's lawyers. I'll put them in some sort of order for you, and then you can leave everything to them. You need to rest.'

'I can't!' she said. 'If I don't do something with them, Mark will think he has to. He was here this morning when I came in. I don't blame him—he is the next in line, after all. But he is still a comparative stranger. And those papers were the last things...the last things Papa was reading when he...he died. I want to be the one to deal with them.'

'Would you let *me* do it for you?'

She stared at him. 'I would,' she said slowly. 'You were as close to Papa as anyone. But you've already done so much. And I have no real claim on you or your time. How could we explain it to Mark?'

'Easily,' he said, his grey eyes serious. 'Because you're wrong, Alexandra. You have every claim on my time and on everything else of mine.'

She looked at him, wide-eyed, uncertain of his meaning.

He went on, 'I always wanted to marry you—your father knew that. And now I want us to marry as soon as it can be arranged. Will you? And will you trust me?'

Lexi did not hesitate. A flood of joy drowned her heartache and she threw herself into his arms again. 'Richard! Oh, Richard! Of course I will! You know I will! I'll marry you as soon as you like. But won't we have to wait? The neighbours will be shocked... Papa's death...'

'They'll get over it. Your father would have wanted you to be safe. If things had been different, you would have been my wife long ago—we both know that. And now you need someone to look after you, to keep you happy and secure. We could marry in a few weeks, if you agreed. The wedding would be a quiet one, of course. Do you mind that?'

'Mind? Oh, no!'

'Then say you agree. I swear you won't regret it.'

'Regret it? How could I possibly regret being married to you, Richard? I've wanted it all my life, I think!'

And after he had gone, taking the papers with him, she had been so happy even in the midst of all her grief. Richard had at last asked her to marry him. He loved her as she loved him...

Now, just a few weeks later, Lexi groaned and hid her face in the bedclothes. How foolish of her to have been so gullible! Of course Richard hadn't loved her in the way she had loved him! He might have married her out of pity as his aunt thought, or perhaps it had been out of guilt, a last flicker of conscience. But one thing was quite certain. He couldn't possibly have loved her.

She was surprised by the sharp pang this thought gave her—the final traces of illusion gone. How curious that it should hurt so much, after all the other things that had happened.

She turned restlessly in the bed. What did it matter what Richard had felt? She was living in a nightmare, married to a stranger. The Richard she had known and loved no longer existed...

It was too much. She closed her eyes again and escaped from the unbearable present into the past, a world where she had known the old Richard, the one who had meant so much to her.

Richard Deverell had been Johnny Rawdon's friend before Alexandra was born, and, though they were very different in character—Johnny so extrovert and Richard always so quiet—they had remained friends ever since. Lexi's earliest memories were of golden days of sunshine as she watched the two boys catching tadpoles or fishing in the lake at Rawdon, and her own cries of, 'Wait for me! Wait for me!' She fell into streams and out of trees, sank up to her knees in mud, and tripped over rocks, but she never complained except when they tried to go off on their own.

Over the years they got used to her copper head popping up wherever they went, and gradually took it on themselves to protect her from the worst of the tumbles and scrapes. In return she gave them her unstinted loyalty and devotion. The three children had been practically inseparable whenever they were free from tutors and governesses. They rode together, climbed trees together, fought and laughed together, spending long days out by the lake, or in the woods round Rawdon.

Everything had been so simple in their childhood. It had seemed to her then that this idyllic existence would last forever. But it couldn't, of course. Things were changing all the time, and the greatest change came after Richard and Johnny had spent the Season of 1810 in London. When they came back to Somerset that summer they were dashing young blades, with no time for their old pursuits or Johnny's unsophisticated little sister. The six years' difference in age between them had become a chasm not to be bridged by persuasion, or tantrums, or anything else. Lexi was forced to watch from a distance as Richard and her brother flirted with the young ladies of the neighbourhood, took them riding or on the river, escorted them to the many picnics and dances arranged by their hopeful mamas. For a short time Lexi, bereft and isolated, thought her world had come to an end.

But, after a while, she started to derive a certain amount of malicious amusement from watching the efforts made by the young ladies to capture the two most eligible young men in the county. They met with little success. Johnny laughed and teased, and treated no one seriously. And though Richard was courteous to all, though he danced with one, appeared to be amused by another, listened attentively to a third, he remained throughout his cool, level-headed self, singling no one out for any particular attention. But strangely, as Lexi watched, her own perception of her childhood companion slowly changed. She gradually became just as intrigued as the rest by the slightly aloof manner he adopted in company, was just as fascinated as they all seemed to be with the charm of his slow smile, his lithe grace, the restrained power in his movements. The familiar image of the quiet boy of her childhood gradually faded, to be replaced with that of a very attractive man—attractive, and, underneath his quiet manner, very assured. Her feelings towards him changed in a way she found difficult to define, but they remained very possessive. With surprise, she realised that, whatever he was, boy or man, friend or eligible prize, Richard Deverell was hers. Had always been hers. Would always be hers. She was even sorry for the silly females who pursued him. Didn't they know that Richard Deverell belonged to her? Lexi was so certain of this that one afternoon in August she told him so.

Lexi and Richard had left the horses tethered to a fence while they went down to the river to look at the otters who lived in its banks. For a while it was like old times, as they shared uncomplicated delight in the antics of the otter cub and talked of anything and everything that occurred to them.

'Are you home for good now, Richard?' Lexi asked.

'I'm not sure. I might go into the Army for a while.'

'The Army!'

'It's a way of seeing the world, and there's plenty of adventure to be had, especially in Spain. Johnny is talking of it, too.'

'Johnny? Papa would never let him go! He's needed here at home. And so are you, Richard.'

'Oh, come, Alexandra! Needed? You know very well that my father takes no pleasure in my company, and Channings is so well run it really has no need of me, either. No, I don't think I should be missed.' Richard spoke a touch bitterly and Lexi was silent for a moment. Then, making an effort to sound calm, she said in a small voice,

'*We* would miss you, Richard…'

'It would only be for two or three years—I don't intend to make a career of it. But Johnny seems very set on the idea. I think he might go whatever your father says.'

'Oh, if Johnny's mind is made up, then Papa will give in. Johnny always gets his way in the end.' She was silent for a moment, thinking of what it would mean to her father as well as herself. Then she said angrily, 'My brother is such a *clunch*! He gets these ideas, and goes ahead without thinking of the consequences.'

'And you don't?' asked Richard, looking at her with such quizzical affection that she had to laugh.

'I know, I know! The Rawdons rush in without thinking. How often have I heard you say that? But Johnny's much worse than I am, you know he is! It wouldn't surprise me in the least if you had rescued him from any number of scrapes while you were both in London.' She paused, and when she next spoke she sounded unusually bitter. 'Now he wants to go into the Army, and he will. We all do our best to please Johnny, but he doesn't care! He ploughs on quite merrily, not thinking of the unhappiness he leaves behind.'

'You sound as if you don't like your brother.'

'I'm not sure I do at the moment.' She looked up to see Richard frowning. She went on, 'Oh, you needn't worry. I may not like him just now, but I shall always love him. In spite of all his faults.'

'Or perhaps even because of them,' said Richard. 'Because that's the way he is. Isn't that so?' He smiled.

The smile did something to her. She suddenly felt absurdly happy, sure that Richard never smiled at any other girl in that particular teasing, affectionate way. The smile was for her alone and no one else. As he turned to help her over the stile at the end of the path, a sudden impulse stopped her from leaping down as she usually did. Instead, she stood on the step, rested her hands on his shoulders, and looked down at him with a grin.

'Which of my faults do you love *me* for, Richard?' she asked, tilting her head to one side, eyes alight with mischief, her hair falling over her shoulder in a mass of copper, almost touching his face.

His hands were at her waist, ready to jump her down, but he suddenly became very still. His grasp tightened, his eyes grew dark, and he wasn't smiling any more. His gaze rested on her mouth... Lexi suddenly felt breathless, even nervous.

'Richard?' she said uncertainly

It was just as suddenly over. He said something under his breath, then dropped his hands and shook his head. After a moment he said calmly and somewhat distantly, 'I couldn't possibly say. There are so many of them!'

His reaction disappointed her, and she felt an urge to disturb that calm self-possession again. She said, 'Do you know, I thought just for a moment there you were going to kiss me. Did you want to?'

'Of course not,' he said with a flicker of anger. 'What a ridiculous idea! You're still a child, Alexandra.'

Stung, she replied, 'I'm nearly sixteen. Not all that much younger than you! You never seemed to notice the difference in the old days!'

'It wasn't the same then. We were *all* of us children,' he said curtly.

'But…*why* didn't you want to kiss me? Aren't I pretty enough?'

'You're not *old* enough! Alexandra, if you were anything but a child you wouldn't ask such questions! Not of anyone!'

'I wouldn't ask anyone else. I wouldn't want anyone else to kiss me, Richard. Only you.'

He looked at her in exasperation, as if he wasn't sure how to reply to this. Then he shook his head and said abruptly, 'I suppose you think I'm flattered. But I'm not. You really don't know anything at all about it, Alexandra. And, unless you want me to leave you here to go back by yourself, we'll end this stupid conversation right now!'

He sounded as if he meant what he was saying. Lexi nodded.

'Very well,' she said. Then she threw him another glance full of mischief. 'But I still think you wanted to kiss me. I suppose I'll just have to wait till I'm older.'

He seemed to speak almost against his will. 'It's very likely that you won't want me to kiss you then,' he said.

'Oh, yes, I will!' Lexi said confidently. 'And, what's more, you'll still want to kiss me, too. You're mine, Richard Deverell! We belong to one another.'

* * *

For the rest of the summer, though Richard was perfectly amiable, he kept his distance, never showing by look or action that he thought of her as anything but a good companion, his best friend's little sister. But Lexi lay awake at night, imagining the kiss he had denied her and fantasising about the future, and though it was never again referred to between them she never faltered in her conviction that he was hers.

She watched him with the other young ladies and was reassured. No rivals there, she thought with satisfaction. And next year he might consider her old enough… But in the end a greater and more powerful rival took Richard away from her. In the autumn he and Johnny announced that they were indeed going into the Army.

Nothing would deter them, certainly not Lexi's protests. Not even Sir Jeremy Rawdon's strenuous efforts could prevent his only son from embarking on such a dangerous career. Johnny was adamant. Richard was going, and so would he. It would be an adventure, a great lark.

'But don't you see how unhappy Papa is?' Lexi cried one day. 'How unhappy we both are! Why are you doing this to us?'

'Because I want to! Two or three years in a decent regiment would be tremendous fun! I've enjoyed this summer, but I'm not ready to settle down yet! Besides, Richard is going. You don't see his family making all this fuss.'

'You know very well why that is so,' said Lexi hotly. 'Lord Deverell doesn't care! He's never taken the slightest interest in anything Richard does. It's not surprising that his son feels no obligation to him. But Papa loves you, Johnny! You're his only son!'

'Oh, stop it! You're a girl—you can't possibly understand what it means. I don't see why Papa is so worried. Nothing will happen to me. I'll be back in a couple of years and ready to take on those damned obligations you both ram down my throat. Lexi, don't look so worried! I'll be all right—you'll see.'

So in the end Sir Jeremy reluctantly gave in, and by the spring of 1811 Lieutenants Richard Deverell and Johnny Rawdon were serving under Wellington's command in Spain. Johnny's 'couple of years' stretched to three. The two friends did not finally return to England until the May of 1814—after Napoleon had been defeated and safely confined on Elba.

Perhaps she *was* the child Richard had called her, but, curiously, Lexi never doubted that Richard and Johnny would come back safely, was confident that the years would bring nothing but happiness. And, though she missed them, she was determined to make good use of her time in their absence. She had till then regarded the accomplishments expected of the daughter of a wealthy landowner—the ability to dress well, to dance gracefully, to sing, play and draw well—as a waste of time. But she now threw her considerable energy and talent into acquiring every social grace. When Richard returned he was to be astonished, overcome, at the change in her. He would find her irresistible.

Then, a few months before they were due to return, Lady Wroxford, her godmother, somewhat belatedly remembered a promise made long before to Lady Rawdon that Lexi should have a London season. So Lexi spent the first half of the year with Lady Wroxford in her house in Curzon Street, and was introduced to the polite world. To everyone's surprise, including her own, she had a modest success. Her determination to learn how to enchant Richard Deverell on his return served her well in the critical world of the London *ton*, and she soon had a circle of admirers wherever she went.

Her godmother did more than just keep her promise. A woman of taste and wealth, she had taken delight in providing her protégée with a wardrobe of beautiful clothes that flattered and enhanced her unusual colouring. Unusual was a word frequently used of Lexi Rawdon. She had learned to control the impulsive ways and hot temper that went with her copper hair, had moderated her careless stride of the past into the decorous steps of a young lady of fashion, but traces of the old free grace and high spirits remained. She was not beautiful in the accepted sense, but her glorious hair and sparkling lavender-blue eyes made sure she was noticed, and her frank, open ways, her wit, her ready laughter, kept a constant supply of admirers round her. The fact that the Rawdons of Rawdon Hall were an old and wealthy family was, of course, an additional attraction. Soon Alexandra Rawdon's name was on the list of the season's most sought-after débutantes.

But though Lexi was always polite, she showed an indifference to flattery and admiration that the world found intriguing. The world didn't realise—how could it?—that Miss Rawdon's apparent lack of interest in her success was perfectly genuine. Though she was enjoying London life, it was merely an amusement, a distraction, while she waited for *one* man to return from the wars. Charming, well bred, wealthy, and seemingly not unduly eager to find a husband, Lexi was soon declared to be out of the usual run of débutantes, and most attractive. Before the season was very old she had received several flattering offers.

And she turned them all down. Lady Wroxford ex-

postulated, accusing her of being difficult to please.
Lexi listened meekly, but said nothing. How could she
tell her kind godmother the truth? That she was waiting
for *one* man to come to London? That only he, and no
other, would *ever* please her?

Then at last Richard and Johnny arrived. They came
back from Spain, bronzed, fit, no longer boys, but men,
toughened by their experiences on the battlefields of
Spain, and confident of their power. But to her they
were still dear, still two of the three most important
people in her world. For a few short months the future
looked brilliant.

The spell of these happy memories was broken, as
the door opened and Lexi was brought back from the
past to the bedroom at Channings. Someone came in. It
was probably Murdie, Lady Honoria's maid, come to
take her mistress's place.

'Alexandra?'

Not Murdie. Richard. No one else ever called her
Alexandra in quite that way. Besides, she would know
his voice anywhere, deep, calm, sometimes tender. Even
though her own eyes were closed, she felt his grey eyes
examining her, speculating... Her heart started thumping, but she held herself still, pretending to be in a deep
sleep.

'Alexandra, open your eyes. We must talk.'

Why could that voice still enchant her? The temptation to do as he said was almost irresistible, but she
couldn't, wouldn't give in. *Why didn't he go away?*

'Did my aunt upset you again? She's old, Alexandra.
She can't understand...' His voice had a wry sort of
humour in it as he added, 'For that matter, nor can I.
But I'm not as tired or as angry as she is. Don't let her

put you off. You might even feel better after we've talked. And sooner or later we shall have to put the pieces of our lives back together again.'

Put the pieces back together again? That would take a miracle! Lexi rather thought they were beyond repair. Still without opening her eyes, she turned her head away from him.

Richard waited for a moment. Alexandra was not asleep. He knew that. But though it was getting more and more urgent for him to talk to her, he was reluctant to force her before she was ready. The events of the past few months had brought her dangerously close to breakdown. He looked down at his wife. Her eyes were still determinedly shut, but the purple shadows surrounding them, and the hollows in her pale cheeks, showed how badly she needed this time of rest and recuperation.

Perhaps it would help to talk of happier times... He sat down by the bed and thought of her as he had seen her in a London ballroom when he and Johnny had come back from Spain in May 1814. The carelessly dressed child he had known in Somerset had turned into a glowing girl, poised and very much aware of her powers. He addressed the still figure in the bed.

'Alexandra... Do you remember dancing with me in London? Johnny and I had just got back from France after our years in the Peninsula. Napoleon had been packed off to Elba and London was celebrating. Everyone said what a brilliant season it was. Do you remember? London was full of visitors—European royalty, diplomats and couriers, sightseers, and all sorts of hangers-on. There seemed to be far more of them than there were of the soldiers returning from the wars... Johnny and I were two of the soldiers, and I can tell you we felt somewhat outnumbered by all those civilians.'

He paused, but Alexandra gave no sign that she was listening. He went on, 'I saw you first at the ball in Northumberland House, I remember. Johnny and I had arrived in London not long before, and had come there hoping to find you.'

Richard fell silent. The occasion was still vivid in his memory. He had seen Alexandra as soon as they had entered the ballroom, but it had taken Johnny a few minutes longer. The sight of his sister then had stopped him in his tracks.

'There she is!' he had said in amazement. 'Over there. Good Lord, Dev, she looks stunning! I would never have imagined she'd turn out so well! Just look at her—if you can. She's damned near surrounded!' Richard remembered his own feelings as he looked at the laughing girl on the other side of the room. Tall and graceful, her hair twisted into a shining knot on top of her head, she looked completely self-possessed, and quite at home in the sophisticated world of London society. Though the smile was as enchanting as ever, she looked very different from the girl with the mane of copper hair who had stood on top of the stile and tempted him to kiss her almost four eventful years before. He could still remember the scent of that hair as it had brushed against his cheek, still recall the sensations aroused in him then...

'We'd better go across before she sees us and comes rushing over,' Johnny had said next. 'She's bound to be excited, but it would never do. Not in a ballroom.'

Richard had known Johnny's sister better than Johnny had. He remembered saying wryly, 'Alexandra knows we're here already. She saw us the moment we came in—or very soon after.'

'What?'

'Your sister has grown up, my boy! She won't come rushing over—she's waiting for *us* to join *her*.'

'Well, I'm damned! Come on, then!'

Now, more than a year later, sitting by Alexandra's bed in the aftermath of the disastrous episode in the church, Richard was filled with regret. If only his father had been a more reasonable man... He could have asked Alexandra to marry him then and there, and if he had things might have turned out very differently for all of them. He shook his head impatiently and got up. 'If only', 'could have', if...if...if...what use was that? Going back was impossible. What was clear at present was that Alexandra was not going to acknowledge he was even there. He'd have to leave it for today. Tomorrow he would have a word with Dr Loudon and see what he had to say. Somehow or other they had to move on, attempt to make sense of this mess. She couldn't escape into sleep forever.

His voice cooler, he said, 'Very well. I can see you aren't yet ready to talk to me. But I won't give you much longer, Alexandra. We made a bargain, you and I, and I shall see that you keep to your side of it. I'll be back.'

He walked to the door. 'Murdie? You can come in now. Lady Deverell is still asleep.' Murdie came in, and with a last look at his wife Richard went out, shutting the door quietly behind him.

Chapter Three

The door closed. Lexi heard a rustle of skirts, and felt Lady Honoria's maid gently straightening the sheets. She was safe.

Still keeping her eyes closed, she contemplated the pictures called up by what Richard had just said. She remembered watching the two men enter the ballroom at Northumberland House. Even in a company that was by then well used to officers in its midst, they had attracted attention. The taller one, dark, with cool grey eyes and an air of arrogance about him, had appeared to be indifferent to the interested gaze of the ladies. The other, with a thatch of dark red hair and laughing blue eyes, had returned their glances with enjoyment. Richard and Johnny. They looked so spruce in their dress uniforms that no one could have guessed that they had arrived in London only that afternoon. Lexi sighed and sought escape into the past again...

Though she had been fully conscious of the two men circling the ballroom in search of her, was aware of their every movement, she made a great effort to appear not to have noticed them. No longer was she the impulsive hoyden who had followed the two boys round wherever they went, pleading to be allowed to go with them. She had learned a lot in the past year or two, and now was the time to put her lessons to good use. And she was determined that when Richard finally found where she was, *he* would have to come to *her*. When he reached her at last she was ready.

'Johnny! Richard!' she cried with a surprised look and a warm but not extravagantly affectionate smile. 'Why didn't you tell us you were in London? It's wonderful to see you—and both looking so well.' Before they could say anything she turned to her godmother. 'Lady Wroxford—you know Johnny already, of course, but this is his friend, Richard Deverell. Lady Wroxford is my godmother, Richard, and a very kind one, too.'

Conventional words, covering a tumult of feeling. As they stood and chatted to her godmother she examined them covertly. They were both still handsome, but they looked older, no longer boys, but men in their prime, with an air of command about them, a hint of ruthlessness. Lexi reminded herself that they had spent the last three years fighting under Wellington in the harshest of conditions, that they had faced death and disease, defeat as well as victory. And now, from what they were saying to Lady Wroxford, it appeared they wanted to put it all behind them and enjoy what was left of one of the most brilliant Seasons London had seen for a long time.

In the days and weeks that followed Lexi realised that Johnny had not changed underneath. He was still her beloved, amusing, carelessly affectionate brother, kind when it suited him, but basically selfish. At first it was Johnny who escorted her to the many events during the rest of the month, but, as his circle of acquaintances expanded, he grew less eager to be tied to his sister. He began to ask Richard to deputise for him, to Lexi's great annoyance. It was no part of her plan that Richard should regard himself as a substitute brother. But help came from an unexpected quarter. Lady Wroxford, too, was uneasy at the arrangement.

'My dear, I know from what you and your brother have told me that Mr Deverell has always been regarded as a member of the family, but the truth is he is a handsome and extremely eligible male who is not at all related to you. Unless you wish to provoke undesirable gossip, you will not be seen in his company as often as John suggests.'

When she put the same point to Johnny, however, he roared with laughter. 'Oh, forgive me, ma'am, but that is nonsense!'

'Indeed?' said Lady Wroxford icily. 'I think I know the world of the *ton* better than you, John. And, while I am in charge of your sister, I will not allow her to be compromised, however close she and Mr Deverell have been in the past. That was when she was a *child*, not the very attractive young lady she now is.'

'You mean people might say Dev ought to marry her?'

'I am sure neither Mr Deverell, nor your sister, would do anything to encourage the gossips to go as far as that, but one cannot be too careful.'

Johnny frowned, then his face lit up and he said eagerly, 'But that wouldn't half be a bad idea! It's never occurred to me before, but Dev would be a first-rate catch for Lexi! They've known each other for ever, and they've always got on well. What do you say, Lexi? Would you like to marry Dev? I think he would be willing if I asked him to. I don't think he has anyone else in mind, and now the wars are over he'll soon have to think of marrying.'

Lexi's face flamed and she had difficulty in speaking. After a moment she said fiercely, 'Don't you *dare*! I'm not so short of offers that I have to rely on you to find me a husband, Johnny Rawdon!'

Johnny shrugged his shoulders and appeared to give up the idea. But Lexi was so worried that he might say something, however harmless, that she began to adopt a much cooler manner towards Richard. Richard was hers, but she was determined that he must come to her of his own free will because he had discovered that he loved her—not because of any nonsense about duty or obliging an old friend.

So though they frequently danced together when they met at the many balls and routs during that glittering Season, though she even went for the occasional ride in the Park with him, she was careful to refuse more of his invitations than she accepted. It was very hard. With every day that passed she fell more in love with him. Even in a crowded ballroom, dancing a formal dance with the rest of the world looking on, she felt a secret harmony between them, which no other man could ever begin to match. The world saw and respected Richard as the heir to an old and wealthy family, a distinguished soldier, a man of honour. But Lexi knew that part of him which the rest of the world did not see, hidden as it was behind his air of aloof courtesy—his wry sense of humour, his compassion, and his vulnerability. And the more she loved him for it all, the harder she worked to hide the fact.

One warm evening Johnny took them all out to Vauxhall Gardens. Lady Wroxford was content to sit in one of the booths, gossiping with her friends, and she made no objection when Richard took Lexi off for a set of dances. But then, instead of joining the dancers, he asked Lexi if she would prefer to walk about the gardens for a few minutes instead. The evening was warm and the dance floor crowded. A few minutes in the peace of the gardens with Richard was very tempting, so Lexi gave way and they walked in silence along the lamplit paths for a minute or two. Then he stopped and said quietly,

'Have I done something wrong, Alexandra?'

'Wrong?' Lexi turned an astonished face towards him. 'This evening? Of course not!'

'Not this evening. But…' he hesitated '…in general.'

Lexi grew cautious. 'What makes you think that?'

'You seem to have changed. Recently I have the impression that you are…wary, in a way you never were before I went into the Army.'

Lexi bit her lip. 'We're both older, Richard…' she said slowly.

'But we're surely still friends? Shouldn't the past still count for something? Do you know, in Spain, at night, after a hard day's fighting, I used to lie and look at the stars, and think about the days at Rawdon when we were children. The pictures I conjured up then helped to keep me sane amongst all that blood and noise and killing. You were always part of them. I used to imagine the way you looked, remembered your laughter, the way you had of wrinkling up your nose, that mane of hair, which was always getting in the way—' He broke off.

This was so unlike his usual tone that Lexi was at a loss to know what to reply. She said somewhat abruptly, 'Lady Wroxford thinks I should have it cut.'

'No!' Then, seeing her surprise at the force with which he had spoken, he went on more calmly, 'No.

Don't give in to her, Alexandra. Your hair is one of the things that make you...special.'

The old Lexi would have instantly demanded how and why, and what else made her special to him. But now, though the colour rose in her cheeks, she suppressed the *frisson* of delight at his words and said with a cool smile, 'Come, sir! You mustn't flatter me! Spain must surely have been full of raven-haired señoritas only too willing to comfort you all! I don't suppose for a moment that you very often thought of your friends in England, not even the copper-haired ones!'

'I wasn't intending to flatter! Damn it, that's what I meant a moment ago! The cool smile, the remark meant to put me off. Why are you treating me as distantly as you do all the others? Surely our old friendship deserves more?'

Lexi said with some feeling, 'But this is not Somerset, nor are we children any longer. You may still regard me as your little sister, but that isn't the way Society sees us!'

'Has Lady Wroxford been talking to you?'

'Yes, she has. But she said nothing I could disagree with. I have no wish to be the subject of conjecture and gossip.'

'Gossip?'

'Yes, Richard! Gossip!' said Lexi sharply, losing her patience. 'Surprising as it may seem to you, the world sees me as a young woman of marriageable age who, unless she wishes to set tongues wagging, should not spend too much time alone with one of London's most eligible bachelors! As I am doing at the moment. And since gossip is the last thing I wish for, I think we should return to my godmother. She will be wondering in any case what has happened to me.'

She started to walk away, but he took her hand and pulled her back. She stumbled and fell against him. His arm went round her and he pulled her closer, his eyes holding hers. A shiver of delight ran down her spine, but she managed to say fiercely,

'Are these Spanish ways, Richard? Let me go!'

'Not yet. And they're very old English ways, my love.' He bent his head and kissed her.

Since the episode by the stile four years before, Lexi had often imagined what it would be like to be kissed by Richard. But nothing had prepared her for this. She felt as if she was suspended in space; her heart was hammering, the blood rushing through her veins to every inch of her body. 'R...Richard?' she said, her voice a mere breath. He laughed and kissed her again, this time more deeply. The kiss went on and on until she thought she would die with the pleasure of it. He held her so tightly, his arms cradling her against him so closely, that she was made aware of his manhood, the strength of his desire, and for a brief moment she responded tumultuously to the new and previously unknown feelings it aroused in her. She put her arms round his neck and held his lips to hers, inviting further caresses....

The sound of laughter nearby brought her suddenly and cruelly to her senses. Full of horrified shame, she wrenched herself out of Richard's arms and tried to escape, but her legs refused to carry her more than a step or two. She stood with her back towards him, fighting for control.

'Alexandra—'

'Be quiet! Don't say a word!'

'I must! I had no right—' He stopped, then began again. 'This isn't the time or the place—' He stopped again and gave a little laugh. 'At least you know I don't regard you as a child any more,' he said ruefully.

No word of love, nothing to show he had been as affected as she had been by what had happened. He was probably well used to such encounters. But what could he be thinking of her? Lexi swallowed. 'No,' she said stiffly. 'I'm no longer a child. And I should never have behaved as I did, least of all with you. Shall we go back to my godmother?'

Richard looked at her searchingly. 'Are you all right?'

'Of course I am,' she said with a brittle laugh. 'Ashamed, perhaps, but otherwise unharmed.'

'I'm sorry, Alexandra.' He stopped and shook his head. Then he said decisively, 'It won't happen again.'

Still nothing that she wanted to hear. The pain in her heart was growing by the minute, but pride came to her aid. Concealing her bitter disappointment, she said as lightly as she could, 'Even old friends can get carried away, can't they, Richard? Perhaps the world is right after all to disapprove of my spending time alone with you. And now please take me back to Lady Wroxford.'

They went back, and for the rest of the evening he behaved impeccably, not ignoring her exactly, but not singling her out for any particular attention either. No one could have guessed from his demeanour that for a few breathtaking moments such a short while before he had taken Lexi to Paradise and back.

In the days that followed Richard remained just as distant. Lexi was left confused and even somewhat angry. Did he think she was in the habit of allowing men to take her to such a secluded situation, to hold her so closely, to kiss her? Was this what he thought of her?

The sole excuse for her disgraceful conduct was her love for Richard Deverell, but it was clear that there was no such reason for the way *he* had acted. He had not even claimed to love her. Perhaps he had found her earlier coolness towards him a challenge? For whatever reason, he had behaved in a manner she would never have believed possible. Had his time in the Army made him cynical?

She hid her sore heart and bruised pride and sought consolation in the company of other, less complicated, admirers. During the last weeks of the Season no one was as gay, as apparently carefree, as Miss Alexandra Rawdon. One young man refused to listen to her when she assured him she was not interested in his offer of marriage. He was so persistent and so obviously eligible that London began to speculate whether Miss Rawdon would finally succumb. When she assured her god-mother that there was no question of it, Lady Wroxford grew really angry with her.

'Mr Transden has everything to recommend him to the most demanding young lady, Lexi. He may not have a title, but his family is a distinguished one. Moreover, he is comparatively young, in good health, and enormously wealthy. And devoted to you! What more can you possibly ask for?'

'I don't love him,' said Lexi.

'Love? Pshaw! I have never approved of gambling, and marrying for love is the greatest gamble of them all! Marry for comfort, girl. You can fall in love later, if you want to—after you've given your husband an heir or two.' When Lexi remained silent Lady Wroxford shook her head. 'I might as well talk to that table leg for all the attention you will pay me, I know. It's that

''old family friend'' of yours, isn't it? You're in love
with Richard Deverell.'

'Is it so obvious?'

'Not at all! Your behaviour towards him has been
admirably discreet.' Lexi had a sudden vision of herself
in Richard's arms at Vauxhall and her colour rose. Little
did her godmother know! Lady Wroxford went on, 'But
I have no idea what *he* feels about *you*—or anyone else.
That's a man who keeps his own counsel, Lexi. No one
would guess from his recent demeanour that his father
is not expected to live much longer.'

'Lord Deverell ill? Are you sure?' asked Lexi in
astonishment. 'I hadn't heard anything of that, and I'll
swear Johnny doesn't know either.'

'Mrs Shackleton told me—she had it from Honoria
Standish, who is some kind of relation. It's a very odd
situation. Apparently Lord Deverell refuses to see anyone, even his own son. What sort of father is that?'

'There was never much affection between them,
ma'am. Lord Deverell has persistently ignored his son's
existence. That is why Richard has been so much part
of my...of our family.'

'I see. It might also explain Mr Deverell's marked
air of detachment...'

Afterwards Lexi found that she was badly hurt by
Richard's silence. They had had few private moments
since that scene at Vauxhall, but if he had wanted to,
he could surely have found the time to tell her about
his father.

However, the next day he called to take his leave of
Lady Wroxford and her goddaughter. Lord Deverell had
sent for him at last, and Richard was leaving London
more or less straight away. He would probably not re-

turn before the end of the Season. Lady Wroxford expressed her concern and wished him a safe journey. Then she threw a quick glance at Lexi, and took pity on her.

'I think my goddaughter might well have some messages you could carry to Somerset for her,' she said, with a smile. 'You'll excuse me, I'm sure, if I leave her to give them to you. Goodbye, Mr Deverell.'

After she had left the room there was a short, difficult silence. Then Lexi broke it with a touch of her old impulsive style. 'Did Johnny know about your father's illness, Richard? Or did you keep it from him, too?'

'I didn't tell anyone.'

'Why not? I thought Johnny was your best friend. I thought you and I were friends, too.'

Richard heard the hurt anger in her voice and said quickly, 'Of course you are! You Rawdons are the only real family I've known.' He frowned. 'I'm sorry. I suppose I should have explained, but it's a painful subject... I don't find it easy to talk about it.'

'Not even to us?'

'Not even to you, Alexandra. You must have realised long ago that my father rejected me almost as soon as I was born. That's no secret. We have always been strangers to each other. His illness was not serious at first, and though it was regrettable it was not important to me. But it now looks as if he might die. Have you any idea what that would mean?'

His bitter tone puzzled Lexi. 'You inherit the title?' she said uncertainly.

'There's much more to it than that. In spite of all the evidence, I've hoped all my life my father would one day finally accept me, that he might even show me a little affection. Stupid of me, I know.' He raised his eyes, and they were for once unguarded. The pain in them made Lexi gasp. He looked away immediately. 'If he dies now, any hope I might once have cherished about getting to know him will be lost forever...'

'Richard...' Quite forgetting her own feelings, Lexi went to him and put her hand on his arm. He looked down at it, but made no move to take it.

'Then there's the question of my future,' he went on.

'How?'

'The Deverell estates are not entailed. My father is free to leave Channings and everything else he owns to anyone he chooses. The only certain income I have comes from what my mother left me.'

'No! He couldn't cut you out of your inheritance! It wouldn't be right! You love Channings even more than he does!'

Richard said wearily, 'He resents my very existence. How do I know what he might or might not do?'

'But you haven't done anything to justify such a terrible thing!'

'Except to be born. To survive, when my mother didn't.'

Lexi's heart twisted at the bitterness in Richard's voice. But she rallied and said passionately, 'I don't believe for one moment that Lord Deverell will cut you out of his will! He must at least be aware of what he owes to his name, if not to you personally. Channings would never survive without you! No, Richard, you must not even think it! And there's still time for him to make some gesture towards you.'

'A deathbed reconciliation? Most unlikely. But I'll try. Alexandra, I'm sorry if I hurt you. Will you forgive me? We've always been friends. I wouldn't want to lose you.'

'Friends?' She gave a wry smile. 'Always, Richard. Forever.'

The Season came to an end and Lexi thanked her godmother and went back to Somerset. Lady Wroxford was reluctant to let her go.

'I've enjoyed your company, my dear,' she said. 'Johnny is all Rawdon, but you... You may have the Rawdon hair, but you have the same lovely eyes as your dear mother. And you are like her in so many other ways.' She hesitated. 'I'm sorry I couldn't find a husband to please you. I had great hopes for you when you came.'

'Ma'am, please don't blame yourself. No one could have been kinder or more concerned. But my heart was given away before I really knew I had one. There will never be anyone else for me.'

Lady Wroxford nodded sadly. 'I hope Mr Deverell will eventually realise what a treasure he could have in you, but you'll have to be patient. At the moment his future is so uncertain that no man of honour could ask a girl to share it. From what Honoria Standish says, his mother's estate would hardly give him enough to live on.'

Lexi stared at her, then her face lit up. 'You think that's the reason he...? What a fool! What a great fool he is! As if I cared about his wretched inheritance! Oh, just wait till I see him!'

Her godmother looked very worried. 'No, no, you mustn't say anything, Lexi! Mr Deverell may be very fond of you, in fact, I'm sure he is, but love...? That I do not know. But I am also sure he's a proud man, willing to ask favours of no one, not even someone he loved. You've learned a lot of restraint since coming to

London, and my advice is to hold on to it now. This isn't a child's game, and you mustn't think it is. No rushing in in your old style, do you hear? You won't gain anything by it.'

'Yes, yes! But Richard and I are *friends*. I can say anything to him. He won't be offended. If only I were sure he loved me…'

Her godmother sighed. 'Well, remember, Lexi… If anything should ever go wrong, don't wait to ask if you can come here. I should be very glad to help you all I can—for your own sake, as well as your mother's.'

Lord Deverell died without any attempt at reconciliation, but he *had* after all left everything to his son. However, the situation between Richard and Lexi was not to be resolved for another year. Channings itself had been well looked after, but the rest of the Deverell estates—some of them in Scotland—had been neglected for so long that Richard was forced to travel for the rest of the year to make the acquaintance of managers and stewards who had never seen him before, in order to satisfy himself that his possessions were in good hands. For the most part they were. The late Lord Deverell had been better served than he merited.

So Lexi saw little of Richard during this time, and when he came back she had no time herself. Her own father was taken ill and they thought for a while that he was going to die. He needed weeks of careful nursing and Lexi spent long hours in the sick room with him. Richard frequently came to sit with Sir Jeremy, chatting to him about local affairs and his own plans for Channings, but after taking a look at Lexi's pale cheeks and heavy eyes he always insisted she should go out for a ride with Johnny, or a walk in the grounds. They seldom spent more than five minutes in each other's company, and hardly any time alone.

Then, to the consternation of all those who had rejoiced in his defeat the year before, Napoleon escaped from Elba. Out of the blue, Johnny and Richard were recalled to service by the only man who could have persuaded them to come back to the Army—their commander in the Peninsula, Wellington himself. Because of his father's recent illness, Johnny was given a post in London, but Richard was sent all round Europe with letters for Vienna, Brussels and the headquarters of other Allies as they all prepared for Napoleon's attack.

He returned to London in the spring of 1815 and joined Johnny, who was acting as one of Wellington's Liaison Officers at the Horse Guards. And at Easter they came down to Somerset for a whole week.

It was not altogether a happy visit. Richard seemed more than usually reserved, and Johnny was frequently moody, on edge and irritable. He was drinking more than he should, too. Lexi tried once or twice to ask him what was wrong, but he always put her off, and in the end she decided that if anyone was in Johnny's confidence it would be Richard. But she had to wait till the day before they left before she could ask him about her brother.

They had all three planned to visit the river bank again, but at the last minute Johnny lost his temper over some triviality and decided not to come. Lexi made no attempt to dissuade him. She could not afford to miss this golden opportunity to have a private chat with Richard…

The weather was warm and the Somerset countryside was at its loveliest—the lanes around Rawdon were lined with hedgerows full of greenish-yellow catkins and the bridal white of blackthorn. The banks and verges below were even more colourful with spikes of purple orchids surrounded by clumps of pale yellow primroses and the delicate wood anemones of spring. The river was full of activity as small animals and birds enjoyed the Easter sunshine and prepared to set up their families. Richard talked a lot of the old days, and, though she felt it was cowardly, Lexi was content to let him. Her own heart was full as she remembered how they had laughed years before at the antics of the otters, how she had wanted Richard to kiss her...

'This is wonderful!' he said, breathing in the fresh, sweet-scented air. 'You've no idea how much I've longed for it. After all my travels, to come home to this...' He turned to look at her. 'And to you. How are you, Alexandra?'

It was so unexpected that Lexi felt herself colouring. 'I...I...I'm well,' she stammered. 'But you know that. Why do you ask?'

'What about Transden? Is he well, too?'

She looked at him in astonishment. 'Transden? Mr Transden? I have no idea.'

'Really?' He sounded sceptical.

'Well, of course I haven't! Whatever made you think I should? I haven't seen or heard of Mr Transden since last summer.'

'Is that true?'

'Of course it is! He was a delightful dancing partner, but nothing more. What is all this? Why are you so curious about him?'

'Last year most of London thought you would marry him.'

'I can't help what people thought last year! But I assure you that I never had the slightest intention of marrying Mr Transden.'

'Lady Wroxford—' Richard began. He stopped and began again. 'When I saw Lady Wroxford in London recently she implied he was…he was still interested in you. She even seemed to think he might eventually persuade you to change your mind.'

Lexi could guess what Lady Wroxford had been up to. Her godmother had been seeing what a touch of jealousy might do. She said firmly, 'My godmother can't really think anything of the kind. She knows very well who—' She stopped short. She had nearly betrayed herself. 'She knows I have no interest in Mr Transden,' she said firmly, then went on, 'We shall stop talking nonsense and discuss something more important. I want to ask you about Johnny. There's something wrong with him and I want to know what it is.'

'What do you mean?' he asked. His tone was guarded.

'Don't put me off. I've asked Johnny himself, but he won't talk to me. I'm worried about him, and I was hoping you'd help. He's been so…so short-tempered, especially this morning. Not only with me, but with my father and the servants as well.'

'He probably had a hangover,' said Richard easily. 'We talked till late last night, and the wine flowed pretty freely. Don't worry, Alexandra. He'll come round.'

'Will he?' She was still doubtful. 'I wonder… I'm sure there's more to it than that.'

'A lot of the work we do at the Horse Guards is devilish dull, and Johnny gets bored. You know what he's like. He enjoys fighting in the open, where you can see your enemy, and the dangers are obvious. Chasing secret documents and looking after them is not the sort of activity he joined the army for.'

'I can quite see that. But why are you and Johnny doing such work? I thought you were still on active service?'

'We are! This is *very* active service, but it's not the kind Johnny is used to. Napoleon's spies would give their right arm to know some of the details in the Duke's letters—where he needs the men, what sort of defences, all the rest.' He added with a touch of impatience, 'I sometimes think Boney's spies are more interested in what Wellington needs than those fools in charge at the Horse Guards! And there's always someone willing to sell information...'

He stopped, and they walked for a moment on in silence. They came to a halt at the stile. Here she paused. 'Tell me, Richard,' she said abruptly. 'Is Johnny drinking?'

'Of course. We all do!'

'Don't be so evasive! You know what I mean. Is Johnny drinking too much?'

Richard hesitated. 'Perhaps. Certainly more than he used to. But don't worry, Alexandra. He's restless, but he'll be himself again as soon as we rejoin the regiment. It can't be long now—this break has come just in time. I doubt we'll still be here in England after next month.'

This was a shock. Lexi swallowed and said, 'I suppose that means you'll both be going into battle.'

'It looks very likely. This time it will be against Napoleon himself, not just his seconds-in-command the way it was in Spain. It won't be quite so easy. Wellington is up to it. If he gets enough men.'

'And I expect you'll both feel happier. But it's...it's hard for us. We can only sit at home and hope you don't get yourselves killed!' She tried to laugh, but it turned into a sob halfway through.

He stopped in surprise and turned to face her. 'Johnny and I will be all right, I promise. My dear girl, you mustn't cry! Don't, Alexandra! Please!'

'I know I'm stupid,' she replied, trying to wipe away the tears with her hand. 'You and Johnny came back unharmed from Spain. It's just…it's just that Papa and I had hoped the wars were ended, and that Johnny would soon be at home for good. Papa is getting old and…and *needs* him.' She scrubbed more vigorously as another tear rolled down her cheek.

'Here, let me do that!'

He took out an immaculate handkerchief and, taking her chin in his hand, wiped her cheek. He finished, but the hand stayed under her chin, and he gazed at her intently. 'And what about me, Alexandra?' he asked softly. 'Do *you* need *me*?'

She couldn't stop herself. Looking at him with her heart in her eyes, she said simply, 'More than my life.'

He drew a sharp breath. His lips barely moving, he said softly, 'Do you remember asking me once if I wanted to kiss you, here at this stile?'

'You said you didn't.'

'I lied to you. I wanted to all right, but you were too young. I had to wait. And then I kissed you at Vauxhall, and you were so angry… The kiss was everything I had dreamed of, but the waiting afterwards was even harder. Alexandra, if you knew how much that first time here by the stile has haunted me, how I have tried to forget it… But I never have. And now… If you were to ask me again if I wish to kiss you, I'll tell you the truth this time.' He put an arm round her, and lifted her chin.

Gazing deep into her eyes, he said softly, 'Ask me again, Alexandra.'

'Do you…do you want to kiss me, Richard?'

He smiled and then began to kiss her, at first gently, as if she were something infinitely precious, then, feeling her response, he cupped her face in his hands and kissed her eyes, her chin, her throat, seeking and finding the pulse beating wildly there. Then he took her into his arms and the kisses became more demanding. He seemed to envelop her, holding her so closely that she thought she could feel every bone and muscle of his body. Lexi's own bones were melting with delight. She felt no shame. This was where she wanted to be, this was what she had waited for all her life, or so it seemed. She was impatient to be absorbed by him, become part of him, she was nothing without him…

After a moment he took a deep breath and held her away. 'I…I think that's enough for the moment,' he said somewhat unsteadily. 'Dear God, Alexandra, you have such power over me. No one else can make me forget the world and everything else in it as you do.'

'Richard?' she whispered, unaware of the pleading note in her voice.

'We mustn't go any further,' he said, roughly. He gave an incredulous laugh. 'You are…totally desirable. But we mustn't go any further. You know that, don't you?'

When she looked away from him without saying anything, he gave her a little shake. 'Don't you, Alexandra?'

She nodded. Then, taking her hands in his, he kissed her gently and said, 'We only have to wait a little longer, my lovely one. My lovely, and…very dear Alexandra. Wait till after this business with the French is over. Then at long last it will be time to talk about our future…'

Chapter Four

In her bedroom at Channings, trapped, it seemed, in the marriage she had so longed for, Lexi turned her head frantically to and fro on the pillow. Why couldn't she forget? Those words of Richard's haunted her. They had been so tender, so full of promise. *'My lovely, and very dear Alexandra, my lovely and very dear Alexandra, my lovely Alexandra…Alexandra…'* No one else called her Alexandra. Richard always gave it a special sound… Why couldn't she *forget*?

Lexi groaned and turned over. A deep sob escaped her. Murdie was there. She got up and held a glass to her lips. It tasted bitter, and in a few minutes she felt herself falling thankfully into oblivion again…

The next day Murdie was sitting by the bed when Richard returned to his wife's bedside. 'I thought my aunt would be here,' he said. 'Where is she?'

'Her ladyship went to her own room, my lord. Lady Deverell was asleep, so she decided to have a rest herself.'

'I see. Well, you may go, too, Murdie. I've come to sit with my wife.' When Murdie hesitated he added firmly, 'I'm sure your mistress has need of your services.'

Murdie looked at him, her face carefully indifferent, then curtsied and left the room.

Richard cast a glance at the sleeping figure on the bed, then fetched the wing chair over from the window and sat down to wait. He was weary beyond measure. His careful plans had gone wildly astray, but if he was to save something from the wreck it was time to talk to Alexandra. She still didn't want him to. Even the damned maidservant knew that. But he had Dr Loudon's assurance that she was strong enough, strong enough even to get up, and he had decided not to wait any longer.

He still had no idea what they would say to one another…

So far, at least, there had been no hint of scandal. Only the five who had been there in the vestry knew of the sensational sequel to the wedding ceremony, and since then Alexandra had had no visitors. But if the situation continued as it was for much longer, the gossip would soon start. Some way of living together had to be found, if only for the next six months…

Richard put his head in his hands. After the tumult of the last few years, after so many barriers to his happiness, the prospect of settling down at last at Channings with Alexandra Rawdon had seemed…very attractive. He smiled warily. Attractive? Why couldn't he admit his real feelings, just for once, just to himself? He had longed for it passionately. He had known he was taking a risk in marrying her so hastily, so soon after the shock of her father's death, but it had seemed the only thing to do. That death had changed what had been a difficult situation into a nightmare…

Richard got up and walked restlessly about the room. He had other reasons for marrying Alexandra, but his betrothal and marriage to Sir Jeremy's heiress had given him access to the papers connected with the Rawdon estates. He had sorted out the worst of the problems before the wedding and hoped that with time he could deal with the rest, too, discreetly, before anyone else found out what the late owner of Rawdon Hall had done…

He glanced at the bed. Alexandra was still asleep. That had been the other, more important reason, of course. He had been desperate to take care of her. She had been left so alone in the world, without a home… Mark Rawdon was a pleasant enough fellow, but he was still something of a stranger. Alexandra could not have carried on living at Rawdon after her father's death. No, an early marriage had been necessary. But, in thinking it would solve *his* problems, he had been disastrously over-optimistic…

He looked again at the figure on the bed. What had caused Alexandra's sudden change of heart? Why had she turned against him? There had been no sign of it when he had asked her to marry him, and that had been a bare five weeks ago. She had changed some time shortly before the wedding. When he had tried to find out what was wrong her answers had been evasive and she had afterwards avoided him. Aunt Honoria had talked of pre-wedding nerves, and he had accepted that as the probable explanation. Not in his worst nightmares had he imagined she was planning anything like the scene in the vestry.

Would she have gone through with it and shot him if he hadn't intervened? He must have thought so then, or he wouldn't have thought it necessary to buy time

with that *lunatic* promise. Six months to prove her accusations wrong. How the devil was he to do it? Telling
her the truth would make nonsense of all his efforts of
the past few months. But one way or another he must
find a way of satisfying her. One thing was quite obvious. Someone, somewhere, wanted to make mischief
for the Rawdon family, and the sooner he found out
who it was the better it would be for everyone, Alexandra, Mark Rawdon and himself.

Damn the troublemaking villain, whoever he was.
Who had told Alexandra about that card game between
Richard and her father? She was far from stupid. She
wouldn't let it rest there. When she was herself again
she was certain to ask *why* her father had risked everything on the turn of a card. And what the devil would
he tell her? Jeremy and Johnny Rawdon were now both
dead, but what would it do to her to learn why her father
had been so ready to risk disaster and disgrace?

Richard shook his head. His plans may have gone
badly wrong, but he had at least succeeded in protecting
her father's reputation. No one now need ever know that
Sir Jeremy Rawdon, a former magistrate and a pillar of
society, had broken the law. It had taken a great deal
of his skill and time between Sir Jeremy's death and his
own marriage to Alexandra to straighten it all out, but
he had succeeded. Ironically, she now apparently held
his efforts against him.

It was even more ironic that she had accused him of
meddling with the evidence of Johnny's death. In that
instance she was perfectly right, of course... He had.

The figure on the bed sighed and stirred. Richard
moved over to the bedside and sat down.

'Could I have a drink of water?' she said in a cracked

voice. 'Dr Loudon's draughts always leave my mouth feeling so dry!'

Richard got up and poured a glass of water. He put his arm round her shoulders and held her upright. 'Here,' he said, holding it to her lips. 'Drink.'

Lexi's eyes flew wide open and an expression of horror appeared on her face. 'You!' she said with loathing. She struck the glass away with such force that water splashed down her nightgown and over the bedclothes.

'You stupid child, Alexandra!' said Richard irritably, as he picked up the glass and put it on the table. 'What do you think you're doing? I'm not an ogre!'

'I don't want anything to do with you! Fetch the maid! Fetch Murdie!'

'I'll fetch no one. I want to talk to you.'

She made a move to get up, but he pushed her back against the pillows and held her there, firmly. His face just inches away from hers, he said softly, 'You might as well listen, my dear. I've waited long enough. You're not leaving this room before we've had our talk, even if I have to use force to keep you here.'

'You can't do that!'

'Oh, yes, I can. We are man and wife, Alexandra. Had you forgotten? Short of murder, I can do anything with you. Anything at all. Do you understand? No one would dream of interfering with what I do here in your bedroom.'

Lexi slid down in the bed, her eyes dark with fear. 'Lady Honoria—' she began, with a quaver in her voice.

'Aunt Honoria won't help you. She's more likely to recommend a whipping if you're strong enough.'

Lexi's eyes grew larger and darker.

'But you needn't worry,' Richard said. 'I won't listen to her.'

She swallowed and drew the sheet up higher. 'Then...then what *are* you going to do?'

He pushed himself up and away, and stood regarding her for a moment. He said with a touch of bitterness, 'You surely don't really believe I'm about to join you in that bed and make love to you, do you?'

'You...you said we were man and w...wife,' she said nervously.

'My dear girl, I don't regard myself as particularly squeamish, but it would take a stronger stomach than mine to make love to a wife who has just threatened to kill me. What do you think I'm made of?'

Lexi gazed at him sombrely. 'I don't know,' she said eventually. 'I thought I did, but I was mistaken. For a while I *longed* for you to make love to me, I couldn't imagine anything I wanted more, but now I think I would *kill* myself if you even tried.'

Richard moved away abruptly and went to the window, where he stood, staring out. There was a short silence.

Then Lexi said, 'If it's not that, what *do* you want, Deverell?'

He turned round. 'We have an agreement. Are you prepared to discuss it with me?'

'It appears I have no choice.'

He nodded, then turned to the chest of drawers next to him. After a moment's search he came back with a fresh linen nightgown in his hands, which he put on the bed in front of her. 'Put this on before we start,' he said. 'You must be uncomfortable in that wet nightgown.'

'No!'

'Are you not yet strong enough to change your own nightgown?'

'Of course I'm strong enough! But I'm not going to undress while you're here!'

'Shall I remind you? I'm your husband. I have every right to be here. I could take every stitch off you if I chose, and no one could object. Do you wish me to do it?' His voice was perfectly even.

'No!'

'Then do as I say. Oh, if it makes you easier I'll look out of the window. But I'm not leaving this room, Alexandra.'

She sat up and hastily changed her gown, then lay down again, pulling the sheets up almost over her face. He turned and gave a grim nod when he saw her. 'I think you're quite strong enough to sit up. In fact, to-morrow you will *get* up and start your new life.'

Lexi stiffened. 'And what is that to be, pray?'

'That is what I want to discuss, my dear. Sit up like a good girl. If I give you another glass of water, will you throw it at me?'

'No, I'd like one, please,' she said sullenly, sitting up. 'I'm thirsty.'

When she had drunk he took the glass again and sat down in the wing chair. 'So far, so good,' he said. 'Now! We have to decide how we are to manage for the next six months, but I should like to sort one or two things out first.' He paused and eyed her curiously. 'Tell me when you first decided that you wanted to kill me. I don't think you had it in mind when you accepted my offer of marriage.'

'No,' she said in a low voice. They were both silent for a moment as they remembered her relief and happiness when he had asked her to marry him. There had been no doubts then. When he had insisted that the wedding should take place as soon as possible she had made no objection. Marriage to Richard had seemed then to be a safe haven in a time of distress.

'So…when did you…change your mind about me?'

'Very soon after. I heard two of the servants gossiping, and, though I know I shouldn't have, I listened.' She stopped. 'I almost wish now that I hadn't… They had seen you and Papa playing cards the evening before he died. Papa had been very angry, they said. He had accused you of ruining him and all his family.' She turned and looked straight into his eyes. 'And you haven't tried to deny it, have you, Deverell?' she said bitterly. 'You killed Johnny, and I suppose you might say that you killed my father, too. You took Rawdon from him, and he died the next day.'

'If you knew how much I regretted that whole business!' Richard's voice was constricted. 'I don't often make such disastrous mistakes. I wanted to help, I assure you.'

'Help? How "help"? By taking away everything my father lived for? By leaving him with *nothing*? You *knew* how much he loved Rawdon, how proud he was of his name, his inheritance! You *knew* how much he suffered when Johnny died. You even helped him to trace Mark Rawdon, so that he could invite his heir to live with us, to get to know and love Rawdon as much as he did! And what was left of Rawdon after you had done your worst? What was there to leave to Mark? The house, and a small farm, that was all! How could Rawdon possibly survive on *that*? My father died of a broken heart! And you are to blame!'

By this time tears were running down Lexi's cheeks as she stammered out her accusations at him. Richard got out of the chair and held up his hand.

'Don't! Don't, please! You'll make yourself ill again,

and I—' He stopped for a moment. 'I don't like to see you in such a state. We'll continue this talk another time.'

'No! We'll finish it now! I accepted your offer in good faith, Deverell. I wanted to marry you because I thought I loved you. But after I heard about that game I wanted never to see you again.'

'Why didn't you ask *me* about it? I thought you trusted me.'

'I wanted to. I tried to. But after that day you were never there! You were always closeted with the agents, the lawyers and all the others. I could never get near you!'

'That's not good enough, Alexandra. I had a lot of business to get through, which had to be finished before our marriage. But I would have made time for you if you had asked me. Why didn't you try harder to see me?'

'Because I thought of something better.'

'I can guess what it was. You decided not to break our engagement but to marry me after all, and ask for Rawdon as a wedding present. Was that it?'

'Yes. It was the only way to save Rawdon. I would get you to give the lands back to Mark, and…and my father's ghost would be happy.'

'And what about you in all this? Did you see yourself as a martyr to the cause?' he asked with a touch of bitterness. 'Was a lifetime in my contaminating presence a price you were prepared to pay?'

'I…I…Yes! Yes, I was.'

'And at what point did you decide that you couldn't face it after all? That killing me was a better solution?'

'No, no, you're wrong! It wasn't my plan to kill you

at all at first. I would have lived with you and been as good a wife as I could—'

He got up again. 'How very noble of you!' he said sardonically. 'Did it never occur to you that I might not want such a wife? Did it never cross your mind that I might, just might, have given what I had won back to you, out of friendship, without any strings at all? Did you never ask yourself *why* I had done such a terrible thing to your father, a man I had looked up to all my life? A *friend* of mine! Of course not! You never were strong on logic, were you?'

'What do you mean?' she demanded. He turned away and went back to the window. Lexi waited, then got out of bed, flung on her wrapper and came over to join him. 'What do you mean, Deverell? I don't believe you would have given it all back as easily as that! Why would you do that? Explain what you meant!'

When Richard turned his expression was not encouraging. Lexi stood and faced him. Her mane of hair had escaped from its ribbons and lay in wild disorder over her shoulders and down her back in a stream of copper curls. Below the nightgown and wrapper could be seen slender ankles and bare feet. But there was no sign of self-consciousness or fear as she demanded yet again, 'What did you mean?'

He looked down. 'Of *course* I never intended to keep what I had won! If your father had lived, I would have returned it all, once he had recovered his senses. But he…he was not himself. He had done something…foolish, something that would have damaged his reputation. I decided—on an impulse, I admit—to do what I could to put it right, or at least to cover it up, but he died before I could tell him what I intended to do.'

'What had he done?'

'You needn't concern yourself. It's all been taken care of since. That's why I was so busy before our wedding.'

'Tell me what it was! I demand to know!'

'I'm sorry. I can't tell you.'

Her eyes narrowed. 'It must have something to do with money,' she said reflectively. 'I know he had been borrowing a lot, and I didn't understand why he had to—Rawdon has always been so wealthy. But borrowing doesn't damage reputations...' She wandered back to the bed and sat down on the edge. She looked up. 'It wasn't the entailed land, was it?' When he made no reply she exclaimed, 'Oh, it can't have been! My father would *never* borrow against entailed land! It's not only dishonourable, it's against the law!'

'Alexandra, either get back into bed or ring for the maid and get dressed. It is not...sensible to wander about in your nightwear. And your hair—' Richard stopped. 'Your hair is very untidy.'

His sudden criticism distracted her as he had known it would. She looked at him with a touch of her old spirit. 'But we're man and wife, Deverell. Surely you cannot object to my being *déshabillée* in my own room?'

'On the contrary, my dear,' Richard said softly, coming closer. 'I find it very...appealing.'

Lexi hastily got back into bed and pulled the bedclothes around her. 'No, you don't,' she said defiantly. 'You haven't the stomach for me, remember?'

He gazed at her for a moment, then said, 'I think you must be feeling better. I'll send your maid to you. Tell her you wish to go downstairs for dinner. It would do you good to get out of this room for a while this evening. I'll call for you, and we'll go down together.'

On his way to the door he said, 'Aunt Honoria will be there this evening, so we'll postpone any further talk till tomorrow. Tonight we'll practise a little social behaviour, instead.'

'Aren't you afraid I'll make another scene?'

He stood at the door. 'I am quite sure you won't. I have your promise, remember?'

'There was nothing in that agreement about my behaving as your wife in company!'

'I was talking of the one you made in the church, Alexandra. The marriage service. Part of what we promised each other—till death us do part—was mutual society, help and comfort. I don't ask for any of the rest you promised me then, not for the moment, at least. So, can't you meet me halfway? You're not a girl who breaks promises willingly, and here is one that is easy enough to keep.'

'Why do you want me to keep you company? I would have thought you'd be happy to leave me to myself.'

He paused. After a moment he said, 'We don't wish to stir up gossip, especially as there are still so many unanswered questions between us. Let's put a brave face on our marriage in public, pretend it was for the right reasons. It may only be for six months. Can you do it?'

She looked at him, her eyes dark with unhappiness. 'I'll try,' she said. 'But don't attempt to tell me it will be easy. And if what you say is true, then I intend to find out what it was my father did, Deverell. Don't think you can put me off a second time!'

After Richard had gone she lay down again. For a moment she had forgotten his perfidy. He could be very persuasive when he exerted himself, and she...she was still so vulnerable, in spite of what she knew... She wondered if he had been speaking the truth about the card game. Richard's phenomenal success at all card games was a family joke. Her father must have been desperate indeed to risk playing with him for such high stakes. But why had Richard suggested it? It had seemed so out of character at the time that, as soon as she had heard of it, she had looked for Richard, to demand an explanation. But he was out for the day, talking to the lawyers.

Her maid came in at that moment and her chatter put an end to the debate in her mind. She needed quiet, solitude before she could think any more. After an hour of preparation Lexi was bathed and scented with lavender water, and her mass of hair had been brushed into a knot of silken copper on the top of her head, with a graceful cluster of curls falling down to touch the nape of her neck. A pale lilac gown, delicately embroidered in silver, a silver gauze shawl and silver slippers completed her toilette. She was nearly ready when Richard returned carrying a velvet case.

'I'd like you to wear these,' he said, opening the case and taking out a string of pearls. Lexi looked at them—the string was long, and the pearls perfectly matched. 'Another wedding present,' he said with a wry smile. 'There are earrings as well. They belonged to my mother.'

'I...I can't wear these,' said Lexi in a low voice.

'You can and will wear them, Alexandra.' Richard's tone of voice was pleasant, but there was an undercurrent of steel. He dismissed the maid with a nod, then sat Lexi down in front of the dressing table and stood behind her, looking at her reflection in the mirror. She gazed back defiantly.

'Put them on,' he said, unmoved. 'I'll fasten them for you.'

After a moment her eyes fell and with a slight shrug she wound the pearls twice round her neck. Richard took the ends, moved her hair to one side and fastened the clasp. The touch of his fingers on the back of her neck sent a shiver down her spine. He sensed it and looked up. Their eyes met. For a moment she saw the face of a stranger in the mirror, a man of feeling, of passion, even. A man suffering deep hurt. Then the moment passed and he was Richard again, calm, impassive Richard. He handed her the earrings.

'I think you can do these better than I. Or shall I fetch the maid back?'

'N...no. I can manage,' said Lexi, making an effort to speak normally. It took several attempts before her trembling fingers could manage to hook the earrings in. When she had finished she stood up and turned to face him.

'You look beautiful,' he said. 'Are you ready to play your part?'

Chapter Five

Lady Honoria was waiting for them in the saloon when they appeared.

'Well!' she said. 'You've made her come. I suppose you know what you're doing.'

'Let us say that I persuaded my wife she was well enough to come downstairs, Aunt Honoria. I told her how much we missed her.'

Lady Honoria shot him a glance. 'That's the way it's to be, is it? Well, I must say, Richard, she looks very well. That dress is particularly becoming. I see she's wearing your mother's pearls?'

'Of course. They are now hers. I see Kirby is at the door, Alexandra. Do you think he is indicating that we should go in to dinner?'

Lexi cast a glance at the butler, then looked at Lady Honoria, who said briskly, 'Don't look at me! You're now the lady of the house. It's entirely up to you when we dine, but I shouldn't keep Kirby waiting too long if I were you. He has to keep the cook happy.'

Kirby gave a disapproving cough. 'The cook will serve dinner when you say you are ready, my lady. Not before. May I say how pleased we all are to see your ladyship downstairs?'

Something of the old Lexi returned. 'Thank you, Kirby,' she said with a smile. Then she turned to Lady Honoria. 'Shall we go in?' she said.

Over dinner they kept up a flow of easy conversation, mostly between Richard and Lady Honoria, though Lexi joined in occasionally. In the absence of any large party to celebrate the wedding, they discussed who should be invited to dine with them during the next few weeks.

'There's no need, if you don't wish it, Lexi,' said Lady Honoria finally. 'It is perfectly acceptable for a recently married couple to wish to be alone for a time. Indeed, I think I ought to return home now that you're downstairs again. If Richard has decided to keep you here, that is to say.'

Even with this sting in the tail the thought of being left at Channings alone with Richard so appalled Lexi that she cried, 'No! No, don't go!'

'Of course we don't wish you to go,' said Richard. The servants had cleared the table and had now left the room, closing the doors behind them. He went on, 'You know very well that this marriage is different from most, Aunt Honoria.'

'Ha!' she exclaimed. 'Is that how you describe it? Different? I've seen some extraordinary marriages in my time, but this one beats the lot! Not many start off with the bride attempting to murder the groom. You're quite right, Richard. I would certainly call it different!'

'Aunt Honoria, you would do me a great favour if you could forget what happened in the vestry. Alexandra has agreed to act in public as if this marriage were normal, and I should like you to do the same. I shall have enough to do to keep the promise I made to her. I don't wish to cope with a tide of scandal as well.'

'What do you mean?'

'He means he has to be free to think up a story to account for the way he cheated my father,' said Lexi coolly.

Richard regarded her for a moment. 'I refuse to waste time on that,' he said. 'You don't think for one moment that I cheated.'

'Am I to understand that what Lexi said was true? You *did* play cards with her father, with Rawdon as the stake?'

'Yes, Aunt Honoria. That was perfectly true.'

'Then it was shameful! You must both have been drunk! It's no wonder she was angry, though nothing would excuse what I saw in that vestry! Is that why you gave it back as a so-called wedding present?'

'They weren't drunk,' said Lexi suddenly. 'But my father was desperate. He must have been.'

'Desperate?' asked Richard guardedly.

Lexi leaned forward. 'You can't have it both ways, Deverell. Either, you are a villain, and cheated my father out of Rawdon—and when I say cheated, I mean that you somehow tricked him into playing with you. No man in his right mind would play cards for high stakes with you, least of all my father, and *especially* not for Rawdon. Or, what you told me was the truth—Papa was in debt and you were trying to put things right. But if that was the case, why didn't you simply lend him the money—?'

Lady Honoria interrupted. '*Jeremy Rawdon?* In *debt*? I don't believe it! He was the most prudent of men, and Rawdon has always been a very prosperous estate! That is impossible!'

Richard got up from the table and walked over to the fire. He stared down at it for a minute or two, then he said, 'Not impossible. True. Jeremy Rawdon *was* in debt. The reason I couldn't lend him the money was that he refused it. And that's all I propose to tell you about it. Your father is dead, Alexandra, but his reputation is safe. Rawdon is still in the family, and clear of debt, which you say is what he would have wanted. We shall leave it at that. And now it is late. I suggest we bid each other goodnight.'

Lady Honoria got up. 'I know that voice. There's no point in arguing with Richard when he talks like that. We shall go to bed. But it must have cost you a fortune to rescue Jeremy Rawdon's reputation, Richard, though I don't suppose you'll tell me how much.'

'More than you can possibly imagine, Aunt Honoria,' said Richard somewhat grimly.

Lady Honoria turned to Lexi. 'Richard shouldn't have played cards with your father, but he doesn't lie. I believe what he says. I still think your behaviour in the vestry was unpardonable, but if he is prepared to forgive you then I suppose I shall have to as well. But I'd like to know whether you intend to carry on living here in Richard's house, eating Richard's food, accepting Richard's protection, without releasing him from that monstrous bargain he made with you. I don't believe even you can do that. You must forget it. Goodnight!'

She went out. Richard came over to Lexi, who was still sitting at the table. He held out his hand. 'She's gone. There no need to say anything. You've done very well tonight, but you look tired now. May I escort you upstairs?'

As they approached the door of Lexi's room Richard

said with a touch of impatience, 'I can feel you stiffening by the minute. You needn't worry. I don't expect you to invite me in—nor do I intend to demand any privileges of a husband. Not yet, anyway. When this is all over—'

'You sound very confident,' she said sharply, more from relief than from any real feeling of anger.

'I have to be. But you needn't worry. In spite of what Aunt Honoria said, I shan't try to renege on our bargain.'

She looked at him for a moment, her eyes full of painful doubt. 'She's right. I wish...I wish we hadn't made it. I'm still not sure how you intend to keep it, or even if I want you to...' Her voice tailed off. She began again. 'I believe you meant what you said about trying to prove me wrong, and I wish I could believe the rest, but I can't, Deverell! I *can't*. Did you really mean to save my father, not ruin him? Or are you telling me a pack of lies? I don't know! I just don't know!' Her voice rose a fraction. 'I'm not sure any more *what* to believe!'

'Come! We're making progress. Two days ago you were quite certain. Go to bed, Alexandra. We'll talk about it tomorrow. Goodnight.'

'Goodnight,' she murmured in a low voice. He waited till she had gone in and shut the door, then walked away to his own rooms.

The next morning he came to her just as she had finished dressing.

'I see I've timed it well,' he said with a smile. 'Shall we talk here, or would you prefer to use the library?' He examined her dove-grey dress, its white collar a foil to her vivid colouring, its simple lines flattering her slender figure. 'That dress is very becoming, by the way.'

'I'll come downstairs,' she said.

'Have you had breakfast?'

'In *bed*? Of course not!' The scorn and surprise in her voice made him laugh.

'It was a harmless enough question! My aunt never stirs out of her room before noon, and I believe she usually has chocolate and rolls before she gets up. I thought the housekeeper might have done the same for you.'

'She did, but I sent them back. I've had enough time in bed.' She dismissed the maid with a nod, then said, 'I've been thinking, and I've decided you're right, Deverell. Whatever may happen at the end of six months, we have to find a way of living together till then. So I agree. In public, at any rate, we shall be a normal couple. I know I can trust you not to take advantage of it in private.'

'Do you, indeed?' he murmured with a wry smile. 'For once you have more faith in me than I have, my dear. But I'll do my best to live up to it.' He laughed as she stared at him and went on briskly, 'This sounds more like the old Alexandra. You must be feeling better. But I was hoping for more than passive toleration from you. I shall need your help if we are to sort out our differences before my six months are up. First let me take you down to the breakfast room, and then we shall talk.'

After breakfast they went to the library. It was a handsome room with a leather-covered desk and comfortable chairs, and a fire was burning in the hearth. Lexi had never been in the room before. Her previous visits to Channings had not been frequent, and had usually been confined to the stables, kitchens and similar places, with the occasional foray into the saloon or dining room. When Richard's father had been alive the library had been his private domain, and not for visitors of any kind, not even his son. She walked over to the windows.

They overlooked a lawn that led down to a lake with an ornamental bridge over the river which fed it at the far end. At this time of year the huge banks of rhododendrons that edged the lawn were a mass of leaves, their early summer flowers only a faint memory. Magnificent beeches, limes, chestnuts overhung the edges of the lake, their branches, covered at this season with leaves of green, gold, and bronze, almost touching the surface. A large number of ducks, coots and moorhens busied themselves, quacking and squawking, on the banks and in the water, all ignored by two swans who were sailing gracefully towards the bridge.

'I hadn't seen this view before,' she said. 'It's beautiful.'

'For years I've planned to make Channings into the family home it could be,' said Richard. 'It was always beautiful, but somehow, compared with Rawdon, it was…soulless. After my mother died my father spent a great deal of time in this room, but he didn't care about the rest of the house—or indeed anything else.'

'When did she die?'

'Just after I was born.'

'You don't remember her, then?'

'No. I knew your mother much better.'

'She died early, too, but I can at least remember her. As you know, I was ten at the time.'

'She was very kind to me. All your family were.

Rawdon was more of a home to me than Channings ever was. My father hardly knew I existed, and certainly didn't care.'

She gave him a fleeting look. They were drawing close to dangerous ground here. The memory of Johnny suddenly hovered like a ghost between them.

He nodded. 'Shall we sit down? I've told the servants not to disturb us.'

They sat by the fire, and after a moment or two Richard, who was now looking very serious, began, 'You accused me of two crimes, Alexandra. Unlike Aunt Honoria, I don't think you were suffering from a brainstorm when you threatened me. You really believed I was guilty of both. Why were you so certain? You said you heard the servants talking about the card game. Did anyone else hear them?'

'Mark was there.'

Richard stiffened. 'Mark Rawdon? What did he say about it?'

'He didn't say anything to me. He didn't know I was there. He was down below in the hall with the servants. I was upstairs on the landing.'

'Mark Rawdon was *gossiping* with the servants about your father?'

'No, no! Mark came along in the middle of their conversation and asked them what they were talking about. When he heard what they had to say, he couldn't believe it, and made them repeat it to him, particularly what Papa had said and how he had looked. But they were quite sure about it all. He…he told them not to talk about it to anyone else in case it came to my ears. That I would be very distressed. But it was already too late, of course. I had heard it all.'

'I see.' Richard was deep in thought. At last he said,

'So you looked for me and couldn't find me. Did you really try?'

'Of course I did! I had trusted you. But then when you seemed to be avoiding me—'

'You concluded that there was something in it after all.'

'It seemed clear enough. The night before he died you and Papa had quarrelled, and he was very distressed. Don't forget, he died the next day.'

'As if I could.' Richard got up and went to stare out of the window.

Lexi went on in a low voice, 'Hearing about that game was such a shock. A further shock on top of so many others... I felt at first that I wanted nothing more to do with you, certainly not to marry you.'

'But then you thought up your plan to save Rawdon. Did you...did you discuss that with anyone else? Mark, for example?'

'A little. It was difficult. As he said, he couldn't really give me an unbiased opinion—he stood to gain so much personally. He saw it from a man's point of view, of course. My father had played with you knowing the risks, and had lost, and he thought it was perfectly correct that you took what was yours—a debt of honour. But he eventually understood how much I wanted Rawdons to continue living at Rawdon Hall and he agreed.'

'I see,' said Richard thoughtfully. 'Very understandable, all of it. Though I can't help wishing your damned cousin had not questioned those servants so very thoroughly!'

'He didn't know I was listening! And I think it was fortunate I heard what I did. At least my eyes were opened and I knew the sort of man I was marrying.' After a silence she added, 'Or I thought I did. But if I

was mistaken about that game, why can't you tell me
what was really wrong with Papa?'

'I...I can't.'

'Are you trying to protect me?' Her voice hardened.
'Or was I right after all, and you're just *pretending* to
protect me, to hide the fact that you're guilty?'

He swung round and said violently, 'God damn it,
it's no pretence, Alexandra! Do you seriously think I'd
put myself through this...this painful and humiliating
process just to save my own face? In an effort—vain,
as it turned out—to preserve your good opinion of me?'

Richard's passion was so unusual that it shook Lexi.
It convinced her as nothing else could have. She said
slowly, 'You really mean it. You *are* trying to protect
me, aren't you? From what?'

But Richard had recovered. His manner was a touch
abrupt, but perfectly normal as he said, 'It doesn't matter. I thought for a while there was some malice afoot,
that someone had tried deliberately to make mischief.
But now it's clear—you heard about that game by pure
chance. There's no need to examine it further.'

'*You* began this discussion, but now that we've
started, we'll carry on till *I* think it's finished! I may
have suffered some body blows recently, but I'm still
the same Lexi Rawdon, still able to use my wits. If I
have been wrong, Richard Deverell, I want to know
more than the fact that my father played cards and lost
to you. I want to know why he risked it!'

'So you haven't forgotten my name.'

'What?'

'You've been calling me Deverell ever since we married. You just called me Richard again.'

'I didn't. I called you Richard Deverell. And it has
been quite intentional. I'll call you Deverell until I'm

satisfied I was wrong about you. Completely and absolutely wrong! Richard belongs to the past and I loved and trusted him. But at the moment he doesn't exist any more—not for me.'

Richard set his jaw. 'I *shall* prove you wrong, you know. You'll learn to trust me again.'

'Well, start by telling me the whole story!' She waited, then went on, 'You said yesterday that Papa had done something foolish. But if you're telling the truth, then it was more serious than that, wasn't it? Papa had broken the law by borrowing against the Hall and Home Farm, hadn't he? Entailed land. Don't look at me so impassively, I know I'm right. It's the only explanation.'

Richard shrugged his shoulders and said, 'Yes. And that's enough. It's all sorted out now. I tell you it's over, Alexandra!'

'No, it isn't!' She got up and came over to join him at the window. 'You must tell me *why* he was in debt. What he had done.' She paused, waiting for him to respond. When he stayed silent she went on more persuasively, 'You needn't be afraid that it will change my feelings for Papa. *Whatever* he did, I wouldn't love him any the less for it. Loving people doesn't blind you to their faults. You love them in spite of them. I remember saying that to you once before. Do you?'

'Yes. Of course I remember. I remember very well. But what you said then doesn't apparently apply to me.' In her eagerness to convince him Lexi had put her hand on his arm. She stared at him, feeling the tension in the muscles of his forearm, and her eyes widened as the truth of what she had just said hit her. She might hate Richard Deverell, might truly believe him to be a cheat and a liar, responsible for her brother's death, but he was wrong. Deep down, in spite of it all, she loved him still. He looked at her hand, and she snatched it away. She mustn't weaken...

'You're different,' she said scornfully. 'Your faults are rather more serious. But I won't let you distract me. Had Papa...gambled the money away?'

'No. Aunt Honoria told you. Your father was no gambler.'

'But he was willing to risk *Rawdon* on a thousand-to-one chance that he could beat you. Rawdon meant more to him than anything else. He must have been absolutely desperate. Why wouldn't he let you lend him money? It can't have been pride—he regarded you as family.'

'I...I wanted to make conditions, which he wouldn't accept. Look, Alexandra, this isn't what I want—'

Lexi said fiercely, 'It's what *I* want, Deverell. If we are to work together at all, I want to know everything! Otherwise I shall simply wait out the six months in my own way.'

'That sounds serious. No co-operation? No company?'

'None! I shall make it more than clear to everyone what I really think of you. I'll even tell them all how I tried to kill you! *I* don't at all mind creating a scandal, but I don't think *you* would like it. The great Lord Deverell nearly shot by his wife at their wedding! What an item for the scandal sheets! You hushed up the business in the vestry pretty effectively, but I could soon let it all out. So tell me about my father, or I swear I will!'

Richard shook his head. 'Oh, no! You can't get your way by threats, my dear. You're making a big mistake, if you think *I'm* the sort of man to submit to blackmail.'

Lexi was quick. Something in his voice, something

he hadn't quite been able to prevent, alerted her. Her eyes widened and she gazed at him in dawning comprehension. Richard started to say something, but she shook her head.

'No! Be quiet! Don't try to distract me again! I won't let you. *You're* not the sort to submit to blackmail. No, not you. But...is it possible Papa *was*?' She stopped and thought a moment. 'Yes, of course, that was it! *That's* why he was so desperate. And you refused to lend him any money because, as you've just said, you don't believe in submitting to blackmail. No, Deverell! Don't shake your head like that! Don't try to put me off. I'm not a child! Trust me with the truth. If my father was ruining himself by paying some blackmailer everything he had, I have a right to know!'

Richard's expression was a mixture of admiration and doubt. After a moment's thought he shrugged and said briefly, 'Yes, he was. He didn't know where to turn next for money.'

Lexi was thunderstruck. 'I didn't really think it could be true,' she said in a daze. 'What had he done? What could Papa possibly be blackmailed for? It's impossible!'

'He was, but I won't tell you what for, whatever you threaten. Your father suffered for months to keep his secret. I won't betray him now.'

Lexi nodded. She had not really expected any other reply, though she fully intended to find out sooner or later. Instead she asked, 'What were you going to do about it?'

'By winning all he had left I had effectively made it impossible for him to pay any more. Rawdon had already been drained practically dry. Anything more and it would have gone under. I had at least saved a little.

But my plan didn't stop there. I intended to find out who the villain was and put an end to his game.' His mouth tightened and he suddenly looked dangerous. 'One way or another.'

Lexi nodded. She could guess what Richard meant. If she ever found out who the blackmailer was, she would do the same.

He went on, 'I didn't think that would be too difficult. Only a small number of people could possibly have known enough about the…the affair. But your father didn't believe I could.' He frowned and was silent for a moment. 'I hoped the blackmail would stop after his death, and I think it has. Alexandra, my dear, I wanted to spare you the pain of knowing all this. I'm sorry.'

Lexi looked at him bitterly. 'Why didn't you tell me before? Why didn't you trust me?' she asked. 'You didn't *spare* me pain, Deverell, you caused me so much more!' She turned away and went back to the fire. The room was silent for a while.

Richard looked at the dejected figure in the armchair by the fire and came over to her. His voice was gentle as he said, 'I'm sorry. I should have realised…'

Lexi jumped up and faced him, blue eyes burning in a white face. 'I don't want your pity!' she said fiercely. 'And if you're trying to apologise, then I suggest you apologise for the right fault! You should never have kept me in the dark as you did! Why didn't *I* see how unhappy he was? He was my father and I loved him! But he, too, kept it from me. You and I together might have saved him. Now it's too late, and I don't know what to say or do! I hate being treated like a child, Deverell! I hate feeling so dependent on you!'

'Believe me, Alexandra, I do not regard you as a child. Not any more.'

'Then treat me as a responsible being! In future share the problems with me, don't shut me out!'

'Just a moment! Was that melodramatic scene in the church the act of a responsible being? I hardly think so!'

'I…I was under stress. It wasn't just about my father—there was Johnny, too.'

'Ah, yes. Johnny.'

'You won't find it easy to explain that away, Deverell.'

He regarded her in silence. 'I can hope,' he said. 'After all, I've convinced you about your father, haven't I?' When she stayed silent he repeated it. 'Haven't I?'

'Yes, damn you! I misjudged you. But it was your own fault!'

Richard looked at her flushed cheeks and overbright eyes. 'Perhaps. Shall we leave the question of Johnny for another time? I think you've had enough for now. I'm not ducking the question, Alexandra. I've told you—I had nothing to do with Johnny's death, whatever you may or may not have heard. But I think we both need a pause from all this drama.' He waited, then added, 'I intend to ride over to Rawdon in about half an hour. I still have one or two things to do there. Do you wish to rest or will you come with me? The fresh air might do you good.'

Lexi sensed that her answer was important to him. Though she was not tired, she was desperate to be alone for a while, to think over what she had just learned. But she hadn't been out for the past three days, and a ride to Rawdon would undoubtedly do her good. She hadn't seen Mark since the wedding. Lady Honoria had been right, too—she *had* done Richard a grave injustice, and perhaps she owed him something. But then she thought of Johnny and her feelings hardened. They hadn't even started on the question of Johnny...

She stole a glance at him and saw that he had taken her hesitation for a refusal and gone back to the window. 'Thank you,' she found herself saying. 'I'd like that. At two?'

Chapter Six

That afternoon Richard watched Lexi coming down the steps in front of Channings. She looked business-like, and very beautiful, in a dark blue riding dress, a fall of white at her throat. She was holding up the long skirt over her arm. Her glorious hair was caught up in a net under a stylish hat, and she wore tan gloves and boots. He saw that the dark shadows under her eyes had faded a little and she had some colour in her cheeks again.

The sun was shining, the air cool but fresh in a slight breeze. It was a lovely afternoon. For the first time since that disastrous scene in the vestry Richard allowed himself some hope. They had made considerable progress that morning. Alexandra was no longer so sure of his guilt in the matter of the card game, and with luck he might be able to weather Johnny's affair, too. By God, she was quick, though! He had never doubted her wit, but he had been surprised at the speed with which she had reached the conclusion that her father had been being blackmailed. Something Richard had said, or perhaps in the way he had said it, must have betrayed him. He must remember to take more care in the future.

They set off towards Rawdon, the horses still fresh, and dancing and curvetting in the breeze. As they came to the fields at the end of the drive Richard caught Lexi's eye, and saw she was remembering, as he was, how often they had ridden this way between Channings and Rawdon in the past. Happy occasions. Johnny had made a third, of course… Johnny. Always a ghost in the background…and a very troublesome ghost, too. Even now, the shock at what Johnny had done, the feeling that he had never really known the man who had been his closest friend, was always there at the back of Richard's mind, bedevilling his own efforts to conceal what he *knew* to be true. Against this background, convincing Alexandra that he was innocent of Johnny's death was going to be far more tricky to manage. How the devil was he to do it?

'Come on, Deverell! Let's get rid of their fidgets! I'll race you to the mill pond!' Lexi swirled her horse round and set off at a fair pace. Temporarily dismissing his doubts and troubles, Richard decided to enjoy the present. He raced after her, his powerful stallion making short work of the distance between them. They reached the end of the fields together.

'That was wonderful!' Lexi cried, as they reined in at the approach to the village. 'It seems an age since I rode like that. Castor hasn't lost any of his speed, I see.' No shadows now. Her eyes were sparkling jewels, her cheeks glowing with colour.

Richard patted the stallion. 'No, he's good for a few more years yet. But I shall have to buy more horses. We'll need a new carriage and pair, perhaps a phaeton. And if we go to London next spring we'll need more than that.'

'Next spring?' she faltered.

Richard took a breath and said firmly, 'We can't keep stopping and starting because of what might happen in six months, Alexandra. Shall we ignore that date in March for the moment? Shall we pretend we are an ordinary couple with an ordinary couple's plans for the future? That would include a visit to London for the Season next year, and the purchase of more carriages and horses. Life will be impossible if we keep reminding ourselves of what might happen before we get there. Don't you agree?'

'You seem to be able to manage such things better than I can, Deverell. But I'll try. Shall we go on?'

Some of the enjoyment had gone out of the day, but when they arrived at Rawdon, Mark Rawdon's welcome made them both feel better. He was unaffectedly pleased to see them, complimented Lexi on her looks, and congratulated Richard on his success in handling the situation at the church.

'I haven't heard a single breath of rumour,' he said, as they settled down in the salon. He looked from one to the other and smiled. 'You cannot imagine how delighted I am to see that matters between you appear to have been happily resolved. Will you now admit, Lexi, how wrong you were to judge Richard so badly? And allow me to wish you both every joy?'

'Yes,' she said. 'Thank you. Tell me, Mark, how is Rawdon faring?'

'Very well! It's early days yet, of course. The estate has suffered somewhat during the past year, but no lasting damage has been done. No, I hope you will soon be satisfied with what I shall do with Rawdon, Lexi. And I owe it all to you.' He gave Richard a deprecatory nod. 'And, of course, to Deverell!'

'Mark, what do you know about Papa's debts?'

He looked surprised at the sudden question. He threw a quick glance in Richard's direction, then said gravely, 'Not a great deal. Your father was already short of money when I came on the scene after…after your brother died. He was already borrowing against the estate then. I was never very sure why. I suppose I assumed he had made some unfortunate investments—something of that nature. Why?'

'Nothing, really. I was just trying to understand what happened. He loved Rawdon so much…' Her voice faltered.

'I shall work hard, Lexi. I shan't let you or your father down.'

'I'm sure you won't! You know, when…when we heard that Johnny had died, the only consolation Papa could find was that there was still a Rawdon to carry on at the Hall. That's why he sent Richard to look for you.'

Mark smiled. 'I wasn't hiding! I had already written to your father to say how sorry I was to hear of your brother's death. He knew where I lived.'

Richard spoke for the first time. 'Sir Jeremy was surprised to hear you even existed! He hadn't heard of his cousins for so many years.'

'Yes, well, my grandfather, Harcourt Rawdon, was a bit of a black sheep. My father wasn't very proud of him. After Harcourt married my grandmother, he spent all her money then deserted her, leaving her alone to bring up their baby son. I believe he died soon after in a drinking bout.'

Lexi's voice was full of sympathy. 'I didn't know this. You haven't spoken of it before, Mark.'

'I'm not exactly proud of it. And I'm not sure why

I'm boring you with it now,' he said with an apologetic smile.

'No, no! It's not boring! What happened to your grandmother and her baby?'

'They lived on charity from her relatives until Father was old enough to make a living, then he looked after her himself until she died. Afterwards he was fortunate enough to meet and marry a highly respectable young lady in Northampton, the daughter of one of the manufacturers there, and did his best to forget his connection with the Rawdons of Somerset. It was pure chance that I read about Johnny in one of the newspapers, and wrote my letter of sympathy. My own father had died the year before and I thought it time to heal the rift.'

'So you had no idea that you were the next in line, so to speak?' asked Richard, idly.

'Not the slightest! I suppose I ought to have, but I'd never really thought about it. Having been brought up in trade, I had imagined I wouldn't be welcome.'

'What nonsense! I am so glad you wrote, Mark!'

Mark nodded. 'So am I, Lexi! Not only for myself, but for your father.' He leaned forward and put his hand over Lexi's. 'And for you, too. I'm glad I was here for you.'

Richard had been looking thoughtful, but at this he got up. 'We all are,' he said briskly. 'Rawdon, there are still one or two papers in Sir Jeremy's desk, which I haven't yet dealt with. Once I've cleared those up I'll hand over the key, and the desk and its contents will all be yours. Would you mind if I looked at them now?'

'Not at all! If Lexi agrees, I shall take her on a tour outside the house while you do that. May I?'

Richard hesitated, then said calmly, 'Of course! I shan't be too long.'

* * *

Lexi had at first been happy to visit what had been her home till such a short time before, but after half an hour she found the associations too painful, and left Mark in the stables talking to one of the grooms. She went back inside in search of Richard, and found him, as she had expected, in the library. She paused at the door. Richard hadn't heard her approach. He was too absorbed in reading what looked like a page torn out of a notebook, and he had an expression of such cold fury on his face that she caught her breath. This was a man who could kill without thinking twice about it. But when he looked up and saw her standing there his expression cleared as if by magic. He crumpled the paper up and thrust it into his pocket.

'I thought you'd be much longer,' he said. 'Surely you weren't bored? Or was it too painful?'

'A...a little,' said Lexi, still dazed by what she had seen. What had been in that piece of paper to make Richard look like a man she had never known? Lexi felt confused. Last night she had seen a stranger in the mirror, a man of deep feeling, so unlike the famously cool Richard Deverell. And now again today...

She went on, 'But I thought you might have finished. I suppose we ought to get back—it'll be dark before we're home.'

'Home?'

Lexi coloured painfully. 'Your home. And I suppose my home, too. I have no other. Not now.'

'My poor girl,' said Richard. He came over and drew her to him, holding her so closely that she could feel his heart beating. 'No, don't push me away,' he said, his voice not quite steady. 'I'm offering comfort, not passion. You're safe.' He rested his cheek on her hair.

'We'll go home as soon as I've packed these papers up.'

Lexi stayed for a moment in his arms, a feeling of bitter regret flooding her. It could all have been so different; she and Richard should be returning to Channings in love and confidence, going back to a home they would make theirs together... A voice deep inside was trying to tell her that Richard *was* to be trusted, but she rejected it. He might well be telling the truth about her father, but there were things he still hadn't told her. The question of Johnny's death lay like a wall of stone between them, and, though he had sworn he was innocent, his reluctance to discuss it had not escaped her. Until she knew the truth about that too, she and Richard could never really be close again.

She released herself. 'Thank you,' she said quietly.

A few minutes later, after making an arrangement for Mark to visit them, they took their leave and set off.

They rode back to Channings almost in silence. Richard seemed preoccupied on the way back, and Lexi's thoughts were busy with what she had seen from the door of the library. Why hadn't she found that piece of paper when she had gone through her father's things? Even from the door she had recognised what it was— another page torn out of his diary. She had found its twin just two days before she had married Richard.

The memory of what that had told her, combined with the look she had surprised on Richard's face just a short while ago, brought back some of the nightmare... She shivered and her horse faltered in its stride.

'Something wrong?' Richard had drawn up beside her.

'No!' she said, forcing herself to speak normally.

He must have sensed something for he went on, 'We stayed too late. I should have remembered you've just spent three days in bed and brought you back sooner. I'm sorry.'

'Don't be,' she said stiffly. 'I'm perfectly all right.'

'Sure?'

'Quite.'

He hesitated then nodded and they set off again.

Lexi's mind returned to the moment she had discovered proof that Richard had killed Johnny. It had been two days before the wedding, and she had been going through the papers on her father's desk, gathering together things she wanted to take to Channings with her. Among them was his diary, and when she had picked it up one page had fallen out. The page was from the beginning of June, a couple of weeks after Johnny's death. She had read the familiar crabbed script again and again, unwilling to believe what she saw. The words had burned themselves into her memory...

Till today I would have said Richard Deverell was the soul of honour. I can hardly believe that a man whom I have regarded as a second son could have lied to us. But it now seems that he was not only there when Johnny died—something he has always denied—but that he tampered with the evidence afterwards to make it look as if Johnny killed himself accidentally. Why would he do this? I refuse to believe that my son took his own life. What reason could he possibly have for such a dreadful act? Did Richard Deverell kill Johnny by accident, perhaps? Did he then cover up the truth to save his own skin? Is that what happened? If that is so, how can Richard Deverell live with him-

self? Perhaps he doesn't expect to for long. To-morrow he leaves to rejoin his regiment in Belgium. The fighting could start there at any time now.

I have sent for him. I must find out the truth before he leaves tomorrow. Did he lie to us or not?

At the bottom of the page was the culminating blow. Her father was clearly distraught, the writing was ill spaced and very uneven, the sentences disjointed. But the message was still devastating.

My heart is heavy this evening. I have spoken to Deverell. He admits it, but refuses to say why. What am I to think? My poor boy! My poor, poor boy!

Lexi had not slept for weeks beforehand. Her nerves were already at breaking point, haunted as she had been by Richard's betrayal of her father and the necessity to marry him in order to save Rawdon. The discovery of that page had tipped the balance and driven her out of her mind. Accident or not, Richard had killed her brother! And, since he had not died at Waterloo, it was up to her to kill him in return. Full of rage and grief, she had gone about her plans with the obsessive cunning of a madwoman—her father's pistol concealed in the vestry beforehand, the marriage, the signatures, the handing over of the all-important deed, then the climax when Richard would suffer retribution. But in the end she hadn't been able to do it. She doubted now she could ever have done it, even if Richard had not offered her a way out.

Now, riding back along the lanes to Channings, Rich-

ard at her side, Lexi realised that she had been lucky.
Hours of sleep during the past three days, and freedom
from weeks of stress, had restored her to reason, and
she was suddenly sure that Richard had been telling the
truth about her father. There *was* a blackmailer, and
Richard *had* been trying to do something about him.
The bargain he had offered in the vestry had saved her
from an act of insanity, for, if she had killed Richard
as she had planned, not only would she have been a
murderess, but her father's persecutor would have gone
unpunished.

She stole a glance at him. If she had been wrong
about his dealings with her father, had she been too
hasty to condemn Richard for Johnny's death, too? But
that was sheer wishful thinking, she thought sadly. The
diary entry had been quite explicit. She would have to
wait till Richard chose to explain—if he could. But first
they must find the criminal who had blackmailed her
father. *Then* she would examine the story behind
Johnny's death.

Where had Richard found the page he had stuffed
into his pocket? She was quite sure it hadn't been anywhere near the desk before. She was consumed with
curiosity about it. Richard had looked very dangerous
indeed when he had it in his hand. Lexi made up her
mind to see it somehow or other, and soon.

They dined together that night, and the next. Richard
was out most of the next day on the estate, and Lexi
spent the time examining the boxes and trunks that had
been sent from Rawdon before the wedding. She had
taken little interest in them before, but now, it seemed,
she would need her clothes and possessions for a while.
She avoided thinking about what would happen after-

wards. Richard had taken trouble to prevent gossip about his marriage, and, in spite of her threats on that first morning in the library, she was grateful to him. She would do her best to keep up the fiction of a happy marriage.

So far Lady Honoria's maid had attended to her in the sickroom—Murdie was experienced, and, moreover, could be trusted to keep her own counsel on what happened there while Lady Deverell was ill. But now that Lady Deverell was herself again, it was time Murdie went back to her mistress, and Lady Deverell's own maid, Cissie, took over. Life must be returned to normal at Channings. So, together with Cissie, Lexi sorted out dresses and shawls for use in the coming months, and arranged some personal possessions on the chests and tables. Then, leaving her maid to put the rest away, she went downstairs to join Lady Honoria.

She had reached a kind of armed neutrality with Richard's aunt. The old lady was still not sure what to make of the situation, but, in spite of her sharp tongue, she was sincerely fond of her nephew and had no desire to make life any more difficult for him. She had decided therefore to forget everything to do with the scene at the wedding, including Richard's promise. And she vaguely hoped, indeed, that everyone else would, too.

So she began their conversation by saying, 'You seem to have made a complete recovery from your... your illness, Lexi. I'm delighted. A day or two more and you will be ready, I dare say, to take up the reins at Channings. There's a great deal to be done. It's years since anyone took an interest in the house. Richard's mother was full of plans, but she died, poor girl, before they could be carried out.'

'Did she write them down or have any drawings?'

'Yes, I'm sure she did. They must be somewhere in the library—probably in the big desk there. I'm sure Richard would find them for you.'

Lexi's heart jumped. 'Is that where he keeps his important papers?' she asked, trying to speak casually.

'Some of them. He has others somewhere in his bedchamber. Not the one he's in at the moment. The master bedroom.'

'Where is that?'

'Why, two doors away from your own, of course! The suites are connected.'

'Of...course...'

'Now that you are recovered,' said Lady Honoria, fixing Lexi with her eye, 'I expect he'll move back into the master bedroom. You are so recently married it would soon cause gossip if he didn't. These things always get out.'

'Yes, of course,' said Lexi slowly. 'I hadn't realised...'

'Now, what other plans have you? Will you spend Christmas at Channings?'

Lexi pulled herself together. 'I expect so. Though Richard was talking of buying a new carriage. And horses. I don't know whether that will mean a visit to London.'

'Ah, yes! London! I was surprised to hear from Mary Shackleton the other day that you had a highly successful Season there last year.'

'Moderately would be a better choice of word. But why were you surprised, ma'am? Am I such an antidote?'

'Not at all! No, I wouldn't have questioned your looks, though you'll agree they are somewhat unusual. No, it was your behaviour I doubted. The *ton* are very ready to criticise anyone who steps out of line. If you had a successful Season, you must have changed considerably since I last saw you. You were always such a hoyden in the past.'

Lexi's colour rose, but she replied calmly, 'Everyone changes with age, ma'am. Were you as outspoken as this when you were a girl? I hardly think so.'

Surprise kept Lady Honoria silent for a moment. Then she gave a bark of laughter. 'I would have been whipped if I had been.' She shook her head and said in a more conciliatory tone, 'You'll have to excuse me. I'm very fond of Richard. I wanted him to have the best. He's an important figure in the county now—he needs a wife who can live up to important occasions, run Channings, and, of course, play a part in the social life of London. I confess I was worried about his choice at first. But from what Mary Shackleton says, you're capable of all that. And now that you've recovered from that brainstorm I see no reason why you and Richard should not be perfectly happy together. I shall leave Channings tomorrow.'

'No!'

'I must—I've already sent a message to my people to expect me. We're agreed, I think, that we don't wish to cause gossip. When you were ill it was reasonable that I should stay. But now that you're well again I must leave you and Richard to yourselves. Don't look like that, Lexi. I won't change my mind.'

She was not to be moved, and after a while Lexi gave up trying to persuade her. But the thought of being alone with Richard put her in a panic. Lady Honoria was perfectly right. Newly married couples were meant to have at least two or three weeks alone together. It was a time when they could truly settle in to their marriage, get to know each other fully. What a time of delight it would have been, if Johnny and her father had never died, never been blackmailed, if Richard had been the man of honour they had all thought him! Lexi felt so disturbed that she excused herself after a while and went upstairs again.

Her maid had emptied all her boxes and taken them off to the attics to be stored there. She had left a tray of oddments, and a small pile of books and papers for Lexi to sort out on a table in the corner of the room. Among them was Sir Jeremy's diary, rescued the day after his death from his desk. Lexi picked it up and turned to the beginning of June. One of the pages was missing, its torn edges still visible. She knew where that page was—hidden in the lid of her jewel box. She leafed through the diary and just a month later, at the beginning of July, she found what she was looking for. Another set of torn edges, another page torn out. Was this the one Richard had found? Though she patiently turned every page after that, no other one was missing. It must be. What had happened in July that was so important?

Cissie returned, and Lexi put the diary back. Badly in need of fresh air, she announced she was going for a ride. Word was sent to the stables, and in a very short time she had changed her dress, and was standing in the stable yard watching an elderly groom saddle up a spirited bay mare. Will Osborne, the groom, had come with her from Rawdon Hall. She could not have left him behind at Rawdon with Mark—he had been one of her father's most trusted servants and she had known him all her life.

'Will! I haven't seen that one before,' she said. 'She's a beauty.'

'His lordship bought it a week or two back, Miss Lexi—I beg your pardon, your ladyship.' He gave her an apologetic grin. 'I forgot for the moment. Can I say how glad I am to see your ladyship well again?'

'Thank you. But why haven't I seen this creature before?'

'It was only brought here today. I understood it was for you to ride.'

Lexi's eyes glowed, her depression momentarily forgotten. 'Whether it was or not, my man, I intend to do so. I can't wait to try her.'

'She's got plenty of go, but there isn't an ounce of vice in her. You'll do very well with her, my lady. But then his lordship always had a good eye for a horse. He and Mr Johnny both.'

'Yes. I'm sure. Come! Help me up!'

They rode out of the stable yard, Osborne a few paces behind Lexi. But they had hardly reached the gate when Lexi saw Richard coming towards them on Castor. He smiled when he saw her, his old familiar, half-teasing, half-affectionate smile. Her heart leapt, and, for a fraction of a second, she had to restrain herself from spurring her horse forward to meet him. Instead she pulled up and waited.

'How do you like her?' he asked.

'She's lovely.' The words came out stiff, but for the life of her she could not have spoken with spontaneous feeling. Her heart was still thumping. She tried again, conscious of the groom behind. 'It's a wonderful surprise. What's her name?'

'I thought we might call her Faith. Or should it be Hope? Were you about to go for a ride?'

'I wanted a good gallop. But I need to find out about

this beauty first. Perhaps I'll decide on a name for her after that.' She patted her horse's neck.

He wheeled round. 'May I come with you?'

'Of course. Shall we go up to the Castle? There's a good stretch of turf there.'

'A good idea. But I think we can dispense with Osborne's services. I'll look after you.'

The groom was suppressing a knowing smile as he left them. You are so wrong, my friend, thought Lexi. I would have welcomed your company—I have little desire to be alone with my new husband! This is no honeymoon.

The Castle was not any sort of building, but an old set of earthworks surrounding a flat-topped hill. Its original occupiers were long since gone, but the vantage point from which they had seen enemies approaching provided magnificent views of the surrounding countryside, and on clear days it was possible to see the coast of Dorset curving round in the distance. As children Richard and the two Rawdons had often toiled up its slopes or scrambled down its sides. They had come home in high summer stained with blackberry juice, and in autumn their pockets had been full of hazelnuts or chestnuts, or they carried wild mushrooms tied up in anything they could find. In winter they had gathered pine cones for the fires at Rawdon, and in spring they had looked for the first celandines, primroses and other wild flowers. It had been a constant source of delight to them and one of their favourite places.

Lexi and Richard had their gallop, then reined in and dismounted. Lexi's hair had come out of her net and she took off her hat to put it right.

'Has she passed the test?' Richard asked with a nod towards the mare.

Lexi forgot her hair. Still holding her hat, she turned a glowing face towards him. 'She's beautiful! A perfect lady. I'd like to call her "Doña". That's a Spanish lady, isn't it? And Doña sounds like a gift, too. Thank you, Richard.'

They were standing very close. For a moment they stared at one another, then Richard lifted his hand and caressed the side of her face. The feeling of his long fingers touching her ear, his thumb cradling her chin, sent shivers down Lexi's spine. She dropped her hat, but made no effort to retrieve it. Instead she stared up at him, her eyes wide and questioning. He gave her a little smile, and his fingers slid behind her ear, tangling in the hair at the back of her neck, touching and feeling the bones of her skull. When she moved her head like a cat, welcoming his caress, his hand moved round and held it firmly and his lips were suddenly on hers.

Lexi had no time to protest, nor did she want to. She was under the spell of the past and the kiss was a perfect culmination of all those years of friendship and laughter on this hill. Richard made no effort to pull her closer; she was free to escape if she wished. But her arms moved of their own accord to wind themselves round his neck, and in the end Richard, not she, was the captive. His response was immediate, but still very controlled. He did not kiss her again, but took her into his arms and held her to him as if she were infinitely precious, his cheek against her hair. 'Alexandra,' he whispered.

They stayed like this for several moments, letting the peace and solitude of the place seep into them, feeling the stress and bitterness of recent weeks slowly fade away...

After a while Richard released her. 'Thank you,' he said quietly.

They stood on the edge of the slope looking down at the countryside laid out before them. Lexi took a deep breath. 'I should have come here long before this,' she said. 'It's hard to feel depressed or angry up here, when you're surrounded by such a...such a wide expanse of sky and land.' She raised her arm and pointed. 'It's even clear enough today to see the sea.'

Richard had been looking at her, but now he too turned his eyes to the scenery. 'It's still so green! In Spain this would have been one vast spread of brown and orange. I used to feel starved for a sight of a green field. Johnny felt the same.'

He had spoken without thinking. For those few minutes he had forgotten the dangers and difficulties of the present, and, like Lexi, he had been moved by the magic of the past, remembering those three children who had spent such long happy days up here together.

He was shocked and angry with himself when he felt Lexi's instant recoil at the mention of her brother. He turned to her, and though his voice was even, he spoke with intense feeling. 'Alexandra, I wish I could give you chapter and verse to prove what I say, but that is impossible. I swear to you on my life that I did not kill Johnny! Neither accidentally, nor deliberately.'

She stared at him in silence, her expression suddenly hostile. 'My father said you had,' she said.

'Your *father*? But he *knew*—' He stopped.

'When we get back I can show you, if you wish,' Lexi said stonily. 'Shall we go back?'

The spell was broken. He picked up her hat in silence, and in silence they mounted and rode back to Channings.

Chapter Seven

When Lexi and Richard got back it was time to dress for dinner. Richard escorted her upstairs and then left her without mentioning Johnny again. Except for being more silent than usual, he had behaved as courteously, as calmly as ever. But Lexi was learning to look beyond the grown man's calm, courteous façade, and tonight she sensed angry frustration behind the mask. She was neither surprised nor sorry. Richard did not often exert himself to charm, but when he did he could always succeed—his Aunt Honoria had said so more than once. He had nearly succeeded this afternoon, too. For a few moments up there at the Castle, he had almost seduced her into believing he was innocent. How disappointed he must have been when she recovered her senses in time and refused to succumb to his charm, after all!

Although she needed no reminders, Lexi went to her jewel box. The page from her father's diary was tucked into a special compartment in the lid. She took it out. The words were the same as ever, as convincing as ever. *I have spoken to Deverell. He admits it…*

Tears came to her eyes. Damn him, oh, damn him! Why was it that Richard could still wrench her heart, still bewitch her into forgetting his treachery, still seduce her into *inviting* his kisses? She looked down at the page from the diary. Incontrovertible proof. Small wonder that Richard hadn't taken up her offer to show him this evidence. Faced with this he could hardly carry on denying that he had lied, that he was still lying to her. She put the page back in its hiding place. It could stay there until the right moment arrived. Then she would produce it, and wait to see what he had to say!

Given a choice, Lexi would not have gone downstairs again at all, but it was impossible to absent herself from the dinner table tonight. She could no longer claim she was ill, and this was Lady Honoria's last evening. So, when the maid came in Lexi forced herself to concentrate on dressing for dinner. In keeping with her sombre mood tonight she chose to wear black, and she ordered Cissie to draw her hair back into an unadorned knot. But if this was an attempt to look her worst, it was unsuccessful. The ride that afternoon had brought back some of the sparkle to her eyes, and put a little colour into her cheeks. The severity of her hairstyle gave prominence to the finely drawn bones of cheek and jaw, and, far from subduing her looks, the matt-black crepe enhanced Lexi's colouring, her creamy skin, the deep smoky blue of her extraordinary eyes, and provided a dramatic foil to the shining coronet of copper hair.

Richard was outside her room when she emerged, and they walked down the broad staircase together. An observer could have been forgiven for thinking they were casual acquaintances who happened to be guests in the same house.

'Your aunt tells me she is leaving us tomorrow,' she said in the tone of one making polite conversation.

'Yes, she is. She is of the opinion that you are now

well enough to manage without her help. Are you?' His tone was equally formal.

Lexi drew a breath. 'As well now as I shall ever be able to,' she said. 'From what I have seen, Channings very nearly runs itself. And Lady Honoria is no doubt anxious to see to her own establishment again.'

'That might well be the case.'

After a short silence, which he made no attempt to break, Lexi began again. 'Your aunt also said that your mother had plans to redecorate some of the rooms here. Do you still have her notes? And, if so, may I see them?'

'Certainly. I'll look them out for you. But I am surprised. I can't imagine why they should interest you.'

'Why shouldn't they?'

His voice was cool as he said, 'From the way things are going, your time here is likely to be so limited I didn't think you would be interested in anything to do with the house. Six months is too short a span to achieve very much in a house of this size.'

They had reached the bottom of the stairs. She looked round at him. 'It was your suggestion that we should act as if the date in March had no particular significance, Deverell. Have you changed your mind?'

He was silent for a moment. Then he said, 'Of course I haven't. Forgive me. I sometimes find it difficult to remain optimistic—or even patient—in the face of your fixed determination to regard me as a villain.'

'Not determination, Deverell,' said Lexi as they went into the drawing room. 'Conviction.'

Later, after the meal was over and the servants had withdrawn, the talk returned to the former Lady Deverell's plans for the house. 'It's no use talking of them in the abstract, Lexi,' said Lady Honoria. 'You'll have to ask Mrs Chowen to take you over the house first. You'll have a better idea of what is needed then.'

'I'll ask her tomorrow after you've gone. You are still determined to go, I take it?'

'Absolutely. From now on you and Richard will have to sort out your differences by yourselves. I've done what I can to put an air of normality into this marriage. I can't do any more.'

'What do you mean? What differences?' asked Richard coolly.

'Don't try to tell me that all is now sweetness and light between you, for I shan't believe it! I don't know what has happened to put you at odds again, but tonight you can hardly bear to look at each other.' She eyed them severely for a moment, then her expression softened and she went on, 'But I'm sure you'll come about. Anything else would be unthinkable. Richard needs to set up his nursery before too long—Channings badly needs an heir.' She looked at their set faces and sighed. 'I suppose you don't exactly have to like each other for that, but I'm sure it helps.'

Lexi had to stop herself bursting into hysterical laughter. At the moment it would be hard to imagine anything less likely. Richard and she were, if possible, further apart than ever. But any desire to laugh died at Richard's next words.

'You're right, of course, Aunt Honoria,' he said, toying with his wineglass. 'And I agree. It's something I always intended to have. Children at Channings.' He smiled without amusement at the shock on Lexi's face. 'What's wrong, Alexandra? Whatever our feelings for each other, you surely didn't imagine I would let Channings fall into the hands of a stranger?'

'I...I hadn't thought about it at all,' said Lexi in a strangled voice.

'I don't suppose you'd admit to it if you had,' said Lady Honoria. 'Girls are not supposed to know much about such things.' She chuckled. 'But what they don't know, they soon learn. Don't worry, Lexi. Richard will see you through—I've no doubt he's had a certain amount of experience. And if you *do* learn to like him again, you might even enjoy it.'

Richard watched Lexi's face turn from white to scarlet and said gently, 'You must forgive my aunt's forthright way of expressing herself. She was brought up in a more robust age. Try not to be embarrassed by her lack of delicacy.'

'Robust or not, when I was a girl we knew what our duty was,' said his aunt trenchantly. 'Lexi won't shirk it. She knows what it means when an old title is in danger of passing out of the direct line. Or an estate passes out of the family. Why, look at the lengths she went to to secure Rawdon for Sir Mark!'

There was a small silence as they all remembered. Lexi bent her head. She was ashamed. In all her planning, all her later confusion, she had thought only of Rawdon. She had never stopped to ask herself what it would mean to Channings and all the other Deverell possessions if Richard died without an heir. The estate was not entailed as Rawdon was, but Deverells had lived at Channings for nearly as long as Rawdons had been at the Hall. They had always been known as good landlords and, in spite of the previous Lord Deverell's indifference, Channings had kept its reputation. And she was sure from everything Richard had ever said to her that he intended to continue that tradition and build on it.

She looked at him now. Sitting at the head of the table, slowly twisting an empty wine glass in his hand, the candlelight highlighting the taut planes of his face and making pools of darkness of his eyes, he looked every inch an aristocrat, the latest member of an illustrious line. She looked at his hands. Slender, with long fingers and narrow wrists, but very strong. What would it feel like to have those hands on her body, to acknowledge his right to create new life inside her, to have Richard's children...?

She jumped as she heard her name. 'I...I beg your pardon?'

'I said, Lexi, that if I'm to be up early tomorrow I should be off to my room now,' said Lady Honoria. 'Goodnight, both of you. Remember what I've said. And now that Richard has moved back to his old room it should be easier to manage!' She gave him what in a lesser mortal would have been a wink, and went out.

After a short silence Richard said, 'That must have been embarrassing. I'm sorry, Alexandra.'

'What for? She's an old lady, she speaks her mind. And she's proud of her family, just as I was of mine. She was right, too. I did do all I could to keep Rawdons at Rawdon Hall.' She paused and her voice rose as she said, 'I just don't know what to do now!'

'At the moment neither do I.' He looked up and said deliberately, 'But I meant what I said. Channings will not be left to strangers.'

Lexi sat in silence for a moment. Then she said, 'Is that why you've moved back to your old rooms? I don't believe I gave any orders to the housekeeper to prepare them.'

Richard sighed. 'No. If I had known, I would of course have told you before it was done. But when I first brought you here, I told Mrs Chowen that I wished to sleep in the other wing in order to give you the complete rest and quiet Dr Loudon said you needed. It was a useful fiction. And I'm afraid she assumed I would move back as soon as you were up again. I could hardly say that was the last thing you would wish for, could I? But don't worry. It will make no difference to our...situation.' He paused. 'Until you are ready, that is.'

Lady Honoria departed the next morning, with her maid, her coachman and two grooms in attendance. Richard and Lexi accompanied her to her carriage, where she paused to thank them for their hospitality and wish them well; then, to their relief, she left without giving them any further advice.

Richard stood watching the carriage disappear down the drive. 'What a lot has happened since she arrived for my wedding!' he said lightly. 'Once or twice even Aunt Honoria wasn't sure what to do. And God knows what will have happened by the time she's ready for her next visit.' He waited, but when Lexi said nothing he went on, 'Come, Alexandra. I'll show you my mother's plans. They're in my room.'

Lexi followed him into the house, up the stairs and into his bedchamber. It was the twin of her own, with two windows overlooking the lake. She hesitated at the door, recognising the faint, very masculine scent she had learned to associate with Richard. Between the windows was a handsome table, and on it a mirror and an array of silver brushes and other male dressing aids. A dressing gown in a rich, dark red brocade lay over the back of one of the chairs, and the bed was hung with the same dark red material. To the right of the bed was the door that led into his dressing room, and from there into her own room. Opposite the bed, between the fireplace and the window, was an exquisite marquetry cabinet dating from the reign of Queen Anne.

Richard did not wait for her, but walked swiftly to the table by the windows, picked up a small silver object that lay open, carefully closed it and put it down again. Then he took a key out of the tray nearby and went to the cabinet. When he opened it Lexi could see interesting-looking little cupboards and drawers surrounding a central slot in which a collection of folders and papers were neatly stacked. Richard took one of the folders out, then turned round and saw that she was still standing just inside the door.

'Ah!' he said with a twisted smile. 'I've lured you into the lion's den. Is that what you think?'

'Of course not,' Lexi stammered. 'I was just…just looking at the room. Has it the same outlook as mine?' To hide her nervousness she walked over to the further window and stood with her back to him, concentrating on the view. It was practically identical—a sweep of lawn leading down to the lake. She jumped when he touched her shoulder.

'I have my mother's notes here,' he said, moving away. 'Shall we take them downstairs? Or would you prefer to look round the house first?'

Lexi pulled herself together. It was ridiculous to let Lady Honoria's words affect her so. This was an excellent opportunity to find out where Richard might have put the page of the diary he had been reading in the library at Rawdon, and she must not waste it. The marquetry cabinet was an obvious place—and at the moment it was open.

'This is lovely,' she said, moving over to touch it.

'I've always liked pieces like this where you could hide particular treasures—love letters and so on.' She fingered the drawers, traced the lines of the marquetry, stretched out a hand to the folders—

'I'm afraid there's nothing so romantic there,' said Richard, coming back to close the doors of the cabinet. 'Any letters are mostly business ones left over from my army days.'

'What? No secret drawers? No passionate missives from a Spanish *condesa*?'

'None,' said Richard firmly. 'There is a secret compartment, but I'm afraid there's nothing incriminating in it.'

'Show me!'

'Don't be silly, Alexandra. If I showed you the secret compartment, it wouldn't be secret any more! Shall we go downstairs?'

He moved purposefully to the door and Lexi had perforce to follow.

Though the late Lady Deverell's schemes for redecoration were thirty years old, they were comprehensive and very attractive. Lexi pored over them for an hour, exclaiming and commenting, occasionally throwing a question at Richard, who was sitting in an armchair nearby. She was entranced. She had never been involved in anything like this before. Rawdon was an old manor house with thick walls and small windows. Warm in winter and cool in summer, it was comfortable but dark. It could never be stylish in the modern manner, and Sir Jeremy had never attempted to change it.

But Channings had been built on the site of a previous building by the third Lord Deverell, Richard's great-great-grandfather, and it was a gracious mansion in the Palladian style, with large windows and airy rooms. It was perfectly suited to the delicate but clear colour schemes devised by Lady Deverell, and for a few moments Lexi forgot the uncertain future in her delight at the prospect of carrying them out.

'What a gifted woman your mother was!' she exclaimed. 'I can't wait to see what the house will look like!'

Richard got up. 'Shall I ask Mrs Chowen to show you round the house this afternoon? There are still quite a few rooms you haven't seen.'

'Thank you. But before you go, can you explain these extra sheets?'

He came to stand beside her. 'My mother planned to add a ballroom to the side of the house.'

'A ballroom?'

'Oh, yes. She loved company, and had plans to fulfil the third Lord Deverell's ambition to make Channings famous for its grand occasions. But then she died.'

'Poor lady,' said Lexi softly.

Richard nodded, but said merely, 'Have you seen what you want of the plans? I'm afraid I promised to see one of the gamekeepers this morning, and it's past midday already. I'll send Mrs Chowen to you before I go.'

He was already at the door. 'Thank you,' said Lexi again.

Channings was much more extensive than Lexi had realised, and the tour took most of the afternoon. Mrs Chowen insisted on taking her to every corner—even to the stillrooms and butler's pantry. It was a well-run household. The servants went about their tasks as if they knew what they were doing, and their smiles were respectful but friendly. Mrs Chowen was proud of her management. She had risen to the post of housekeeper through forty years of service, and clearly regarded her new mistress in a somewhat motherly light. This made her more inclined to talk. She had been with the family since before Richard was born, and had of course known the late Lady Deverell.

'A lovely lady! And his late lordship was that in love with her. I wish you had seen them together, my lady. You could say he worshipped the ground she walked on! He was forty when they married and she was only nineteen, but after he met her no one else would do. Then, when she died, he wouldn't talk to anyone, or see anyone. He was like that for the rest of his life, but you know that already, you being local. Mind you, they do say that the Deverell men have always been like that. Once a Deverell makes his choice, it's for life.' She gave Lexi a little nod and a smile as she added, 'I'm sure his present lordship is just the same.'

'I...I hope so,' said Lexi nervously. 'What do you call this room?'

'This is the blue parlour, my lady. It was her ladyship's favourite room, and the late Lord Deverell wouldn't let anyone else into it after she died. But Mr Richard gave orders before you came that it was to be aired and dusted. He thought you might like to use it.'

'He...he's very thoughtful.'

'That he is! We never thought he would live, you know. Such a tiny baby he was. It was a miracle he survived.'

'I think he survived very well, Mrs Chowen,' said Lexi, smiling in spite of herself. 'You couldn't call him small now!'

'Oh pardon me, my lady! My tongue does run on so.

Of course he couldn't! He's a fine man, and a very good master. Things have turned out very well indeed for him—and for all of us at Channings. His lordship safely home from the wars and now happily married. Oh, yes! It will all be different now.' She had a look at Lexi's pale face. 'But I'm afraid I've kept you too long, my lady. His lordship asked me particularly not to wear you out, and you've been on your feet for well over an hour! Would you like me to have a fire lit in the blue parlour for you? And perhaps have cook send up something tasty for you to eat?'

It had been a strain keeping up the pretence that Richard's marriage was the ideal match Mrs Chowen thought. Lexi ate what she could of the delicacies sent by the cook, and then lay down on a day bed by the long window and looked out. On this side of the house the ground rose to a small wood. Beautiful specimen trees were planted at intervals in the lawns that led up to it, their spreading branches there to give shade in summer. At this season their leaves were beginning to fall, leaving a brilliant carpet of crimson, copper and gold on the grass below.

Lexi sighed. Channings could be everything she would ever desire—the beauty of its setting, the house itself with all its potential, its atmosphere of an orderly, settled household...and life with Richard. The temptation to forget the past was very strong. For a moment she allowed herself to dream. Visions of herself and Richard floated through her mind, living together, and loving each other more with every year that passed. There would be picnics on the lawn, sounds of laughter and music on summer evenings, candlelight casting a glow over faces round the dinner table in winter... And there would be children. Babies to cuddle, toddlers walking unsteadily along, waiting to be swept up by their father when they fell... Smiling, Lexi fell asleep.

When she next opened her eyes it was very nearly dark outside, though the room was lit by the flames from the fire. Someone must have been in to make it up. A pair of long legs could be seen stretched out in front of it. The rest of the figure was hidden by the wings of the chair it was sitting in.

Still under the spell of her dream she said softly, 'Richard?'

For a moment she thought he couldn't have heard, for he stayed quite still. Then he got up and came over and sat on the edge of the day bed. 'You've woken up at last,' he said in his deep voice. 'I was just wondering whether to wake you—it's nearly dinner time.'

'Was I asleep?'

'You didn't stir when I came in.'

'It was you who made up the fire?'

'I tried to do it without disturbing you.'

'I was dreaming.'

'They must have been pleasant dreams. You were smiling.'

'Richard...'

'That's the second time you've called me ''Richard'' in as many minutes. You called me ''Richard'' yesterday, too.'

'Did I? I sometimes forget to hate you.'

'Do you really hate me, Alexandra?'

'I try to! But it's hard. Hatred is such a destructive emotion. And the future looks so bleak...'

The flickering firelight, the lingering memory of her dream and the silence that followed these words had a strange effect. She wondered whether there was, after all, a way for them to live together. Taking a deep breath she said, 'Richard, I wonder... What if...what if we drew a line under what has happened? Tried to forget the past and make our marriage a normal one? Could we do that, do you think?' She waited tensely for his answer, wishing she could see his face, but it was in shadow. The silence went on for longer than she wanted.

Finally he said, 'Tell me why you've changed your mind.'

'Something Lady Honoria said. I was so young when my mother died that I was never taught how girls should regard marriage. But not all marriages are love matches. People...people can live together without feeling romantic about it. Lady Honoria was right when she talked of duty and the rest, when she reminded me of the way I'd felt about Rawdon, how important it had seemed to keep it going. And...and Channings has been in the Deverell family for almost as long as the Rawdons have owned the Hall. It made me think. Then this afternoon, being taken round the house by Mrs Chowen, listening to what *she* said... I hadn't considered before what it would mean to Channings if you died without an heir.'

'But what about your aversion to the man who ruined your father and killed your brother?'

'You didn't ruin my father. I believe you were telling the truth about the card game. You were trying to save him.'

He went on relentlessly. 'What about your brother? Do you still believe I killed him, in spite of anything I can say?'

'That's...that's different.' Lexi felt him stiffen. 'I'm

sure it was an accident,' she said desperately. 'I'm sure you didn't mean to. And I think I could forget. Or at least put it behind me. In time.'

Richard stood up. 'Tempting though the prospect is,' he said with an unusually harsh note in his voice, 'I'm afraid that isn't the sort of marriage I want. I don't want a wife who "does her duty" by me for the sake of the estate. And I certainly don't want a wife who shudders and looks away every time her brother's name is mentioned between us. Johnny and I saved each other's lives more than once in the three years we spent fighting together. He was closer to me than any brother could have been. When he died I did my best for him and for your family, Alexandra. I did *not* kill him, and I'm damned if I'll father children—for that's what you're saying, isn't it?—whose mother will always believe deep down that I'm a murderer and a liar.'

Lexi scrambled up and faced him. 'But what else *can* I believe?' she cried. 'You refuse to tell me *anything*! I have my father's *word* that you killed Johnny, *and* that you admitted it! Are you saying that *he's* a liar? Is that it?'

'I don't believe your father said anything of the sort. He couldn't have!'

'I have evidence!'

'You said that before. Where is it? Show me!'

'I will!'

She stormed out of the blue parlour and up the stairs, without even looking around to see if he was following her. Cissie was in her room, laying out a dress for the evening, but Lexi told her to leave, and, after one look at her mistress's face, Cissie wasted no time in obeying. Richard strode in as Cissie scuttled out.

'Now, where is it?'

Lexi went to the jewel box and took out the page. There were a couple of tear stains on it, and it was crumpled with much handling, but the words, her father's fateful words, were still legible. Richard took it from her and she watched him while he read it. His mouth tightened and he took a deep breath before he said,

'And *this* is your "evidence"? The reason for the scene after our wedding?'

'Isn't it enough?'

'No, damn it, it isn't!' he said angrily. 'It's not nearly enough! To think that you—' He walked away from her, then turned and came back again. His voice still trembling with rage, he said, 'You were prepared to call me a liar and a coward, kill me, destroy us both—for how could you have escaped punishment for shooting me?—on the basis of this scrap of paper? A page torn from a diary written by a man beside himself with grief at the death of his only son? I could kill you myself for this, Alexandra!'

In the silence that followed his outburst Lexi said slowly, 'How did you know that?'

Richard was still very angry. 'What do you mean?' he asked curtly.

'How did you know that it was from my father's *diary*?' She went over to the pile of books on her table and picked it up. 'You're right, of course,' she said leafing through the pages. 'Here's the gap. But how did *you* know that, Deverell?'

He paused. 'It was easy enough to recognise a page from a diary. And in your father's handwriting…'

Lexi was turning the pages to the month of July. 'There's another page missing. See?' She regarded him closely as she showed him the torn edges. 'But I haven't found that. I wonder what could have happened to it.'

Richard had calmed down again. To Lexi's disappointment he didn't respond to her deliberate provocation, but asked instead, 'Where did you find this page? And when?'

'Two days before the wedding. It was tucked inside the diary, but it fell out when I was packing some of the books and papers on his desk.'

He frowned. 'I had been working there the day before,' he said slowly, 'but I don't remember seeing either the diary or this page.'

Richard's refusal to own up about the second page infuriated Lexi. She cried, 'What does it *matter* whether you saw it or not? You're trying to distract me again, aren't you? But I won't let you! That paper is proof enough for me that you killed Johnny! How can you possibly deny it? How else can you explain what my father wrote?'

Richard said carefully, 'There's nothing on that page to say that I admitted killing Johnny, nor even that I was there when he died. I confessed to Sir Jeremy that I had interfered with the evidence. And that is all I shall say on the matter.'

Lexi took a moment to work this out. 'What you're claiming is that you changed things *after* Johnny was dead. Is that it?' Richard looked at her in silence. 'But why should you do that? Unless...' Lexi's voice died away. She looked at Richard in horror. 'You're telling me that Johnny killed himself *deliberately*?'

'I don't propose to tell you anything.'

'No, no! I won't believe it! It's absurd! Unreasonable! You *can't* leave it at that. Why would Johnny do such a thing?'

'I…don't know.'

'You're lying! One way or another, you're lying, Richard Deverell! Either you killed my brother or you know why he killed himself. Anything else is impossible. Tell me! I demand to know the truth!'

'Believe me, Alexandra,' said Richard heavily, 'you are much better off *not* knowing.'

There was a tap on the door. When Lexi called, Cissie came nervously into the room. 'Excuse me, your ladyship. But it's getting late. Are you meaning to change before dinner?'

Richard went to the door. 'We'll continue this discussion another time,' he said. 'I have to go out again this evening.'

She ran to the door and caught his sleeve. 'But you *can't* leave it like this!'

'I must, I'm afraid. I met Canon Harmond while I was out this morning, and promised him that I would come down to the Rectory tonight. The matter is urgent, so I can't put him off.'

'I don't believe the state of the church tower, or whatever it may be, is more urgent than what we were talking about!'

'I'm sorry,' he said, removing her hand. 'Can you be ready to go down for dinner in half an hour?'

Richard was clearly determined not to stay, and the presence of the maidservant prevented an angry protest. Lexi bit her lip and forced herself to say calmly, 'Of course.'

During the meal Lexi tried several times to reopen the subject, but Richard evaded her questions every time, again using the presence of the servants as a pretext. And, as soon as they had left the room, he too excused himself and left. It was quite clear that he was determined not to answer her questions. Lexi picked up her glass of wine and went upstairs. She had already drunk more than usual without feeling noticeably happier, but hoped this last glass would help her to sleep.

Cissie helped her to undress, then Lexi sat at the dressing table while her maid brushed out her hair and tied it with a white ribbon. After the maid had gone Lexi put on her robe and walked impatiently about the room. The wine had not helped, after all. Her afternoon nap had been a mistake—she had no desire to sleep. The feeling of impotence in the face of Richard's refusal to discuss her brother's death was making her restless. Or was it something worse? Was she afraid deep down that he had been telling the truth all the time? Was she reluctantly coming to the conclusion that Johnny, her laughing, carelessly affectionate, much-loved brother, had been driven by such despair that he had taken his own life?

Lexi picked up the diary and looked at the place where the missing page had been. The beginning of July... Weeks after Johnny's death. What had her father written during that first week in July to cause Richard to look so angry when he read it? If Johnny *had* killed himself the answer to the riddle might well be on that page. She suddenly made up her mind, put the diary down, opened the door in the wall in the corner by her bed and walked through into Richard's dressing room. She waited a moment but heard nothing. Her husband would be out for an hour or more yet, and the valet had probably gone to his own quarters. There was time to search that cabinet for the missing page. She opened the door and went through.

Richard's room looked different by candlelight. The

curtains matching the bed hangings had been drawn, giving the room a rich, if somewhat sombre, air. There was no sign of Phillips, but the bed covers had been drawn back and he had laid out Richard's robe and night things ready for his master's use. Richard must have told him not to wait up. Lexi shut the door carefully behind her, waited for a moment to calm her nerves, then walked resolutely to the cabinet. It was locked. A nuisance, but it wouldn't stop her. Richard had fetched the key from his dressing table this morning. She went over to the dressing table and saw a key lying in a small tray at the side of the mirror. That must be it. On the point of going back to the cabinet, she paused. What was it Richard had taken such pains to shut before she saw what was inside? Could that be a clue? She cast her eye over the table. The only likely object was a chased silver watchcase...

Lexi opened it. A beautifully made, but perfectly ordinary watch. Why had Richard been at such pains to hide it from her? She turned it in her hand and pressed a small catch on one side. The cover of the watch clicked open to reveal a separate compartment. On one side was a small head-and-shoulders sketch of herself, and facing it, protected by a delicate glass disc, was a copper-coloured curl. She stared at it. How long had Richard been carrying this around with him? Johnny had made several sketches of her over the years—he had quite a talent for it. Her picture must have been cut from one of them. And the curl—she remembered about the curl. Johnny had teased her about her hair some years ago and she had been in such a temper with him that she had taken her sewing scissors and started to cut it off. Richard must have kept one of the bits that had fallen before he had stopped her.

The discovery had a strange effect on her. She would never have imagined that Richard was at all sentimental. And about *her*! Perhaps he had just recently put her picture in his watchcase—a token gesture to his new bride? That was more likely. She stared at it for some minutes, but eventually came to with a start. Time was getting short and she still hadn't looked inside the cabinet. Lexi closed the watchcase and returned it carefully to its place, then picked up the key and went back to unlock the doors of the cabinet. She was so nervous that when she first tried she fumbled and dropped the key. With a small cry she bent down, picked it up and inserted it, this time successfully. Now! She stretched out her hand, took one of the folders from the middle section and leafed through the papers inside—

'Looking for love letters? I've told you. You won't find any.' Lexi froze. The voice was Richard's.

Richard had arrived back from the Rectory some minutes before. Far from discussing the state of the church tower, he had been listening to Canon Harmond's plea for help with his grandson, who was in the Army and in serious trouble with his senior officers. The good Canon was in some distress and it had taken Richard quite a while to reassure him, and promise what help he could.

As he rode home through the dark he felt jaded and weary. The Canon's wine, though a good vintage, had not cheered him as it should. Life seemed to hold nothing but problems, not least the enormous problem of his relationship with his wife. For every step forward they seemed to take two steps back. Why the devil couldn't she accept what he said, trust him? Knowing the truth would only bring her yet more grief! Why couldn't she just accept his word? But, in spite of himself, a smile came to his lips as he thought of her. Because she was Alexandra, that was why! In all the years he had known her, she had never been content to accept the easy way out. She had always made her own judgements, fought for what she believed in. And he had loved her for it.

This afternoon she had forgotten her animosity, and smiled at him. She had looked so beautiful in the firelight...had called him Richard. He had started to hope all over again at her first few words. And then she had gone on to make her offer, and hope had died. Had she really thought he would happily accept such a travesty of a marriage, a marriage of convenience, merely to beget heirs for Channings? Did she think he would be content to make love to her, knowing what she really thought?

But then...could Alexandra have offered anything else? Believing what she did, how could she possibly love him as passionately, as all-embracingly as he desired? Perhaps he had expected too much. God knew, he should have learned by now that nothing was ever perfect, especially not any relationship involving love.

When he got back the house was silent, the servants all in their own quarters. As he went quietly up the stairs he wondered if he had been too hasty that afternoon in rejecting her offer. It wasn't the sort of marriage he would have chosen, but unless a miracle occurred it might be the only one possible, for, even at the risk of losing her, he would never willingly tell Alexandra what had really happened with Johnny.

He went directly into his dressing room from the landing and sat down to remove his boots, taking care to make as little sound as possible. The last thing he wanted was to disturb Alexandra—he had no stomach for further discussions about her brother tonight. Then he shrugged himself out of his coat and removed his cravat. He was in the process of undoing his shirt when he heard a sound. He stopped to listen. Someone was in his room. It wasn't his man—Phillips had been told not to wait up for him. Richard moved quietly to the door to his bedchamber and carefully, silently, opened it. Alexandra was at his cabinet, so absorbed in what she was doing that she wasn't at all aware of him. For a moment he watched her leafing through the folder in her hand, and felt desire rising in his loins. She was so beautiful... Her hair was a stream of bronze in the light of the candles. The robe she wore was almost transparent in the firelight, its delicate folds giving more than a hint of the slender curves and long legs underneath it.

Richard drew in a breath. What was she doing, this wife of his, in his bedroom at this hour? Obviously looking for something, but what? It didn't matter. What mattered was that she was in his bedroom, and very suitably dressed for what was rapidly filling his mind to the exclusion of everything else. To hell with patience and restraint and all other considerations! They could be dealt with some other time. Tonight he would claim what had been his right and his desire for so many years. Alexandra and he were married. It was time to make her his in every sense of the word. But he would have to proceed cautiously at first. A little strategy was called for...

'Looking for love letters?' he asked. 'I've told you. You won't find any.'

Chapter Eight

Lexi swung round. Richard was leaning against the door from his dressing room, arms folded, watching her. He must have been back for some time, but she had been so absorbed in the watchcase and her search through the contents of the cabinet that she hadn't heard him.

He had taken off his coat and boots before coming through into his bedchamber, and his shirt was open at the neck. Her throat was suddenly dry. She croaked, 'I…I thought—' She swallowed and tried again. 'I thought you were out for the evening,' she said more normally.

His eyes went to the open cabinet, then to the folder in her hand. 'Evidently.'

'I…I saw the f…folders and…and things this morning when you had the doors open. I wondered if some of my father's papers might be among them.'

'And you couldn't sleep until you had made sure,' he said sympathetically. But Lexi was not taken in. His eyes were about as sympathetic as a black panther's, she thought. They had a similar predatory gleam in them.

She was suddenly conscious that she was in her nightdress and robe. The nightdress was a shift of fine linen, the robe a delicate, flimsy confection of silk and lace, aimed to entice rather than to conceal.

He came closer still. 'Shall we look together?' he asked, taking the folder from her.

'No!' said Lexi, desperately conscious of his nearness. She swallowed again. 'I...I can do without them. For the moment. Thank you. I...I think I'll g...go back.' She tried to move away but his hand was suddenly at her waist, holding her where she was, its warmth burning through her thin garments.

He put the folder back without releasing her, then pulled her to face him. 'You disappoint me,' he said softly.

'I...I do?'

'Yes. I've been wondering whether I was a little over-hasty this afternoon. About your plan for our future. Children and so on. I had started to reconsider your suggestion.'

'Oh, but I don't think this is the moment—' She started to move again but he drew her back against him without any visible effort.

'When I saw you here I thought for a moment that you'd decided to seduce me into agreeing to it.' His arm slid right round her. 'I quite liked that idea,' he said, nuzzling her left ear.

'Richard,' Lexi said, finding it difficult to sound as firm as she would have liked, while her heart was pounding and her knees threatening to give way. 'I don't believe you thought anything of the sort. And I am *not* trying to seduce you!' She tried to lean away from that insidious mouth, but found that the movement merely brought their lower bodies into closer contact.

She discovered with a shock that, whether she believed him or not, Richard was quite definitely more than ready to be seduced.

'Hush!' he said, putting a finger against her lips. 'Of course you are. Why else would you come into my room?'

Resisting a mad temptation to take his finger into her mouth, Lexi said in a strangled whisper, 'I...wanted... to look for some papers.'

His reply to this was to pull gently at the ribbons of her robe. Lexi tried to stop him, but her heart wasn't in it. He caught her hands easily and held them while he kissed her, gently, sweetly, coaxing her into breathless acquiescence. She gave a sigh of pleasure, then nearly stopped breathing altogether when his fingers found her breast and stroked its sensitive centre into instant response. Her robe fell to the ground in a slither of silk, but Lexi was past caring.

Punctuating his words with kisses, Richard lifted her just enough off the ground to walk her slowly backwards, away from the cabinet, as he said, 'You must tell me about these papers, but first—' He put her gently down, then joined her on the bed.

'Richard, I—'

'No, no! It's just a conversation, Alexandra,' he said, pulling his shirt free. 'It's more comfortable here, that's all. Are you cold?' He drew her closer to him, trapping her legs under one of his.

'N...no,' said Lexi, who was feeling as if she might well melt in the warmth generated by their two bodies, now so close, so very, very close. 'B...but—'

'Good.' His fingers slipped down to the edge of her nightgown and drew it slowly up. 'You were saying?'

She couldn't say anything. His lips were on hers, his

hands were sliding up her bare legs, filling her unbearably with a strange, aching excitement. He lifted up her hips, easing the nightgown further, and then his mouth was on her body. Lexi was lost in a surge of shocked delight, unable to escape even had she wanted to. 'You shouldn't do this!' she managed to whisper as his lips slowly burned a path up to her breasts.

'Why not?' he growled against her throat. 'We're married. You're my wife, Alexandra! I told you once, remember? Short of murder, I can do anything I like with you. But if you're not enjoying it, I'll stop.' He lifted his head and looked at her with a wicked little smile. 'Do you wish me to stop?'

'No!' she cried. 'That is… Yes! Oh, I don't know. I ought not to! Richard, *please*!'

'Richard pleases you? Isn't that what you mean? Don't be afraid to admit it. There's nothing wrong with enjoying your husband's caresses. Come, let me take this off. It's very much in the way, wouldn't you say?' He raised her shoulders and removed the nightgown completely. She would have covered herself with her hands, but he held them away while he gazed at her.

'My wife,' he said softly.

Then he gave her a swift kiss and got off the bed. For a moment Lexi felt bereft, but then she saw that he was only taking off the rest of his own clothes, before joining her again. The sight of his naked body took her breath away. The boy she had grown up with had turned into a superb man—lean, powerful and strong. She lay there, tense and unsure, not certain what to do, only knowing that she wanted him to come back to her again, to take her further into the unknown territory of love. There was no turning back now, nor did she wish to. She felt she had been waiting for this moment all her life—nothing existed but this room and this man, and a mysterious longing inside her that she felt nothing but Richard's body next to hers could assuage.

When he lay down again the teasing expression had quite gone, and for a moment he looked a stranger, not Richard at all, but a man at the edge of his control, caught in the grip of some intense emotion. She whispered his name and touched him, seeking reassurance, and the look of blazing passion in his eyes was instantly veiled. He bent over her, holding her tenderly, murmuring her name, until she relaxed again in his arms. Then he started to kiss her—gently at first, then more intimately, until he lifted her against him and their bodies were meshed in each other. Soon she lay beneath him, twisting in his arms with frantic desire, seeking his invasion, feeling incomplete without it, and yet still afraid of the final step.

At the last moment Richard sensed the fear and held himself back. He took her head in his hands. Looking deep into her eyes, he said fiercely, 'I love you, Alexandra. I loved you when you were a child, and I love you now. Trust me. Give yourself to me, my darling.' There was a brief moment of panic, of pain, and then he was hers, all hers, completely, triumphantly, hers. As she was his. Completely. No longer Richard and Alexandra, but one being, as it had always been meant...

Lexi woke up and stretched like a cat against the long body next to hers, feeling sensuously warm and cherished. Richard had made love to her again more than once in the night, each time carrying her along with the intensity of his passion, fulfilling her desires as completely as his own. She had known an ecstasy that had surpassed anything she could possibly have imagined, had wondered whether she would die with the joy of it, and then had turned to him, eager to respond again to his every caress. Finally he had taken her in his arms and held her till she fell asleep against the slow, powerful beat of his heart.

She pulled away and looked at him now. His black hair and bronzed skin were in stark contrast to the white of the sheets. He was handsome, so handsome... Not even the scar on his cheek had spoiled his looks. Her finger traced it, then moved on to the dark line of an incipient beard along his jaw and upper lip...

Suddenly her finger was caught and held between his teeth. His eyes opened and, letting her finger go, he gave her a smile. It was so sweet a smile that Lexi's heart melted with tenderness.

'Good morning,' she whispered. He kissed her for an answer, drawing his thumb across her breasts, and sending a shiver of delight down her spine. Still without speaking, he raised an eyebrow.

'I...I don't think so,' she said with real regret. 'I can hear noises outside. It must be quite late.'

'Perhaps you're right,' he said. His voice was deeper, more gravelly than usual. Lexi found it very attractive and said so.

'And you, madam wife, are enchanting!' he murmured, kissing her again. 'Enough to make a man forget the world and think he was living among the stars. But the world goes on all the same and you're right. I must get up.' He got out and put his robe on, then padded over to open the curtains. Light flooded in.

'You look...magnificent!' said Lexi, kneeling up in order to admire him. 'Like the Grand Turk. Or a Grandee of Spain. Ought I to go back to my own room before you dress? Will Phillips come in here?'

'He knows better than that!' said Richard, holding out her nightgown. But when she reached for it he drew his breath in, then knelt on the bed to face her, and stretching her arms out wide, held her captive.

'Alexandra,' he murmured, gazing at her, 'Alexandra!' With a groan he bent to kiss her, his lips roving over her body, seeking out the secret centres of delight, tantalising her until she could stand it no longer, but pulled him down with her back into the tumbled bedcovers. There they lay in a tangle of limbs, murmuring incoherently, kissing almost desperately until the world and everything in it was forgotten as they matched each other once again in a climax of passion. Afterwards they lay in silence, Richard's head on Lexi's breast.

'Richard—' said Lexi after a while.

'I know. I know. I must get up.'

'Would you pass me my nightgown? And ought I to go back to my own room before anyone comes? I don't yet know the rules, you see.'

Richard laughed in delight as he got up and handed her the nightgown, kissing her as he did so. 'You broke all the rules last night.'

'I did?'

'It is customary in respectable households for the lady to wait modestly in her own room at night for her husband to visit her there. She doesn't seek him out in his own bedchamber! That is considered extremely forward.'

Lexi poked an outraged face through the nightgown. 'But I thought you were out! I didn't come to—'

Richard kissed her into silence. 'I know. I was teasing. And I shouldn't. It was the greatest surprise…and the greatest delight of my life. Shall I carry you back to your room?'

'I can walk.'

'Can you indeed? Then I'm not such a Grand Turk as you thought!'

Lexi shook her head and stretched up to kiss him back. 'You were everything a woman could wish for,' she said huskily. 'Thank you.'

He swept her up into his arms with a groan. 'I love you!' he said. 'I'd like nothing more than to keep you here all day. But I must take you back where you belong, for now.'

He took her through to her room and put her in the chair by the window.

'Cissie's been here already,' she said, looking round at the open curtains and the tray beside the bed. 'My secret is out. And I don't care one bit!'

Richard kissed her, laughing. 'I'll take you to breakfast when you're ready. Don't go down without me,' he said as he went back into the dressing room.

The days that followed were taken out of a fairy tale. It was one of those times in late autumn when wraith-like fingers of mist in the morning give way to clear blue skies and brilliant sunshine, and the air is like cool, crisp white wine. The trees are making one last great display of colour before winter finally bares their branches, the hedgerows are covered with the downy feathers of travellers' joy, and spiders' webs, hanging with diamond drops, glitter on fences and gates.

Richard and Lexi went out each day after breakfast and wandered about the park surrounding Channings, marvelling at the beauty of the world, and finding it full of joy and laughter. Their sense of companionship was stronger than it had ever been in their childhood, and it had now acquired a totally new and exciting dimension.

They were intensely conscious of one another physically, constantly touching or holding hands. Richard's arm was frequently on Lexi's waist or round her shoulder, and when he helped her over stiles or through gates he now demanded a kiss before he would release her. Lexi had never seen him so relaxed, so freely, openly happy.

At night they made love, fiercely, passionately, tenderly, with laughter and words or, when words were not enough, in silence. They saw no one. When they went riding they went along deserted lanes and byways, and those who happened to see them smiled and nodded their heads and felt lighter-hearted at the sight of such happiness.

The weather held for a week, and on the last day they walked up the hill at the back of the house, where late cyclamen flowered under the trees, and squirrels were busy building up their winter stores. At the edge of the wood at the top Richard stopped and turned Lexi round, holding her against him.

'Look!'

Channings lay spread out below them, white and beautiful, gleaming in the sunshine.

Lexi let out her breath in a long sigh. 'Oh! Oh, Richard, it's so lovely! I hadn't realised just how lovely it was.'

'It's ours, Alexandra. Yours and mine for all our lives. Together we'll make it into the home it should have been, a place where our children will grow up, never doubting that their parents love them, a place where they'll feel secure and cherished. And happy.' To Lexi it sounded like a vow.

Lexi blinked to hold back a tear. 'As you were not. Oh, Richard, I do so want it to come true!'

'It will. Have faith.' A cloud passed over the sun and Lexi shivered. 'You're cold! Shall we go back?'

'No, no! It was only a moment while the sun went in. No, let's go on!' And Lexi deliberately shut her mind to all thought of anything but the present, as they continued to wander hand in hand through the grounds, making plans, exchanging kisses, falling in love more deeply than ever with Channings, and with each other.

They circled right round and came back on to the drive at the front, and were still some distance away when they saw Mark Rawdon standing at the bottom step surveying the house. One of the grooms was just in the process of leading his horse away to the stables.

Richard's hand tightened its hold and he swore under his breath.

Lexi, too, was filled with dismay. 'Oh, Lord, I'd quite forgotten. We invited him over when we were at Rawdon. And now we'll have to entertain him for hours. What time is it? Thank God there isn't a moon! He won't stay more than an hour at the most. He doesn't like riding in the countryside after dark.'

Richard gave an involuntary laugh. 'I thought you liked your cousin?'

'I do! But…but…'

'But you don't want to entertain him today. Is that it?'

The colour rose in Lexi's cheeks. 'There's only one person I want to entertain today, Richard.' She gave him a look, half-shy, half-inviting.

Richard caught her up and kissed her. 'He'll go soon enough, my heart. And then…'

Flushed and happy, Lexi shook her head at him, then with him at her side walked decorously forward to greet her cousin.

'There's no need to ask how you are, Lexi,' said Mark a while later. 'In spite of its...awkward beginning, married life obviously agrees with you. I'm so glad for you both! It can't have been easy.'

She and Mark were sitting in the blue parlour, waiting for Richard to join them. Canon Harmond had called again, looking serious, and, after he had made civil enquiries of them all and chatted for a few minutes, Richard had taken him off to the library.

'It wasn't so hard. Perhaps I haven't told you? Richard was telling the truth about that card game, Mark. He *was* trying to help my father. The servants at Rawdon didn't know the whole story.'

'I see. That's wonderful!' Mark gazed at her with delight. 'And he's explained about Johnny, too? Of course he has! You wouldn't have that very pretty glow about you if he hadn't.'

Lexi got up. 'He hasn't,' she said. 'Not yet. But I'm sure we'll sort it out in time.'

'So am I! Richard is a splendid sort of chap. I never believed for one moment that he couldn't explain it all away perfectly. It was obvious that he and Sir Jeremy were in each other's confidence.' Mark gave a laugh. 'Indeed, I think your father would have been better pleased if Richard had been able to inherit Rawdon.'

'That isn't so! My father was delighted to find that you were there to carry on. He was very proud of our name.'

'But he regarded Richard as a second son. They were very close.'

'Yet you believed as I did, that Richard had betrayed him?'

'Well, the servants did tell a pretty convincing story. But, as you say, we didn't know the whole.'

There was a slight question in Mark's voice. He would clearly like to know what had really happened between Sir Jeremy and Richard, but Lexi did not propose to enlighten him. The fewer people who knew about the blackmail business the better.

'Well, it's all over now,' she said briskly. 'As you see, Richard and I have settled our differences and are perfectly happy.'

'So, no pistols in six months' time?'

'Of course not! It was a ridiculous idea. I must have been mad!'

'No, just distressed and ill. Though if I'd known what you were about to do—'

'Couldn't you have guessed? I was in no state to dissemble during those last few days. I'm sure Richard would have suspected something if he hadn't been so busy.'

'Well, I didn't. I was worried, of course. I knew you didn't want to marry him, after you found out about Johnny. But then you changed your mind. My hands were tied after that—after all, Lexi, in saving Rawdon you were saving me! In any case, what could I have done if you *hadn't* married Deverell? I was in no position to help you myself—you know what a fix the estate was in. Sir Jeremy might have been proud of his name, but he left me nothing in his will. Apart from what was entailed—the Hall itself and the Home Farm—everything was left to you!'

'I'm quite sure he meant to change it,' said Lexi. 'It was made after Johnny died, and before he found you.

But…but he had other things on his mind. He didn't expect to…to die so soon…' Her voice trembled. 'I did my best to put it right…'

'Oh, my dear Lexi! You put it wonderfully right. Rawdon will soon be as it was in the old days, thanks to you. I shall never cease to be grateful. And I cannot say how happy I am that you and Richard have managed to sort things out between you. I always knew, of course, that Richard would protect you.'

'Protect me? That's a strange way of putting it.'

'Hasn't he told you? Your father made him promise he would.'

'You mean when he asked for Papa's permission to marry me? When was that?'

'Er…it wasn't quite like that. Richard wasn't asking to marry you—though if your father had lived I'm sure he would have got round to it eventually, Lexi. Any man would be proud to have you for a wife.'

'So what was this promise?'

'It was about a week before Sir Jeremy died. We were all three discussing the estate. Richard told me how kind you had all been to him and how much he owed to the Rawdon family. Your father brushed it off, and said what I told you before—that he had always regarded Richard as a second son. Then he said, ''But if anything happens to me I rely on you to protect my Lexi, Richard. You know what I mean. Will you promise to look after her?'''

'And Richard promised.'

'Naturally. He could hardly have done anything else, could he?'

'He…he didn't say anything then about wanting to marry me?'

'Not then, no. Just a promise to look after you. He

can't have foreseen—none of us could—how soon he would be unhappily called on to keep it. A week later your father died, apparently ruined by Richard himself—the very man who should have saved him...' Lexi uttered a protest and Mark hurried on, 'But as you say, that wasn't so—I understand that now. And I must say, Lexi, Richard has more than kept his word to your father. He has looked after you to marvellous effect. I've never seen you looking better.'

'Thank you,' said Lexi. She looked towards the door. Where was Richard? Surely the business with Canon Harmond was not as complicated as this? She needed his presence. Mark meant well, but somehow or other his words had cast a cloud over the day. For the past week she had managed to forget the unanswered questions about Johnny. She had built a wall in her mind to protect her idyll with Richard, but now it was showing cracks. She needed him here to repair them with his love, to be reassured by the unmistakable delight he had shown in her company...

She walked to the door. 'Excuse me, Mark. I'll just see if I can rescue Richard—by inviting the Canon to tea, if nothing else will work! You've hardly had a chance to talk to him, and it will soon be getting dark.' She shut the door behind her and took a deep breath. Much as she liked her cousin, why did he have to come today of all days? He brought too much of the past with him. She and Richard had been wrapped in a world of their own for such a very short time. She wanted more of it, more of the perfect happiness only he could provide. She gave a gasp of pain as a small voice inside her told her she was deceiving herself, that her happiness had never been completely, unequivocally perfect.

It had only been achieved by wilfully ignoring the can-ker at its heart. Johnny.

A sob escaped her. Why did Mark have to come with his questions, his assumptions that everything had been cleared up? Before he came she had been managing to keep the demons of doubt at bay. But now the spectre of Johnny had risen again. And there was more... Rich-ard loved her as much as she loved him! He must! He had said so dozens of time in the week that had passed, and she could have sworn that his joy in her company was genuine. He *couldn't* just have been pretending, doing his duty, keeping a promise to her father. He would have to be a consummate actor if he had!

But the niggle of doubt would not go away. Lady Honoria's words came back to her to haunt her. *'Why the devil did he have to settle on you?... Well, I'll tell you why...! It's all of a piece with his present behav-iour. Because he was* sorry *for you, that's why! He thought he owed it to your family to protect you.'*

Had Lady Honoria been right? Men were not like women, she reminded herself. Richard wouldn't nec-essarily have to *love* her before he could enjoy sleeping with her.

Lexi's anger and disappointment grew when she heard that Richard had gone down to the rectory with Canon Harmond. The church tower had been standing for centuries—it would surely not fall down if it had to wait a day or two longer! How could he simply go out and leave her to cope alone with their visitor? How could he leave her at all for so long for a piece of unimportant business?

She went back to Mark. 'I'm sorry. Richard appears to have gone out without telling me. Canon Harmond's errand must be more urgent than I thought.'

'I quite understand, Lexi. I had one or two questions for Richard, but they can wait. I'm beginning to know what it's like to be a landowner and at everyone's beck and call—even on one's honeymoon, apparently!' He looked closely at her. 'You seem to be upset?'

'No, no! I'm sorry you couldn't talk to Richard, that's all.'

'What for? To give him an account of my stewardship?' Lexi was surprised at the slightly acid note in Mark's words.

'Mark! Why ever did you say that? You own Rawdon, fully and completely! You're no steward of Richard's.'

Mark shook his head and laughed. 'I'm sorry. It's sometimes difficult. I always feel that Richard is critical of me. I suppose I'm too conscious of the fact that I'm a novice in these matters. Forgive me, Lexi, I ought not to be so touchy about my dignity. And I'm sure Richard has a very good reason to spend his time with Canon Harmond rather than with me.' Then, to Lexi's relief, he added, 'However, I don't think I'll wait for him any longer. Once the sun goes down your country lanes are a little too dark and narrow for this city man!'

'I'll certainly talk to Richard when I see him,' she assured him. 'And we'll arrange to meet again soon.'

As Mark was taking leave of her, he held on to her hand and said with a look of concern, 'You're quite sure everything is all right, Lexi?'

'Of course,' she said perhaps a shade too emphatically.

He frowned. 'You know I would do anything for you. I owe you everything.'

'That is nonsense. You owe me nothing. Rawdon is

yours by right, Mark. In any case, there is nothing for you to do. Richard and I are very happy together.'

Mark was clearly not altogether convinced. 'Well,' he said doubtfully, 'If there should ever be anything… I'd like you to regard me not just as a cousin, but as a friend.'

Lexi took her hand away. 'I do. Goodnight, Mark. Ride safely.'

After Mark had gone Lexi was left alone with her thoughts. They were not as pleasant as they had been earlier in the day. She paced to and fro in the pretty room that had once belonged to Richard's mother, a prey to renewed uncertainties, willing Richard to come back to kiss away her doubts, help her to forget everything else in the delight of his lovemaking. When one of the servants came to tell her that Richard had been delayed and would not be in till much later, she almost lost her temper with the poor man, restraining herself with difficulty from ordering him to go to the rectory and not to return without his master. She only just managed to thank him with reasonable civility before she started pacing the floor again.

After a while she came to a decision. It was no use, she had to know. Deliberately or not, Richard had managed to make her forget her curiosity about the page from the diary. She had to see it! The valet would be in Richard's room at the moment, it was his time, but he would finish after a while. She would go upstairs and change her dress, then she would look inside that cabinet again.

Upstairs she found that Cissie, who had been almost as happy as Lexi about the recent situation, and was inclined to be a touch sentimental, had plans to dress her hair with flowers. She had looked out a bride-like confection of a dress, too—white gauze over a petticoat of white silk, with roses round the hem and lovers' knots of ribbon at the neck and sleeves.

'Not that one,' said Lexi abruptly. 'Put it away and fetch the plain lilac silk. I'll wear that tonight. And I haven't time to wait while you fuss with my hair. Dress it as usual. Please.'

Cissie looked crestfallen, but did as her mistress ordered. Lexi was unusually silent. She could hardly wait till the maid had finished, and as soon as Cissie had gone she went through to Richard's room again. On the way she was lucky enough to meet Phillips, who was in the dressing room collecting his master's clothes for the evening.

'Lord Deverell is going to be late,' said Lexi. 'You'd better come back in an hour.'

The valet bowed and went out, and, now sure she would be undisturbed, Lexi went on through. This time she did not hesitate. She collected the key, opened the cabinet and started to search feverishly through the folders. The missing page must be somewhere inside them, it must! One folder after another was searched, then discarded, hastily stuffed back, and another collected in its place. She was beginning to despair when she suddenly found what she was looking for.

Almost at the same moment she heard Richard's voice, not, thank heaven, at the door this time, but on the stairs, calling for her.

'Alexandra! Where are you?' He was back! Lexi slipped the page inside her bodice, pushed all the folders further in, then closed and locked the doors of the cabinet on them. Then she ran over to the dressing table and replaced the key. She could hear Richard in her room. He would be through any moment. She snatched up the watchcase that was lying in its usual place, and was turning it over in her hands when he entered.

'This is very nice,' she said, holding it up as he strode towards her. Ignoring her words, he pulled her into his arms and kissed her thoroughly. 'Oh Lord, I thought I should never get back to you,' he said. 'I was supposed to be advising poor Harmond, but all I could think was that you were here, waiting for me. Have you missed me?'

Held fast in his arms, her feelings in turmoil, she nodded without speaking.

'You can't imagine how I've longed for this,' he said, his face buried in her hair. 'Time away from you is wasted time. Did Mark stay long?'

'Till it was almost dark. He waited as long as he could.'

'I suppose I'm glad you had company. But now he's gone and we're alone again. I see you're dressed for dinner. I had thought we might have it sent up here— would you like that?'

'But the servants—'

'Hang the servants! I want to be alone with my wife, to be close to her, not sitting with yards of dining table between us, and hundreds of servants marching in and out!'

Lexi was forced to laugh. 'Richard! The dining table is reduced and we have Kirby and one footman when we're alone! And what would Mrs Chowen say if she heard of such goings-on?'

'Chowen is a sentimental old soul at heart. She wouldn't turn a hair. But why are we talking about servants? If I wasn't so hungry, I'd toss you on to that bed right now and ravish you on the spot! What do you say?'

Lexi was torn. The thought of an intimate supper for two in that bedroom was extremely enticing, but at the moment her feelings were so confused she was not sure she could bear it. It occurred to her, too, that she had to get rid of the page she had stuffed inside her bodice before Richard saw it. 'I…I don't think you ought to go hungry, Richard. And…and I think I should prefer to eat downstairs.'

She could see he was disappointed and almost gave in, but hesitated when she remembered the paper hidden in her dress. For a wild moment she wondered whether she should take it out and confront him with it there and then. No, he would take it from her, she was sure. She must have time to read it first. After dinner, perhaps.

He was reluctant to let her go, but had to release her when Phillips came in to help him change. Lexi escaped into her own room where she put the page from her father's diary inside the lid of her jewel box, beside the other one.

Lexi found it nearly impossible to behave normally at dinner. Richard had adopted his public demeanour for the occasion—courteous, reserved, slightly cool. But his eyes rested frequently on his wife, and the expression in them was warm and loving. He was full of plans for Channings, and though Lexi did her best she had a hard time responding to his enthusiasm.

'You're very quiet, my love,' he said finally.

'Am I? I'm sorry. I think I must be tired.'

'You've done too much today. We must see that you

An Important Message from the Editors

Dear Reader,

Because you've chosen to read one of our fine romance novels, we'd like to say "thank you!" And, as a **special** way to thank you, we've selected <u>two more</u> of the books you love so well **plus** two exciting Mystery Gifts to send you — absolutely <u>FREE</u>!

Please enjoy them with our compliments...

Pam Powers

Lift

Peel off seal and place inside...

How to validate your Editor's
"Thank You"
FREE GIFTS

1. Peel off gift seal from front cover. Place it in space provided at right. This automatically entitles you to receive 2 FREE BOOKS and 2 FREE mystery gifts.

2. Send back this card and you'll get 2 new Harlequin® *Historical* novels. These books have a cover price of $5.50 or more each in the U.S. and $6.50 or more each in Canada, but they are yours to keep absolutely free.

3. There's no catch. You're under no obligation to buy anything. We charge nothing—ZERO—for your first shipment. And you don't have to make any minimum number of purchases—not even one!

4. The fact is, thousands of readers enjoy receiving their books by mail from The Harlequin Reader Service®. They enjoy the convenience of home delivery...they like getting the best new novels at discount prices BEFORE they're available in stores... and they love their Reader to Reader subscriber newsletter featuring author news, special book offers, book reviews and much more!

5. We hope that after receiving your free books you'll want to remain a subscriber. But the choice is yours— to continue or cancel, any time at all! So why not take us up on our invitation, with no risk of any kind. You'll be glad you did!

GET TWO *Free* MYSTERY GIFTS...

*SURPRISE MYSTERY GIFTS COULD BE YOURS **FREE** AS A SPECIAL "THANK YOU" FROM THE EDITORS*

DETACH AND MAIL CARD TODAY!

Yes!

I have placed my Editor's "Thank You" seal in the space provided at right. Please send me 2 free books and 2 free mystery gifts. I understand I am under no obligation to purchase any books, as explained on the back and on the opposite page.

PLACE
FREE GIFTS
SEAL
HERE

349 HDL EFV4   **246 HDL EFZ4**

FIRST NAME	LAST NAME

ADDRESS

APT.#	CITY

STATE/PROV.	ZIP/POSTAL CODE

(H-H-08/06)

Thank You!

The Harlequin Reader Service® — Here's How It Works:

Accepting your 2 free books and 2 free mystery gifts places you under no obligation to buy anything. You may keep the books and gifts and return the shipping statement marked "cancel." If you do not cancel, about a month later we'll send you 6 additional books and bill you just $4.69 each in the U.S., or $5.24 each in Canada, plus 25¢ shipping & handling per book and applicable taxes if any.* That's the complete price and — compared to cover prices starting from $5.50 each in the U.S. and $6.50 each in Canada — it's quite a bargain! You may cancel at any time, but if you choose to continue, every month we'll send you 6 more books, which you may either purchase at the discount price or return to us and cancel your subscription.

*Terms and prices subject to change without notice. Sales tax applicable in N.Y. Canadian residents will be charged applicable provincial taxes and GST. All orders subject to approval. Credit or debit balances in a customer's account(s) may be offset by any other outstanding balance owed by or to the customer. Please allow 4 to 6 weeks for delivery.

get an early night.' Lexi went scarlet as he looked at her with a familiar gleam in his eye.

'I...I think I'll go up now,' she faltered.

'Come, we'll go together.' He got up and, waving away the footman, came round to help her himself.

'Oh, but there's no necessity for you to leave the table, too. You haven't finished your wine!'

'I don't need it,' he said. 'I shall come with you. There's something I'd like to give you.'

'What is it?' she asked, wondering what she would say if he was at last offering to show her the page from the diary.

'A very special ring. It belonged to my grandmother. You should have had it earlier, but I was waiting for our anniversary.'

'Anniversary?' Lexi said blankly.

'A week ago today we became lovers. One week of perfect happiness. I wanted to spend the whole day with you, but Mark's visit and the business with Harmond made that impossible. But you shall have the ring. It's upstairs. Come!'

He held out his arm, and Lexi could do nothing but accept it.

They went together into his room, where he settled Lexi down in the armchair and kissed her. 'Sit there while I fetch it, my love. And afterwards you can go to your bed and sleep, if that is your wish. You're looking very beautiful, but rather pale. You mustn't be ill again.' As he picked up the key and went over to the cabinet he asked, 'What did Mark have to say for himself? His visit doesn't seem to have done you much good.'

Lexi watched him nervously, as he put the key in the lock. 'He...he talked of my father. And Rawdon.'

He stopped what he was doing and turned towards

her. 'He didn't upset you, did he? I'll have a word with him if he did!'

'No, no. He means well.'

As Richard turned back again Lexi thought she heard him murmur, 'Oh, does he?' but by now she was too apprehensive to take it in.

He turned the key. The doors of the cabinet burst open and a torrent of folders fell out. The floor was scattered with papers and documents of every description.

'What the devil—?' Richard stared at the floor. The silence was dreadful. It grew and grew until it filled the room. Finally he turned his gaze towards Lexi.

'It appears you've been looking for love letters again,' he said.

Chapter Nine

Richard's look was neutral, his voice expressionless. But it was too much for Lexi's nerve.

'Don't play with me, Richard. You know very well I wasn't,' she snapped.

'Then what *were* you looking for?'

'I told you last time. My father's papers.' She hesitated, took a breath and plunged in. 'To be precise, one particular paper.'

His eyes narrowed. 'Did you find it?' he asked.

'Yes.'

He bent down and flicked over the papers that had spilled out of one of the folders. When he stood up again his eyes were cold.

'I think I know the one. But tell me just the same. What was it, Alexandra?' he demanded harshly. What a change from the lover of the past week, she thought. No trace of softness or affection in this man. She lifted her chin and said deliberately,

'I was looking for the other page from my father's diary. The missing one.' She paused, then added, 'The one you said you knew nothing about.'

Richard turned his back on her with a muttered oath.

When he turned round again he looked…dangerous, as dangerous as he had looked in the library at Rawdon. Lexi thought fleetingly this was how he must have looked to his enemies in Spain—perhaps the moment before they died.

'How did you know I had it?' he asked curtly.

'I saw it in your hand, when we visited Mark. When you were reading it you…you looked as you do now, and it made me wonder. You crumpled it up and put it in your pocket. I made up my mind then that I would see what it was.'

'Why didn't you ask me about it?'

'Don't be absurd. You wouldn't even admit you had it. You would never have shown it to me.'

'You're damned right, I wouldn't!' he said angrily. He thought for a moment, then said more slowly, 'It was before dinner, when I found you in this room. You must have taken it then, but I don't believe you've had time to read it. You're pale and nervous, but not distressed. I probably came back too soon. Where is it?'

Lexi stared at him defiantly.

'Where is it, Alexandra?' He came over and took hold of her arms. 'Tell me where you've put it!'

She found her voice. 'I won't, Deverell! You're right, I haven't yet read it, but I fully intend to!'

He gave her a shake. 'For God's sake, don't give yourself more pain than you've already had, girl! *Give me that page.*'

Lexi wrenched herself away from him. 'I've said I won't!' she replied, her voice rising. 'I can guess what it's about. It's what the blackmailer threatened to tell everyone about my father, isn't it? Isn't it, Deverell?'

Richard pulled her back and held her so tightly that she could hardly breathe. He kissed her savagely, plundering her mouth. 'Don't start calling me Deverell again, Alexandra!' he said roughly. 'I'm not an enemy. Why won't you trust me? Don't spoil everything... Please!'

'*Spoil* everything! What is there to spoil?' Lexi was suddenly so choked with angry tears that she could hardly speak. 'Oh, you make love divinely, *Deverell*, I can't deny that,' she said at last. 'You're very clever. A woman can forget everything in the world while she's in your arms—Johnny, the diary, everything! I was fool enough to believe you really loved me. But I was wrong, wasn't I? You wouldn't hide things from me, look at me the way you looked just now if you loved me. You married me because you were *sorry* for me, didn't you? Because you had made a promise to my father. Why weren't you honest with me? A normal, businesslike arrangement would have been enough—the sort of marriage I offered you. You really didn't have to pretend it was something different.'

Richard went very still. 'I don't understand. What promise?'

'Don't pretend you don't know! Mark told me this afternoon. He was there when my father made you promise to protect me. And though he tried not to let me see, it was clear he thought that was the only reason you married me. Was it?'

'I see... Mark told you... Mark *thought*... And now you...you *think* I was lying when I said I loved you? That this past week, when we made such exquisite love, I was *pretending*? And all those plans we made for our future, for a life together at Channings...you thought they were all part of a meaningless *business arrangement* I made with your father?' He stood back from her and shook his head as if to clear it. His next words seemed to be to himself. 'I...I hadn't realised. This week I would have said we had put all our misunderstandings behind us, that we now had faith in one another at last.' He gazed at her with a puzzled frown. 'I thought I had found what I had waited for all my life. But from what you've just said, it isn't so, after all—there isn't any faith. You still don't trust me.'

The pain in Richard's voice twisted Lexi's heart. Full of contrition she came back and put her hand on his arm.

'No, no, Alexandra,' he said, thrusting her away from him. 'I must think... I didn't realise you could still feel like this...' Then, making a visible effort to pull himself together, he said in a different tone, 'But all that must wait. I *did* make a promise, though it wasn't what Mark said it was. And now I must keep it. Give me the page you took from my cabinet *now*, before you read it, and we'll...we'll start again. Try to put the pieces back together. But first you *must* give me that page.'

Richard's rejection of her attempt to comfort, his insistence on her obedience had served to harden Lexi. She lifted her chin and said stubbornly, 'You won't change my mind, Deverell. I have a right to know what it was my father wrote in his diary. I will not hand it over unread.'

'No, damn it, you have *no* right! It was in your father's personal diary, written by him, and not meant for anyone else's eyes.' He held her by the shoulders and looked intensely into her eyes. '*Listen* to me! Mark was wrong. Your father had known for years that I wanted to marry you. He didn't have to make me swear to that. The promise I made him was to protect you from...from learning what the blackmailer threatened to tell. *That* is what I swore to him. He was desperate that you should never know. It's my belief that he tore out those two pages himself, so that there was no risk you would ever see them. God knows how either of them arrived back on his desk after he was dead!' He took a breath, then said with a good deal of force, 'I insist that you give me that piece of paper, Alexandra. You must obey me in this. I command you!'

'*Command* me? *No!* I will *not!*' cried Lexi, staring at him wildly. 'I *will* read that page!' Then she turned and fled into her own room, slamming the door and locking it behind her. She ran over to the one leading to the landing and locked it too. Then she took the page out of the jewel box, and, ignoring the hammering on her door, she started to read its two closely written sides eagerly, holding the page close to the light. After the first few lines her father's words leapt off the page and threatened to stifle her very breath. She had never expected anything like this, not in her most desperate imaginings…

Today Richard has confirmed that it is true about Johnny. My worst fears have been realised and I shall have to pay my tormentor after all. Oh God, I was so sure beforehand that Richard would laugh at me, tell me to dismiss what was in that letter as the work of a crank. But instead he confirmed every detail. How can I bear it? To think that Johnny, my proud soldier, my son, my joy, was caught red-handed selling his country's secrets to the enemy!

I have never seen Richard so angry. He had worked so hard to spare Johnny's family the truth and was furious that I knew it after all. Afterwards he told me the rest of what happened that night, hoping, I suppose, to give me what comfort he could. The safety of our country was never under threat—the documents were rescued before they could be taken away and used. And Johnny had evaded capture in the tavern, though I suspect Richard had a hand in that. By the time he got back to their rooms Johnny was dead, killed by his own hand. Richard seemed to blame himself for not preventing it, but I was glad. Glad! Is that so unnatural? My son's death spared the Rawdons the disgrace of a court-martial and a certain execution. And, thanks to Richard's efforts to give it the appearance of an accident, Johnny has even been decently buried in the family plot. And there he shall stay, whether I am committing a sin in leaving him there or not.

I thanked Richard for all he had done, but when he demanded to know who had told me I refused. How could I confess that I was about to submit to a blackmailer's threats? That someone else knows it all and wishes me to buy his silence. As I will. I must. If the truth were made public, the Rawdons would be disgraced forever. What would happen to Lexi then? Richard has sworn she will never learn what happened from him.

But what am I to do if this villain proves to be greedy, and demands more in the future? Rawdon is rich, but most of our money is bound up in the land. Raising further sums would be very difficult. I must face that when it comes. Meanwhile I must pay. Oh, Johnny, Johnny!

She jumped as the door crashed open and Richard appeared.

'Give me that!'

Lexi handed it over without a word. He looked at her white face. 'You've read it,' he said. He caught her as she swayed. 'You fool, Alexandra! You damned fool! What good does it do you to know the truth?'

But at this she pulled away and looked at him with blazing eyes. 'The truth? You really believe this…this nonsense?'

'You're distraught. I knew you would be. Come, let me send for Cissie. We still have some of Dr Loudon's sleeping draughts, I believe. You'll feel better if you have a rest.'

'Leave me alone! I don't want Cissie. I'm not distraught, I'm *angry*! And astonished.'

'Astonished?'

'*How* could you or my father believe that Johnny was a traitor? It is *impossible*!'

'The evidence was overwhelming. Believe me, Alexandra, if there had been any room for doubt I wouldn't have rested till I had proved him innocent.' He burst out, 'God damn it, do you think I *wanted* Johnny to be guilty? He was my friend, I owed him my life—' He broke off and turned away.

'What evidence was there? You can't have looked hard enough.' When Richard didn't immediately reply she cried, '*Tell* me! But I warn you, Deverell, whatever you say, I shall *never* believe Johnny was a traitor! It just wasn't in him! He had his faults, but *that*? Never, do you hear? *Never*!'

Richard moved restlessly around the room. His own face was pale, and he wore a deeply troubled expression. Finally he said, 'I did my best to keep my word to your father. But I've failed. And now I think it better to tell you the rest. You'll find it difficult to deny then that Johnny…that Johnny was indisputably guilty.'

Lexi came close and stared him in the eye. 'You can give me all the evidence you like,' she said belligerently, 'but I still won't accept it. I only want to know what it is so I can find the fault in it!'

He regarded her with a look of compassion. 'Shall we sit down? And I think I'd like that glass of wine after all. You'd be the better for one, too.'

Richard sent for wine and glasses, then they settled themselves on the chairs in Lexi's room. She waited patiently, while he sipped the wine and collected his thoughts. She wanted to hear every last detail. Eventually he began.

'Johnny had been working for some months at the Horse Guards before I joined him there. When I arrived in April he was restless, unhappy, eager to be in action, not, as he called it, trundling papers round like a messenger boy. You asked me yourself at the time whether he was drinking. He was. Too much. Probably more than you could imagine. He was gambling, too.' Richard gave a hint of a smile. 'You know as well as I do that Johnny hadn't the head for either.' Lexi nodded, her eyes intent.

'I'm telling you this just to give you the background. I wasn't worried. I was convinced that once we were in action again, in Belgium, France—wherever—Johnny would be himself again.' He stopped. 'He was a bonny fighter. One of the best.'

'But that's why I know that he wasn't a traitor! Johnny was absolutely straight. He could be selfish, but he was brave and true. Why couldn't you see that? Why did you of all people condemn him?'

Richard looked grim. 'I'm afraid I had no choice,' he said and went on. 'As soon as I arrived I heard there was trouble at the Horse Guards. We had a rotten apple among us, someone selling information to Bonaparte's spies. Some of the letters and lists Johnny and I were handling were very sensitive—the Duke was desperate for men and weapons and sent a stream of demands, some of them with vital information about his plans for the disposition of the Allied forces. He sent them through us because we knew enough about his strategies to explain what he meant to the right people. So we had to be extra careful.'

'In other words, the Duke knew he could trust you? Both of you.'

'He thought he could, yes.'

'He *did* and he was *right*! Go on. So far, all you've told me is that Johnny was bored and finding amusement in the wrong places. That's not a hanging offence, surely?'

'Alexandra, I'm not enjoying this. You'll have to be patient.' Richard drank some wine. He continued, 'I had been asked in confidence to keep an eye on one particular person—not someone in the Army, a civilian—who was possibly a French agent. One day we got word that he was expecting to be given something of great importance that same night. I took two of my most trusted sergeants—men who had fought under me in the Peninsula—and followed him to an inn among the slums of the city.'

At this point Richard appeared to forget her, forget where he was. He was reliving a scene that had taken place months ago, and his voice betrayed how vivid it was in his mind, how sharp the pain still was. He went on.

'It was dark inside, crowded and full of smoke. The

smell was terrible. We weren't in uniform, so we were able to move about without being noticed. The man we wanted was in a corner, near one of the doors—' He stopped.

'Go *on*!' said Lexi, urgently.

'We waited. Then someone approached our man. He had on a cape, and a hat well pulled down over his eyes. A suspicious character, you might say. We saw them…we saw them haggle for a moment over a parcel the man in the cape had in his hand. Then the parcel was handed over and a purse given in exchange.' He stopped. 'The picture of that purse has stayed in my mind, haunting me. I can still see it. The Frenchman handed it over, and, just as the other took it, some trick of the light caught it, so it was clearly visible in his hand.'

'What did you do?'

'We went after them. We rescued the papers first— saving them was vitally important—and one of my sergeants arrested the French agent. But some of our friends in the tavern thought it was anybody's fight, and in the mêlée that followed the other man, the man in the hat and cape, got away.'

'My father thought that you had made sure he did.'

'Did he?' Richard's face was shuttered. 'Perhaps I did.'

'Why?'

'Because, God help me, I had recognised the man in the cape. It was Johnny.'

'It can't have been! How could you possibly be sure? A dark tavern, the cape, the hat… How could you possibly tell?'

'I caught a glimpse of his face.'

'Pshaw! A glimpse. Under a hat.'

'That hat was Johnny's. I knew it very well. He'd had it for years, a battered felt hat. He wore it a lot of the time we were in Spain to keep the sun off. It was a standing joke with all of us, but he still wore it. Yes, it was his, all right.'

'How can you be sure? There must be *hundreds* of such hats. No, Deverell, you haven't convinced me. And you never will!'

'Wait! There's more.'

'Well, tell me!'

'Your father was right, I was so certain it was Johnny that, once I was sure the documents were safe, I allowed him to escape in the fight. But I kept an eye on him and as he went out of the door one of the fellows in the tavern knocked the hat off. Johnny's hair wasn't as bright as yours, but it was still quite distinctive.'

Lexi was not giving way. 'We're not the only red-headed family in England—and your man could have been Irish! There are hundreds of red-haired Irishmen.'

Richard carried on as if she hadn't spoken. 'I collected the documents and arranged for the Frenchman to be taken away. When I got back to our rooms Johnny was slumped over the table, quite dead. He had shot himself.'

Lexi got up and walked away. With her back to him she said painfully, 'That is the only thing I cannot argue about. Johnny undeniably died that night. And I think…I do believe now that you made it look like an accident, in order to spare us.'

'Thank you,' he said with a touch of irony.

She swung round. 'But I still don't accept your story!'

'Hell's teeth, what more do you need? Why else would he have shot himself? He wasn't expecting to see

me in that tavern. He must have known he'd been recognised, that there was no real escape.' Richard buried
his head in his hands. 'Oh God, Alexandra,' he said in
a muffled voice. 'How do you suppose I felt when I saw
him? If there had been any other way of explaining it
all, don't you think I would have grabbed it with both
hands?'

'Johnny wasn't a traitor,' she said stubbornly.

Richard looked up and said slowly and deliberately,
'The documents that were being sold that evening were
ones that had been in Johnny's possession all day. I had
seen them myself on his table in the afternoon. I was
even annoyed with him because he had been careless
enough to leave them out in full view for anyone to
read.'

This was a body blow. Lexi felt as if her knees would
give way and she sat down suddenly. Richard poured
her another glass of wine. 'Drink this.'

She took the glass and sipped at it. Her hand was
trembling so badly that some of the wine spilled out on
to her dress.

'Here, let me.' Taking the glass from her, Richard
knelt beside her chair, and put one arm round her shoulders. He held the wine to her lips. 'You look paler than
you did in the church at our wedding. And it's my fault.
Why the devil was I so careless with that piece of paper? You should never have seen it!'

Lexi took another sip of the wine then pushed it
away. 'You mustn't say that. If I hadn't, you would
never have thought of proving Johnny innocent.'

Richard put the glass down and sat back on his heels.
He said gently, 'I wish with all my heart that we could.
But you have only just discovered what Johnny did,
whereas I have lived with it for months, thought about

it for months. Johnny was as guilty as hell. It would be impossible to prove anything different. You're shocked at the moment, of course you are. I can't tell you how I felt—still feel. It was almost as if the bottom had fallen out of my world. But I truly believe that the best way to go forward is to accept that he's guilty, and try to forgive him.'

Lexi jumped up, kicking the wine glass over as she did so. 'Don't be so stupid!' she shouted. 'I tell you, there's nothing to forgive! Yes, I've had a shock, yes, I'm distressed. But I have not gone completely mad. And I would have to be *quite out of my mind* to accept what you're saying!'

'Your father wouldn't have agreed with you. He accepted it—'

'My father was old and ill. Johnny's death alone was enough to unbalance him. But even he didn't really believe it, till you came with your tale and your so-called "evidence"!'

Richard drew in a breath, then let it slowly out. 'If you had read that entry more carefully, you'd know that I didn't have to tell your father anything. He already knew the "tale", as you call it. Someone else knew about it and was threatening to tell the world unless he was paid. By the time I found *that* out your father had practically ruined himself meeting his blackmailer's demands. I told you, I did my best to persuade your father to fight, but he wouldn't risk it. I assure you, Alexandra, every detail the blackmailer gave your father was correct.'

'Except the most important. It wasn't Johnny who sold those papers.'

'My God, you're obstinate. How can you be so wilfully blind? Every bit of proof points to Johnny's guilt. It all fits.'

Lexi was silent for some minutes, and Richard could have been forgiven for thinking she was finally convinced. But then she said,

'I want to go to London.'

'London? What can you do there?'

'What can I do in Somerset? There's nothing here to help me.'

'I'm not sure I understand what you are talking about. Help what? How?'

'You're not usually stupid, Deverell. I want to see where Johnny died. I want to meet his other friends, the people he worked with. Above all, I want to talk to the men who were with you that night.'

Richard stared at her in astonishment. When he recovered he said violently, 'On no account! I wouldn't let you near them.'

'Why not?' she demanded.

'You do realise, don't you, that I had to persuade them to keep quiet about Johnny? They recognised him too, you know. And they agreed because they'd known and liked Johnny for years. One or other of them even—' He stopped abruptly.

'One or other of them did what?'

'The Frenchman died in the fight that night. I was never sure who killed him, but I suspect Sergeant Chalmers might have thought he was better out of the way. Dead men don't tell tales. He was always ruthlessly loyal to men he had fought under, and Johnny had been a favourite of his.' He paused and said, 'That's why I found it hard to believe that either of the sergeants was blackmailing your father. But I couldn't think who else would know about it. I fully intended to question them, but then Sir Jeremy died, and I thought it better to leave it alone.'

'If that's the case, I want to talk to them even more!'

'I said no! They are not men you ought ever to meet.'

'Don't talk rubbish, I'll do whatever I have to. But I'm not sure I can do it by myself. You must help me!'

'To do what? To beat your head against the brick wall of Johnny's guilt? I certainly won't help you to do that, Alexandra. And if you start to ask questions about the circumstances surrounding Johnny's death, you could well undo everything I tried to do for him and for your family.'

Lexi was silent again. 'Very well,' she said after a pause. 'If you'll excuse me, I think I'd like to go to bed. Alone.'

The single word hovered like an invisible sword in the air. There was a short silence. Then Richard nodded. 'Certainly,' he said coolly. 'That was to be expected.' He was once again the reserved, formal man of the past. The idyll of the last week might never have been. 'I'll send one of the maids to mop up the wine. Can you wait? I'll see she comes promptly. Goodnight, Alexandra.' He bowed and went through to his own room. He shut Lexi's door quietly, but so firmly that the sound echoed in her ears like a knell.

Lexi's heart was heavy, but she spent half the night making plans. It would have been easier if Richard had agreed to help, but his refusal had neither surprised nor deterred her. She knew her brother was innocent and was determined to prove it. Her godmother had quite a few friends—she might know someone who could help. But Richard had been right in one respect. In making her enquiries she must take care not to raise the slightest doubt about the manner of Johnny's death. An accident was what everyone thought it, and that was what it must remain until she had proof of his innocence. She started to think...

In the early hours of the morning she fell asleep at last, only to wake an hour or two later with tears on her face. Her body was alive with desire, aching with the memory of the previous nights, longing for the warmth of Richard's body next to her, the comfort of his arms, his strength and passion, his love...

But after a while she had herself under control again. What sort of love had it been? How quickly Richard had changed when she had defied him, how firmly he had pushed her away, grown cool towards her, commanded, without any attempt at persuasion, that she should obey him. Could he have behaved like that if he really loved her? And, most significantly of all, could he have accepted her decision to sleep alone so calmly? No, Richard had probably married her out of pity, as his Aunt Honoria and Mark thought.

And now the gulf between them was so deep that she wondered if it could ever be bridged. She could hardly believe that Richard really thought Johnny guilty of treason. How could he? After all those years of friendship, their closeness as children, their life together since, how could Richard, knowing Johnny so well, *possibly* believe him guilty? *Richard* was the traitor, betraying all those special bonds that she thought had held the three of them together. He had condemned her lack of faith. But what of his own? The very foundation of their relationship had been cracked by it.

Lexi shivered. One week of such happiness as she had never before known. And now a chasm had sprung open between Richard and herself, a chasm that could only get deeper after she had begun to carry out the plans she had been making.

Richard fetched a bottle of brandy and put it by his bed. Then he poured himself a glass, drank it in one draught and threw himself down. He gazed moodily at the ceiling. After years of waiting, and the unexpected trauma of the wedding and its aftermath, he had finally achieved his longed-for goal—the prospect of happy years at Channings with the love of his life. Alexandra's warmth, their love for each other, their children, would breathe life into the empty rooms, and break down the barriers he had built up between himself and anyone who could hurt him as his father had hurt him.

It had been a dream, a fantasy, and it had lasted not much more than a week. He and Alexandra were now further apart than ever. How could she believe for one moment that he had married her from a sense of duty? Why couldn't she see that he loved her more than life? Had always loved her. How could she possibly have so little faith in him that she allowed an idle remark from a cousin she hadn't even known for more than a month or two to have such an influence on her? That had hurt in a way he had sworn he would never let anything hurt him again.

And now she had raised the spectre of Johnny, had forced him to relive the worst moments of his life.

He could see with dreadful clarity the scene in that tavern, still feel his incredulous shock when he had recognised the hat, seen the hair, looked at those accursed documents. He had hurried back to their rooms, hoping against hope that there had been some dreadful mistake, that the documents in Johnny's charge were still safely on the table. Or that Johnny himself would be there with an explanation—that it had been a mad trick, a brain-storm, or even a ruse to trap the Frenchman.

He was used to the sight of blood—what soldier would not be?—but he would never forget the shock when he saw Johnny's body in a pool of blood, his own *treacherous* blood.

Richard turned over with a groan and buried his head in the pillow. Why hadn't Johnny died in battle? He would have taken it hard, missed him, but eventually he would have learned to live with it, to be proud of having known Johnny Rawdon. But this...this was like a canker, eating away at everything he thought he had known about his friend, everything he had admired.

And now Johnny Rawdon's sister wanted to bring it all back, prove him innocent. It was impossible.

Richard lay awake for some time, pouring brandy and drinking it steadily. It was one way to seek oblivion. It eventually worked and he fell asleep, but his sleep was disturbed by wild dreams. For one moment Alexandra was next to him, her long limbs entangled with his, responding with all the surprising passion of the previous week. Then he was suddenly back in that tavern, and Alexandra was disappearing through the door, red hair flying, struggling to escape with a purse that was too heavy for her to manage. He woke up with a shout after he had dreamed of seeing Johnny's body, stretched on a table, his head covered in blood... But when he had looked again the face wasn't Johnny's. It was Alexandra's.

Richard got out of bed. He felt terrible. He poured himself another glass of brandy and then sat in the chair by the window till dawn. What was he to do? What the hell was he to do?

* * *

The next day Richard announced he would be out till the afternoon. He did not say what he would be doing, nor did Lexi ask. His absence was an unexpected bonus and she had no wish to detain him. She wrote two notes first thing in the morning and despatched them at speed to the receiving office in Dorchester to catch the early mail. If the groom who took them wondered why the wife of a peer had not asked her husband to frank them for her, he was too well trained to say anything. Then she went to the stables to find Will Osborne and asked him to have the gig ready in about an hour for a brief trip to Dorchester. She also selected one or two items from her wardrobe and concealed them in a bag that she herself fetched from the attics. Lastly she wrote another note addressed to Richard and sealed it carefully. This she put inside the lid of her jewel box.

Richard spent the morning riding on isolated tracks and little-used lanes, and after a while the fresh air and silence began to cure his aching head and he was able to think more clearly. His marriage had begun disastrously, and after a short period of world-shaking happiness disaster had struck again. He and Alexandra had come a long way from that scene in the vestry, but he now suspected he had been a fool to believe that miracles could happen, that happiness in love *was* achievable. The secret of happiness, as he had discovered at a very early age, was to keep one's emotions under strict control, to expect nothing of anyone. He had forgotten this rule this past week—he must take care to remember it in future.

With his usual self-discipline he put aside his own deep unhappiness, and turned his mind to the question of Johnny. Why couldn't Alexandra have had the same blind faith in her husband as she had in her brother? To believe in Johnny's innocence was against all logic, all reason. But she was absolutely certain of it. Richard rode on, remembering her passionate conviction, and found himself beginning to reconsider his own verdict on Johnny. This was absurd! The facts shouted his guilt. It was true that at the time he had felt the same incredulity, had had the same difficulty in believing Johnny guilty, but the evidence was overwhelming. Except for one tiny detail, everything fitted perfectly, incontrovertibly.

Except for one tiny detail... Richard rode on considering that detail. The purse. He had not found anything like the purse of money the Frenchman had handed over to Johnny in the tavern. Johnny was perennially hard up—it had been a joke between them. But afterwards, when he had searched Johnny's room and belongings to make sure that there was nothing to contradict the accident theory, he had not found any large sums of money. Where had the purse gone? He didn't believe one of the servants could have taken it and left without raising an alarm. The sight of Johnny's body would have been enough to send anyone screaming from the room. Besides, the servants had all been out for the day.

Richard frowned. Where *had* that money gone?

After a moment he turned round and set off back to Channings. He had come to a decision. He would do as Alexandra wished, and take her to London. Her unswerving certainty that they had all been wrong about Johnny made it impossible to be at ease while any questions, however trivial, remained unanswered.

When he got back he was disconcerted to find that his wife had gone to Dorchester. He was slightly surprised that she had the energy after the turbulence of the day before, and wondered what she could have to do there. It was market day, of course. Perhaps she thought the excursion would take her mind off her woes? It was annoying that she was not at home to hear of his change of mind, but he could wait. She would be safe enough. Will Osborne was with her, and he was devoted to her. He wouldn't let her overtire herself.

Richard went to the library where he sat down to work. If he and Alexandra were to set off for London at such short notice, there were things to be done. The staff in his house in Brook Street would have to be informed, and the servants here told what to do in his absence, too. One of the grooms was despatched with a letter to his housekeeper in London, another to the Rectory carrying Richard's excuses for a meeting he would not now be able to attend. Soon the household was in a bustle of activity. The decision might seem sudden, but that was no excuse for delay. To the surprise of his household, his lordship was taking his new wife to London.

Chapter Ten

An hour later Richard had accomplished most of what was necessary, and was beginning to wonder where Alexandra was. There was a knock at the library door and Mrs Chowen came in, her rosy face showing unusual concern.

'What is it?' asked Richard.

'I hope you'll forgive me, my lord,' she said with a curtsy. 'But we were wondering about Lady Deverell. There's not that much to do in Dorchester, even on a market day, and she's been gone quite a long time. We all expected her back before now.'

'Oh, I don't think we need worry, Mrs Chowen. Osborne is with her. She's safe enough with him.'

Mrs Chowen did not appear to be reassured. She hesitated and looked as if she was wondering what to say next.

'What is it, Mrs Chowen?'

'Lady Deverell's maid is outside, my lord. I think she'd like to tell you something…'

'Cissie? Send her in.'

Cissie came in, timidly made her curtsy, then looked

at Mrs Chowen and waited. 'Well?' said Richard. 'What is it?'

'Mrs Chowen thought I ought to tell you, my lord...'

'Go on,' said Richard rather impatiently.

'It was when I was asked to pack her ladyship's things, my lord. When I looked for what she would need for the journey I found that some of her things were missing from the dressing table. And one of her nightgowns is missing, too. And some of those books that were on the table in the corner.'

Richard got up. 'Are you sure?'

'Oh, yes, I'm quite sure. I know all her ladyship's things.'

Richard smothered an exclamation and hurried upstairs. When he looked round the bedchamber he saw that the girl was right—the basic necessities for Alexandra's toilet were not there. Nor was the diary. When he opened her jewel box and looked inside the lid, he saw that the loose pages from the diary had disappeared. In their place was a note addressed to him.

Richard—You wouldn't listen so I have to do it by myself. I shall stay with my godmother in London. Please don't come to fetch me back. You would be wasting your time. Alexandra.

Richard stared at the note in growing anger. He could hardly take it in. Alexandra had gone to London without a word of warning, had left without giving him any chance to discuss the matter, or to tell her of his decision to take her himself. But why was he surprised? It was absolutely typical of the girl to act first and think afterwards, with no thought of possible repercussions.

What the devil did she believe she could do on her own in London?

Richard went over to stand at the window while he attempted to get his feelings under control. After a moment anger was mixed with concern. What was she doing, taking off for London with only an elderly groom for company? How did she propose to get there? As far as he knew, she didn't have the resources to travel in anything like safety or style. Anything could happen to her! Anything at all! Will Osborne wouldn't be much use in a real emergency. Richard shut his eyes and told himself that he was being stupid. This was no way to deal with the situation. Getting in a panic was useless, he must think.

After a moment he was sufficiently in command of himself to face his staff. He would have to go after her, of course, and that meant a hasty change of all his plans. He went towards the door where he was met by Mrs Chowen.

She had obviously come up the stairs in a hurry—she was flushed and panting. 'Will Osborne is back, my lord. But he's alone.'

'What?'

'I haven't had a chance to talk to him—he's just this minute arrived.'

Richard brushed past her and ran down the stairs. The groom was in the hall, twisting his hat in his hand and looking distressed.

'What the devil are you doing here, Osborne? Where is her ladyship? Why aren't you with her?'

'Her ladyship is on her way to London, my lord. She caught the stage at Dorchester about an hour ago. She didn't say anything to me about it aforehand, she was off afore I knew. I didn't know what to do for the best, so I came back here straight away to let you know as soon as possible.'

Richard didn't waste time in asking why the groom hadn't stopped his mistress from leaving. He knew his Alexandra—too strong-willed for her own good. He demanded, 'But why the hell didn't you go with her?'

'I couldn't! They were full—they wouldn't let me on!' Will Osborne looked ashamed. 'I'm that sorry, my lord. But Miss Lexi was always able to get the better of me when she had a mind to it.'

Richard paused. 'The stage, you say?'

'To Salisbury, my lord. Her ladyship won't get further tonight—when I asked at the ticket office they said it was a slow one—it won't reach Salisbury till seven.'

Richard stopped to think. 'She won't come to much harm on a stagecoach, though she'll be damned uncomfortable. It was full, you said?'

'Not another place on it—I'd have taken it if there had been.'

'Seven o'clock at Salisbury... I don't suppose I'll be able to catch up with it much before then. Right, Osborne. You may go.'

Osborne stopped at the door. 'I'd... I'd like to go with you if you'll take me, my lord.'

Richard looked at his dusty face and weary stance. 'I think not. I intend to travel as speedily as I can. You need a rest—I don't suppose you spared yourself or the horses on the way back from Dorchester, did you?'

'I was worried about Miss Lexi. I still am.'

'You needn't be. I'll find her, never doubt it. The Rawdons usually stopped at the White Hart in Salisbury, I believe?'

'Yes, my lord. The master always stayed there whenever he was in Salisbury. We're pretty well known there.'

'Then that's where she'll be. Thank you. Tell Coles to saddle up two of the best horses, then see to your own team and get some rest.'

As Richard got ready to go he was once again angry and aggrieved. Alexandra, it appeared, had been so eager to get away that she had run off unescorted on a common stagecoach, and by now was God knew where on the road to Salisbury. He shook his head in frustration. This was so like her! Impulsive to a fault, plunging in without thought for any consequences. It would serve her right if he left her to manage by herself, but that was out of the question. She would be safe enough on the coach, but heaven knew what might happen to her, alone and unprotected in a large town. He *must* reach Salisbury before seven.

The preparations for the planned excursion to London were already well under way. All Richard had to do was to make sure that all the servants knew their orders, and then bring his own departure forward. He sent his valet to pack him an overnight bag immediately, told Mrs Chowen to see to it that Lady Deverell's luggage, together with her maid, were in his lordship's coach before dawn the next morning, and sent reminders to his coachman and head groom that his travelling coach was to be at the White Hart Inn in Salisbury before midday the next day.

Within half an hour Richard had set off for the road to London via Salisbury. He smiled grimly. Lady Deverell was in for a shock.

Lexi had never travelled by stagecoach before, and was not enjoying the experience. The Accommodation

Coach rumbled and swayed through Piddletown, Winterbourne Whitchurch, and Blandford, setting down and picking up, but always remaining uncomfortably overcrowded. She sat squashed between a lady of ample girth and creaking stays, and a thin solicitor's clerk with extremely sharp elbows. The clerk said very little, but the lady never stopped talking. By the time they reached Blandford Lexi's head was aching and so were her ribs. She was glad to get out with all the other passengers to stretch her cramped limbs and breathe in some cool evening air. For those who felt like them, refreshments were to be had. Lexi did not feel like anything at all. Then the passengers climbed in again and the coach lumbered off, swaying if anything more than before. The solicitor's clerk had left the coach at Blandford, but his place had been taken by a farmer twice his size on his way to Salisbury to see his son. The clerk's sharp elbows had been replaced with a farmer's stout haunches. The clerk had at least been silent, but the farmer liked to talk. His voice was loud and penetrating, and he spent the rest of the journey exchanging stories over Lexi's head with the fat lady.

By the time the coach reached Salisbury her headache was worse than ever, her legs were so stiff she felt she might never walk again, and her dress was crumpled beyond cure. She also felt distinctly in need of a wash. She stumbled out of the coach and went to see to her bag.

'Let me do that for you,' said a familiar voice.

With a sense of inevitability she turned to see Richard smiling sardonically at her efforts to straighten up.

'You!' she said. 'How on earth did you get here?'

'More comfortably than you did, apparently. What have you done to yourself?'

Lexi shuddered. 'I can't begin to tell you.'

Richard took her arm and gave her bag to a porter. 'I've taken the liberty of changing your room at the White Hart,' he said. 'You'll be more comfortable in the rooms I've engaged for us both.'

Lexi accompanied him without protest into the hotel and up to their rooms on the first floor. She was horrified when she went to the mirror and saw how she looked.

'Unfortunately I left in too much of a hurry to bring a change of clothing for you,' said Richard. 'But the carriage will be here tomorrow with Cissie. You'll have fresh clothes then. That dress you're wearing looks as if it should be thrown on the rubbish heap.'

'The carriage?' Lexi's face was set. 'I told you in my note. I won't go back with you! I'm going to London.'

Richard, too, had had a hard day, followed by a punishing ride from Channings to Salisbury. He said forcefully, 'If I choose to take you, you'll go back to Channings whether you want to or not, my girl! If you behave like a wilful child, you should be treated like one.'

'Is it so childish to want to clear my brother's name?' cried Lexi angrily.

'At the moment, in the eyes of the world your brother's name is perfectly clear. I worked damned hard to make sure of that. But that won't last long if you rush in asking questions and raising doubts with no thought for the consequences.' He went on with marked irritation, 'My God, Alexandra, will you *never* learn to take time to consider before you act?'

'What do you mean?'

'I would have thought you'd learned your lesson! As you may or may not remember, if I hadn't persuaded you to hold your fire a short while ago I would now be dead. Even you would admit that *that* might have been a mistake.'

She stared at him aghast. So much had occurred she had almost forgotten that scene in the church. The thought now that she could have killed Richard horrified her. Her eyes dropped. 'I was ill,' she muttered. 'I didn't know what I was doing.'

'I would still have been dead,' he said implacably.

Lexi rallied and said defiantly, 'If you and my father had taken me into your confidence instead of treating me like a child it would never have happened.'

'And if you had had confidence in *me* it wouldn't have happened, either! But no. You preferred to listen to your damned cousin—someone you hardly knew. Just as you allowed him to make trouble yesterday.'

'Don't be so unfair, Deverell! Mark isn't to blame for any of this. Why do you condemn him for telling me the truth? You *did* play cards with my father, you *did* quarrel with him afterwards. Mark only told me because I *asked* him to, after I'd heard the servants talking. Besides, I told you, that wasn't why I wanted to kill you that day. Mark wasn't even there when I came across the most damning piece of evidence of all— when I thought you had killed Johnny.'

'You *thought*! Exactly! And you're still leaping to the wrong conclusions, still prepared to believe the worst of me—' He stopped and then went on, making an obvious effort to speak more calmly. 'It won't do, Alexandra. This is not the sort of marriage I want. You must have faith in me or I can't—'

Lexi lost her temper. She cried, 'You can't what,

Richard? Treat me as a grown woman? You don't do that now. You've always treated me as a child! Are you *sure* you didn't marry me because you were sorry for me?'

'For God's sake, Alexandra, don't start that again! Why won't you believe that was Mark's mischief?'

'It wasn't only Mark who made me think so. Your Aunt Honoria said much the same.'

'Aunt Honoria? When?'

'The first time she spoke to me after I was brought to Channings. She was angry with me for being so ungrateful, when you had been so kind. *Kind*! I didn't want your *kindness*!'

'Nor was it what I offered you.'

'I didn't *know* what you were offering. I wasn't sure of anything any more. But she said then that you had married me out of pity. I can surely be forgiven for believing Mark, when he appears to think the same as your own aunt.'

'What the devil does Mark know about anything, damn him? Except how to interfere.'

'Mark has done nothing but support me and try to help me. Why are you so critical of him? Are you sure you're not jealous?'

Richard was astounded. '*Jealous*? Of Mark Rawdon? Good God, no!' With an exclamation of disgust he walked round the room. Then he stopped and faced her. 'Or…am I wrong?' he said. 'Should I be?' He looked at her shocked face and threw out a hand in a gesture of denial. 'No, forget that. I don't know why I said it. Dear God, how did we get to this point?' He turned away abruptly and ran his hand through his hair. 'I think I need some air.'

Lexi did not relent. She said stonily, 'And I would like a bath after that terrible journey.'

'I'll send a maidservant up to you,' he said. He nodded and went out.

The servants brought up water and filled up the bath in the room next door, which proved to be a kind of dressing room. Richard was out long enough for Lexi to take her bath and have something to eat, too. She was bone weary, but she decided to wait up. There was still unfinished business between Richard and herself, and she was determined to settle it that night. When he came in she was sitting ready for bed in the settle by the fire.

'I thought you'd be asleep,' he said coolly.

'I waited for you. I had to make sure you understood. I will not go back to Channings.'

'Not ever?' he asked, without expression.

That gave Lexi a shock. 'Why do you say that? That's not what I meant at all. Channings is my home! I just meant that I had written to my godmother to tell her I am coming to London for a short time and asking her if I may stay in Curzon Street with her. She will be expecting me.'

'Then she will be disappointed.'

'Richard, I tell you—' she began hotly.

'Before you go any further,' he said wearily, 'let me tell you what *I* have in mind. I planned to tell you this earlier today when I got back to Channings—but of course you hadn't waited. The carriage will arrive here tomorrow, and you shall travel with me to London in greater comfort than you'll find in a stagecoach. I've already sent a man ahead to tell the housekeeper in Brook Street to prepare the house for us. I'm sure your godmother will understand after I've explained that I found I could come with you after all.'

Lexi's face lit up. 'Richard!' she exclaimed. 'You've changed your mind!'

But his expression didn't alter, and after a moment the joy faded and she looked away. 'Why?' she asked slowly. 'I don't believe you have changed your mind about Johnny, after all. Why have you decided to come to London?'

'Because, whatever I do or say, I don't doubt that you will find some way of getting there, sooner or later. Someone has to stop you from crashing about, stirring up new suspicions about Johnny's death, so I decided it was better we should go together, where I can keep some kind of rein on you.'

'Really?' said Lexi coldly. 'You *do* think of me as a child, don't you?'

'It's a world you don't understand. A world I know very well.'

'What difference will that make? *You* think Johnny guilty. *I* don't.'

'I'm sorry to say that's true. But...' He walked away and said with his back to her, 'Your blind faith in Johnny is very persuasive. You've reminded me of the Johnny I thought I knew all those years. His actions that night *were* totally out of character. In fact, if he hadn't been drinking so heavily I should be at a complete loss to account for them.' He swung round again. 'I still can't believe him innocent, Alexandra. But I don't think I can ignore what you've said as completely as I thought I should.'

Lexi was touched, though she tried not to show it. Small as it was, it was the first indication that she might have some influence on him. For the first time since that dreadful scene in her bedroom a flicker of hope stirred in her heart.

There was a pause. Then he added, 'Besides, there is one small discrepancy in the events of that night. I don't think it can prove anything at all, but it exists.'

'What is that?' she asked, all eagerness again.

'The purse the Frenchman gave Johnny. I told you I saw it when it was handed over. But it wasn't there when I searched his room afterwards. Nor was there any large sum of money there. What could he have done with it?'

'Johnny couldn't have done anything at all with it,' Lexi said impatiently. 'He wasn't in the tavern at all.'

'That isn't good enough! If he wasn't there, how did it happen that his hat and cape were both back in his room, less than an hour after I had seen someone very like Johnny wearing them in the tavern?'

Lexi sighed and put a hand to her aching head. 'I can't explain. And I don't feel I can think any more tonight, either. I must go to bed. But I'm glad you've decided, for whatever reason, that we shall go to London after all. The answer must lie there—' Then she said in a startled voice, 'What are you doing?'

'Isn't it obvious? I'm undressing.'

'But can't you do that in your own room?'

'This *is* my room, Alexandra. The White Hart hasn't unlimited bedrooms, and that bed is surely big enough for two. We shared one without any trouble quite recently.'

'That was...that was different.'

'Yes, it was.' He paused. 'Indeed it was. But we are nevertheless still married. It is not a crime to share a bed.' He waited again then said impatiently, 'Oh, don't worry! As you said, it is different now. You made that

perfectly clear last night. You are safe from my attentions. At the moment I have no wish for a "business
arrangement", and I assure you, after today's exertions
I have no strength—or desire—to *pretend* I love you.'

Lexi got silently into bed and lay stiffly at the ex-
treme edge of one side. Richard went through to the
dressing room, where she heard sounds of water splashing. Then he came back, blew out the candle and got
in beside her. The only light in the room came from the
flickering fire. Soon the only sound was that of Richard's even breathing. He was asleep on the other side
of a yawning gap in the bed. Lexi swallowed a tear and
composed herself determinedly for sleep.

She woke in the night and found she was cradled in
Richard's arms. Sleepy, warm and comfortable, she
stretched up to touch his face. He moved over her and
soon they were kissing each other passionately, locked
in a close embrace, as he joined his body to hers. But
there were no words of love, none of the lingering tenderness of their recent nights together. And when it was
over he moved away, back to the other side of the bed.
The chasm had been made clearer than ever. It was a
long time before she fell asleep again.

When she woke the next morning Richard was already up, sitting by the fire at a table which was laid
with breakfast. He was reading a newspaper. Lexi got
up and went through to the dressing room without
speaking. Her clothes from the day before had been laid
out over a chair, and after splashing her face with water
from a ewer and basin on a stand at the side she put
them on.

'We'll hold on to these rooms until the carriage ar-
rives. You can change here,' he said as she came

through and sat down at the table. He folded the newspaper.

'Please feel free to read if you wish,' said Lexi. 'We are, after all, an old married couple by now, are we not?' Her voice was sharper than she perhaps realised, and Richard pulled a face and opened the paper again. After a few moments Lexi said stiffly, 'I'm sorry. Please talk to me, Richard.'

'What shall we talk about? If you are expecting me to apologise for breaking my word to you last night, then I will. I can't explain why it happened—except propinquity, perhaps?'

'That's possibly the most insulting thing you could have said. I don't think a great deal of your apology.'

'I'm sorry if it offended you. But I'll see that it doesn't occur again. In future I'll make sure we have separate rooms.'

Lexi swallowed, and changed the subject. 'Have you any plans for our stay in London?'

'It isn't the Season, of course, but there are entertainments enough.'

'I don't want to be entertained,' she said quietly. 'I want to find out about Johnny.'

'And how would you go about that?'

'Talk to his friends? Find out what he was doing in the days before he died?'

'An excellent idea! Where would you find his friends—those, that is, who are in town at all? Were you going to call on them at their rooms, perhaps?'

'I...I hadn't thought...'

'They might well think it strange if you did.'

'I'm sure you could help me if you chose to. But perhaps you don't want to?'

'I do want to. By taking you to the theatre, concerts,

accepting invitations from old friends to evening parties... Shall I go on?'

'Thank you,' she said, biting her lip. 'I think you've made your point.'

His expression softened slightly as he saw signs of her distress. 'Forgive me. I don't think you realise how difficult this is... I'll help you all I can. Will that do?'

Lexi nodded. It would *have* to do. Richard was even angrier with her than she had thought he would be. To be fair, if he had already been planning to bring her to London he had some reason to be furious with the manner in which she had run off without warning. But she had never known him so unapproachable. Lexi began to realise just how badly she had hurt him.

The carriage arrived punctually, and within the hour they had set off for Basingstoke, where they were to spend the next night. They were alone in the carriage. Cissie and Phillips were travelling with the baggage in a second vehicle, which had been hired in Salisbury. For a while they drove along in silence, each deep in thought. Then Richard stirred himself and began to point out items of interest on the way. He spoke as if she were some remote cousin, or a child in need of entertainment. Lexi could hardly bear it. In an effort to break down the barrier between them she said suddenly,

'I've been thinking over our conversation last night.'

'Indeed?'

Ignoring his tone, which was distinctly chilly, she went on. 'There's one particular matter I'd like to make clear.'

'What is that?'

'When I asked you if you were jealous of Mark—'

'Please! I should never have said what I did.'

'I agree. You shouldn't. I might regard him as a brother. It is certainly no more than that. But I suppose we were both angry and didn't stop to consider our words.' She waited for his response to this overture, but when it came it was not quite what she had expected.

After a minute he said, 'If I am at all jealous, it is of his apparent influence over you.'

'How can you think that?' she said in astonishment. 'Mark doesn't influence me in the slightest!'

'Indeed he does! He undermines your trust in me.'

'That's nonsense!' Lexi was troubled. The conversation was not going the way she had hoped.

'Then why do your talks with him always have an unfavourable effect on our relationship?'

'That is absurd.'

'Think again, Alexandra. Remember how you learned about the card game. You may have overheard the servants talking, but, however reluctant he may have appeared to do it, Mark filled out the details for you. I suspect he encouraged you to behave as you did at the wedding, too.'

'Now that really is nonsense! He didn't! He would have stopped me if he had guessed.'

'Do you think so? Why didn't he guess? He isn't a fool, and he knew how you felt. He must have seen that you were beside yourself with grief and anger when you thought I had killed Johnny. If I had been as much in your confidence as Rawdon was, I am quite sure *I* would have suspected something. Then there was the talk you had with him more recently. Before I left you alone with Mark Rawdon that afternoon you were happy and secure. And afterwards...'

'Oh, I think you're wrong! You must be. It's true he made me wonder...'

'Whatever he did, it caused a rift between us, and it is my belief that he meant to.'

Lexi couldn't deny the existence of a rift. She would have called it rather an abyss. But it was out of the question that Mark had caused it deliberately. She said very firmly, 'I am sure that Mark would never knowingly cause me any unhappiness. Furthermore, he must be fully aware of what he owes to you.'

Richard said with cool irony, 'Being aware of an obligation is not always a reason for liking someone, Alexandra. Quite often the reverse, in fact.'

'But you were the one who persuaded my father to answer his letter of condolence. And later to receive him at Rawdon! Mark knows that. Oh, no, I think you're wrong, Richard. Mark would have to be a monster of ingratitude to wish you ill. Why, if you hadn't gone to Northampton to speak to him in the first place he would never even have known he was the heir to Rawdon.'

Richard looked at her thoughtfully. 'You think not?'

'Of course he wouldn't.'

'I wonder…'

'You don't regret bringing him to Rawdon, do you? You mustn't. Just think of how happy it made my father.'

'There is that, yes. But bringing him to Rawdon wasn't really my doing. Once Mark Rawdon's existence was known it was certain that he would come sooner or later. I only ensured it was sooner.' He paused, then said with an effort, 'I'd like you to do me a favour if you would, Alexandra. Be on your guard when you talk to Mark Rawdon.'

'I can't do that. Why should I?' she said obstinately. 'You're being unreasonably suspicious. Mark is my only living relative, and I am sure he is fond of me.

The fact that he sometimes sees things differently from you doesn't mean he is not to be trusted, does it?'

Richard tightened his lips. He said after a moment, 'Trust is altogether a difficult issue at the moment, is it not? I might have known you wouldn't be convinced by anything *I* could say. We'll forget the matter.'

They were approaching a large town. Basingstoke. Lexi sighed. It was no use. Richard was completely unreasonable on the subject of Mark. The prospect of any reconciliation was getting further away by the minute.

The Crown Inn at Basingstoke was not at all busy, and Richard engaged two bedchambers and a private parlour. They walked about the town a little, then had a meal together before retiring. He was polite and attentive, but made no effort to engage in any serious conversation, and when the time came bade her a civil goodnight and went to his own room. Lexi once again found it hard to sleep.

Chapter Eleven

They arrived in Brook Street during the early afternoon, and after taking time for a short rest and refreshment they walked round to Lady Wroxford's house in Curzon Street. Lady Wroxford was surprised. She had received Lexi's hastily written note, and had expected her to arrive alone and in a carriage. It took a while to explain their change of plan. Her brief disappointment that she was not to have her goddaughter for a guest after all was soon outweighed by her relief and delight that Richard and Lexi had come to London together. They assured her that they would be in Brook Street for several weeks, and expected to see a great deal of her.

'Dearest Lexi! Let me look at you, my dear. Still very pretty, I see, though perhaps a little thinner? But that is hardly any wonder. My poor child, what a time you've had since I last saw you!' She turned to Richard. 'I have to thank you, sir. You did say in your letter to me before the wedding that you would bring your bride to see me as soon as you could, but I hardly expected it to be barely a month after the marriage!'

Lexi looked at Richard. 'You wrote to my godmother?'

He nodded. 'I knew she would be disappointed not to be at the ceremony. And at the time you were in no state to deal with such matters.'

'My poor child! I was disappointed, of course. But I understood perfectly. Bearing in mind the sad events of the previous months, the wedding was naturally very quiet. My dear Lexi, what a very dreadful time you had this last summer! But that is all over now, and you must do your best to put it behind you. I'm sure it won't be difficult with such a handsome husband to keep you amused!' Lexi nodded—she could not have responded any other way to such an unconsciously ironic remark. Her godmother went on, 'However, I hope he will not deny me your company altogether! I was looking forward to an orgy of shopping with my favourite goddaughter.'

'Dearest Godmama, as if he could!' said Lexi, rousing herself. 'I absolutely rely on you to take me again to your modistes and milliners. I haven't forgotten what fun we had last year. And I very much hope you will help me to plan one or two dinner parties I intend to give.'

'With great pleasure. Fortunately there are quite a few members of the *ton* in London at the moment. And company to dinner is perfectly acceptable, even if you are still in mourning. I shall look forward to it, Lexi. But I hope you are not too tired to have dinner with me tonight. I have chosen all your favourite dishes. Do say you'll come! I shall expect to hear all about the wedding. Every last detail!'

As Lexi accepted she carefully avoided Richard's eye. She sincerely hoped that her godmother would never hear *all* of the details of that wedding.

* * *

Over dinner that evening Lady Wroxford broached the subject of Johnny. 'I was devastated when I heard about it, Lexi. Such a terrible accident! Your poor father.'

'Yes,' said Lexi. 'Yes, it was a sad blow for us all. I don't think Papa ever really got over it.'

Her manner was so subdued that Lady Wroxford said gently, 'Would you rather not talk about it?'

Lexi shook her head in denial. 'I'd like to hear about Johnny's life in London in the weeks before he…before he died. I know so little of that time, and it might help to bring him closer.'

'Well, if you think so…' said Lady Wroxford uncertainly. 'But surely Lord Deverell has told you—?'

'You forget, ma'am,' said Richard. 'I was out of England for much of the earlier part of the year, so I had seen less of him than his other friends. Can you help us? Did you see much of Johnny?'

Lady Wroxford wore a small frown. 'I wouldn't say I saw a lot of him,' she said slowly. 'He came once or twice to parties I held in the evening, but he had his own circle—young bachelors like himself. I was always pleased when he came—he could be very amusing. Are you sure you want to talk about him, Lexi?'

'Yes, I do. What about his friends? They must have been as shocked as we were by his death?'

'Oh, yes! Young Stephen Hargreaves was deeply affected for weeks. I had never seen him so quiet. He was one of Johnny's drinking companions.' She hesitated. 'I have to say that I wish you had been back sooner from Vienna, Lord Deverell. Johnny would have listened to you.'

'In what way?'

'I thought he was getting a little too reckless. There were rumours that he was badly in debt...' She looked at Lexi uncomfortably. 'I tried to talk to him, but of course I had no authority as far as Johnny was concerned. I dare say he thought me a busybody. He laughed at me, at any rate, teased me—you know the way he had.'

'In debt? But Papa made him a huge allowance!'

'Yes, yes. People exaggerate.'

'Did he seem worried, ma'am? Unhappy?'

'No, no, Lexi! He was perhaps bored, but certainly not unhappy. Why do you ask?' Something in Lexi's face made her hasten to add, 'Oh, my dear girl, no! Johnny's situation was not as bad as that! You mustn't think for one instant that his death was anything but an accident! There was never the slightest hint of anything else.'

'Of course there wasn't,' said Richard briskly, with a brief look of warning for Lexi. 'Johnny's pockets were always to let, but he had never allowed it to bother him. And on the day of the accident he was very much alive and looking forward to the race meetings the following week. But about these friends of his—Stephen... Hargreaves, did you say? Not an Army person, I think?'

'No, Stephen isn't the sort for the Army! He likes his comfort too much! His mother is a friend of mine. Would you like me to invite him here to dinner one night? I always laughed when I saw them together. Stephen's hair is as red as Johnny's.'

'Really?' asked Lexi.

'Yes. They were both teased about it—you know how it is, Lexi. Redheads are frequently teased about their hair. I dare say you've had some teasing in your time.

Johnny always laughed it off, but Stephen is a sensitive soul.'

'Alexandra's hair is a beautiful colour,' said Richard.

Lady Wroxford eyes twinkled as she said, 'It is. But I wouldn't expect you to say anything different.' She smiled at them both, then said, 'So it's settled. I shall invite young Hargreaves to meet you as soon as it can be arranged—I'm sure he will talk as much as you wish about Johnny. And I shall consider who else I might invite. There were quite a few others who were close to your brother, though how many are in London at the moment is another question.'

They talked for a while after that about other things. Lady Wroxford naturally wanted to know more about the wedding, and Lexi had to admire the skill with which Richard answered her questions with perfect truth, but without any hint of the sensational events in the vestry afterwards.

When she heard of Lexi's collapse at the end of the ceremony Lady Wroxford said, 'After such a summer I am not at all surprised. What a blessing it was that you did not allow Lexi's bereavement to delay the wedding. It was hardly an ideal beginning to your life together, but Lexi at least had someone who loved her to see she was properly looked after. Her cousin could hardly have taken on such a task. How have your people received Sir Mark, Lexi? It can't have been easy for them to accept someone they knew so slightly after working for so many years for your father. Do you see much of him?'

'A little. I think he does very well, ma'am,' said Lexi. After their discussion in the carriage she found it difficult to talk easily of Mark in Richard's presence.

But Lady Wroxford did not appear to be aware of

any undercurrents. She went on wistfully, 'I don't suppose I shall ever visit Rawdon again. I have never met Sir Mark, so he is very unlikely to invite me there! It must all be quite difficult for him. Am I right in thinking that he had never been to Somerset before this year?'

'Yes. Papa was not even aware of his existence.'

'How very strange! And he has had no experience of running an estate, either?'

'Sir Mark is very eager to succeed,' said Richard, briefly. 'As Alexandra said, we believe he does quite well.' He went on smoothly, 'But though Rawdon may be closed to you, I hope you will consider Channings an adequate substitute, Lady Wroxford. We would very much like to see you there.'

'I shall come as soon as you give me the word. In the spring, perhaps? I should love to visit you both in your own home, but I am also eager to see Channings—your late father never received visitors.'

'I think you'll find that Channings will be a more hospitable place in the future.' Richard waited, then looked at Lexi's wan face. 'Won't it, my love?'

'What? Oh, yes!' said Lexi, who had been wondering what the situation next spring would be. 'Yes, do come, ma'am!'

Richard smiled at Lady Wroxford. 'You'll have to forgive Alexandra, ma'am. I'm afraid she found today more demanding than she had expected. If she is to be fit to face life in London, it's time I took her home.'

Lady Wroxford looked at Lexi's pale face and heavy eyes and stood up. 'My poor Lexi, I've kept you far too long. I quite forgot the time in the pleasure of having you here. But now you must go. We shall have plenty of time later to talk. I'll send for your carriage.'

* * *

Once inside their own house Richard accompanied Lexi upstairs to her room, where Cissie was waiting for her. But here he paused and said, 'I hope you'll excuse me for a while. It is still comparatively early. If you have no objection, there are one or two calls I should like to make tonight.'

Lexi was so weary that she could think of nothing to say to this. She merely nodded. He hesitated. Then, as if he seemed to feel the need for more explanation, he went on, 'I hope to meet someone who might help us. The sooner we start our enquiries, the better.'

'You really have no need to give me excuses,' Lexi said, coolly. 'I understand perfectly. You cannot wait to visit your clubs. Try not to wake me when you come in.'

His lips tightened and he said, 'That's hardly likely, is it?' Then he bowed and went out.

Lexi submitted to Cissie's ministrations, then got into bed. She tried not to let her mind dwell on Richard. Perhaps he had been telling her the truth when he said that he hoped to meet one or two people who might have information for him, but it was more likely that he wished to avoid her company. The situation between them had been bad enough, but it had been made worse by her refusal to listen to his ridiculous suspicions of Mark. But why couldn't Richard understand that she *had* to believe in Mark, *had* to trust in him. He was the only member of her family left, the only link with her father, with Johnny and with Rawdon itself.

She sighed into the dark. She felt as if she was being split into two. Richard was still the most important person in her life. The rest of the world, including Mark, came a very long way behind, and, whatever happened between them, no one would ever mean more to her. But she *knew* he was wrong about Johnny, whatever the evidence said. And he was wrong to be suspicious of Mark, too. Even at the risk of alienating him further, she would defend her cousin, as she would continue to defend her brother, against his absurd, unreasonable, doubts. But the thought of alienating Richard further was not a happy one, and Lexi eventually fell asleep still worrying over it.

Meanwhile, as Richard was walking in the direction of St James's he was pursuing his own thoughts. It had been made clear to him in the past two days that the foundation of trust on which he hoped to build his marriage had been seriously undermined. For one short week he had been gloriously, foolishly, certain that their love for each other could overcome all obstacles. But Alexandra had evidently not felt the same—at least not for long. At the first sign of difficulty she had rejected him. And now she had given him the impossible task of proving Johnny Rawdon innocent. He squared his shoulders. If that was what it would take to save his marriage, then that was what he had to do! He must have the same faith in Johnny as Johnny's sister had, and start from the premise that Johnny was *not* a traitor.

It wouldn't be easy. Though he had gone over the scene in the tavern again and again, he had never found anything to indicate that the man in the cape was anyone but Johnny. It would therefore be a waste of time to start there. He must find another beginning. That there had been a traitor in the Horse Guards was an undeniable fact. If it hadn't been Johnny, then it must have been someone else. Who? That was the question he would try to answer.

* * *

White's clubrooms were not as crowded as they would have been outside the hunting season, but Richard was greeted enthusiastically by several old acquaintances. Goodnaturedly parrying a good many ribald questions about his recent marriage, he spent an hour or two with them at the tables, where he proved that neither his luck nor his skill had diminished during his absence from London. By the time he eventually left he was not only considerably richer in pocket, but had discovered, to his surprise, that his new approach was to have an immediate result. He had managed to spend half an hour drinking with the most notorious gossip in the Horse Guards, a certain Sir Charles Stainforth. Though the subject was highly confidential, Sir Charles was easily persuaded to talk to him.

'My dear fellow,' he said, stretching for another sip of wine. 'How we missed you! The place was in chaos after you left. Why the devil couldn't Wellington have left you where you were with us? Still, I suppose he had a use for you at Waterloo, eh? I see you escaped with not much more than a scratch. You always were a damned lucky dog.'

'Come, Sir Charles. The place was always in chaos, with or without me.'

'It got much worse, I can tell you. There we were, scurrying around trying to get everything over to you chaps in time, and Wellington never leaving us alone for a minute.'

'As I remember, you had another little matter to deal with, too.'

'Other little matter?'

'I'm talking of the leak of information…?'

'Ah! The spy in our midst. Yes, yes. You had the job of investigating it for a while, didn't you? I'd forgotten

that. But you'd left for Belgium before it all came out.
As I heard it you were very close to catching him, too.
Pity you had to leave before it was all discovered.'

Richard said carefully, 'Discovered?'

'Not that it was ever made public. The wretched fellow wasn't exactly what you'd call a professional. Just
a desperate fool. He did it for the money, of course.
Spent too much time in places like this, playing with
stakes he couldn't afford. He was thousands in debt at
the end.' He gave Richard a grin. 'Pity he didn't have
your sort of luck, eh? Mind you, nothing was ever really
proved against him. It was all kept very quiet. Not a
word was said to anyone outside.'

Richard stiffened. 'What…what happened to him?'

Sir Charles looked slightly guilty. 'Oh Lord, didn't
you know? I wouldn't have said a thing if I hadn't
thought you already knew all about it. I thought he was
a friend of yours?'

Richard's heart sank. Was he about to hear that all
his efforts to save Johnny's reputation had been in vain?
His relief was enormous when Sir Charles went on,
'Ah! I forgot. You were probably too busy dealing with
Johnny Rawdon's death at the time, and then you were
off to Belgium very soon after. Sad business, that.
Splendid fellow, Johnny Rawdon! Did I hear you'd
married his sister? I met her a year or two back during
the Season. A lovely girl. My congratulations, old chap.
You seem to be as lucky in love as you are at cards! Is
Lady Deverell with you in London?'

'Yes. And thank you. But you were saying …?'

'What?'

'About the spy?'

'Oh, that! Not a spy, Deverell. You can't say Henry
Seymour was a spy! He was just damned stupid. As far

as we could tell, he never gave the French anything really important.'

'How the devil could anyone be sure of that? It's just as well Wellington never heard of it. He'd have made sure Seymour was hanged.'

'I say, that's a bit drastic!'

'For a spy? In wartime? What did happen to him?'

'Seymour had one or two pretty powerful connections, don't y'know, and they managed to get things hushed up. To tell the truth, we didn't come out of it too well either, so we were perfectly willing to keep it quiet.'

'So?'

'We asked him to retire. As it happened he wasn't in London at the time—he'd already gone off to his place in Dulwich, so we just told him not to come back. Ever. It was all quite discreetly done.'

'So it was Seymour? I would never have guessed.'

Sir Charles looked worried. 'You'll keep it to yourself, won't you, Deverell? All done and dusted now. Best forgotten.'

'Of course.'

After leaving Sir Charles, Richard went on to Brooks's, where he spent the rest of the night playing for high stakes. He felt little enough temptation to go back to Curzon Street before he had to. Once again, it seemed, he couldn't lose. Wasn't there some saying about being lucky at cards, and unlucky in love...? Whatever it was, it seemed to fit the case. But later, as he walked home through the early light of dawn, he felt that something more than winnings had come out of the night's work. His new approach to the business of Johnny had produced one small nugget of hope. Whatever Johnny had or had not done on the night of his death, he had not been the traitor everyone had been looking for. It wasn't much, but it was something to store away alongside the question of the missing purse.

Lexi woke just before dawn and for a moment she wondered where she was. As she gazed round memory returned. She was Richard's wife in Richard's London home. But where was Richard? Wherever he was, he wasn't with her. She turned over in despair and hid her face. Why wasn't he here? It was easy enough to keep up her spirits during the day, to pretend that she didn't care. But here in the dark hours before dawn it was more difficult. She wanted Richard, she wanted the confident, laughing, passionately vulnerable lover, her heart's delight, her other self, to come back to her. But she had lost him, and in his place was someone who wouldn't let her near him, perhaps not ever again.

She got up late the next morning feeling very low, and her mood was not improved when she found that Richard had already gone out. She was to breakfast alone.

It was fortunate that Lady Wroxford called just after she had finished. Her godmother took one look at Lexi's face and announced that she had come to take her shopping. 'There is no time to waste,' she said. 'Though it may seem a backward way of doing things, you need a trousseau. I don't suppose you thought of such matters before the wedding.'

'I still have some very pretty dresses from my come-out, ma'am!'

'And they are sadly out of date! Now, don't try to tell me you are still in mourning, Lexi. I know you are, but you can still dress in style, and, as it happens, black, grey, lavender and lilac are among the colours that flatter you most. And white, too. Especially white. My dear girl, I can see you are not quite yourself, but shopping gives any woman's spirits a lift. Do come!'

This was the point at which Richard came in. 'You are very kind, ma'am,' said Lexi, giving Richard a significant look, 'but may we postpone our expedition till tomorrow? Richard has said he will take me to find some of Johnny's friends today.'

Her godmother laughed. 'Bless you, girl, you won't catch them till much later in the day! If they are not still abed, they will be at Jackson's, or Angelo's, or Tattersalls, or in some other haunt of young men of the town.'

Richard added, 'And I'm afraid I can't take you anywhere, Alexandra. I have another visit I must make today.'

Lexi began hotly, 'But you promised—'

Richard took both her hands in his and raised them to his lips. He spoke indulgently, but his grey eyes had no warmth in them. 'And I shall keep my promise. But Lady Wroxford is quite right. The *ton* will expect to see Lady Deverell dressed up to the minute. Before we do much entertaining you will need a new wardrobe. I don't want the world to think I can't keep you properly dressed. Go with your godmother today. My visit is to an old army acquaintance who has retired. I assure you you would find it very boring. Visiting Lady Wroxford's modiste would be much more fun.'

Richard excused himself and went out again not long after, and from that moment Lexi put him out of her mind and submitted to her godmother's wishes completely. The two ladies had a most enjoyable day making appointments with modistes and milliners, visiting warehouses and shops and luxuriating in enough fripperies and furbelows to please the most extravagant feminine heart.

Richard meanwhile had travelled to Dulwich, where he requested a shabbily dressed servant to take his card to Mr Henry Seymour. He was left to wait in the hall, which was devoid of furniture. Several lighter patches on the dark green walls betrayed where pictures, presumably now all sold, had once hung. The servant returned and led Richard through several dismal, shabbily furnished rooms to a study at the back of the building. Here, sitting in front of a low fire, was Henry Seymour, a shadow of the man Richard had known, badly shaven, with slack cheeks and unkempt hair. Remembering the sleekly prosperous-looking man, with the air of a well-fed cat about him, his love of ostentation and comfort, Richard was unexpectedly saddened by his present state.

Seymour made no attempt to rise. 'What the hell do you want, Deverell? Come to lecture me on my wicked ways, have you? Or didn't they tell you about me?'

'I've no desire to lecture anyone. I'd like some information.'

'Sit down, sit down! Have a drink.' Seymour made a gesture to the bottle of brandy, which was on a table by his chair.

'Thank you.'

Sunken eyes gazed at him. 'I'm surprised you want to drink with a traitor.'

'We were good friends once,' Richard said evenly. Seymour's eyes turned away to the fire again. 'Why did you do it?'

'What the devil has that to do with you?' Then, after a pause, he said, 'You wouldn't understand. Money,

Deverell, money. I needed money to pay my gambling debts. Not everyone has your confounded luck. In the end, this…' Seymour made a gesture that was meant to encompass the house and its surroundings '…this was all I had left. And what the War Office paid me wasn't remotely enough.' He paused. 'It was wrong, I know that. But I swear I was careful never to give them anything of any real use.'

'How could you know that?'

After a long silence Seymour said, 'You're right, of course. I couldn't. But when they asked me to give them something big…something I knew was vital…I said no. That was when I realised I couldn't carry on.'

'So you refused them. What was it they wanted?'

'You must know what it was. Papers, plans for the Allied points of resistance. You and Johnny Rawdon were looking after them.'

Richard narrowed his eyes. 'How the devil did you hear about *them*?'

Seymour roused himself and gave Richard a pitying smile. 'Come on, Deverell!' he said. '*You* may have been the soul of discretion, but Johnny Rawdon trusted anyone and everyone, especially when he'd had a drink or two. I don't know how my French friend got wind of them. *I* didn't tell him, if that's what you think. He knew of their existence before I did and wanted me to steal them for him. That was when I came to my senses and told him I wouldn't.'

'It was fortunate for you that you did. We were very close to unmasking you. We knew a meeting had been arranged at the Cock Tavern for that night.'

'You wouldn't have found me there. I'd seen Bénuat the day before and he had been so damned unpleasant that I decided never to meet the fellow again. I was already out of London that night.'

'Bénuat was your agent, I assume. We knew about him. Are you *sure* you told him you wouldn't do it?'

Seymour started up in his chair. 'Damn you, yes!'

'It's just that he turned up, you see. At the Cock. I saw him there myself.'

'Not to meet me, I swear.'

Richard gazed at him thoughtfully, then sighed and nodded. 'I believe you. There's just one other thing. Did Bénuat ever mention anyone else? Another agent…or any other connection?'

Seymour smiled grimly. 'We didn't have time for gossip. Our meetings were always rather short, as you might imagine. But when I told him I wouldn't get him those papers, he did say he'd have to look for someone else to do it. I didn't think for a minute he'd find anyone. Did he?'

Richard got up. 'I'm obliged to you, Seymour. You've been very patient with me. Is there anything I can do for you? Anyone you wish to send a message to?'

Henry Seymour gave a twisted smile. 'Thank you, but no. You're the first visitor I've had since it happened. It's no more than I deserve, but it's a damned lonely life. My wife died years ago, and there's no one else.'

Richard nodded. 'I'll call again before I go back to Somerset, though my time is not altogether my own. By the way, did you know I am now married?'

'How should I know that? I hear nothing here. Who's the lucky girl?'

'Johnny Rawdon's sister.'

'The lovely Alexandra? Lucky man! How is Johnny?'

After a moment's silence Richard said, 'You really are cut off, aren't you? Johnny's dead.'

Seymour's shock was perfectly genuine. 'Never! Killed in action, was he?'

It was quite clear that Henry Seymour had no idea of any connection between Johnny Rawdon and the Frenchman. So Richard said evasively, 'Something like that.'

'A damned shame. He was a good chap, Johnny. So you married his sister? Will you…will you bring her with you when you call again?' There was a significant silence and Seymour went on, 'Of course you won't. I was wrong to ask.'

'I have to go, I'm afraid. I will come again. I'll be alone.' Richard got up, nodded, and left his host pouring another drink for himself and shouting for his servant to put more logs on the fire.

Lexi was waiting for him when he got back. She was already dressed for dinner and looked very beautiful in a white silk dress trimmed with heavy lace. She was wearing the pearls he had given her wound into her hair, but no other jewellery. He suspected that she had no other—all the Rawdon valuables had gone to line a blackmailer's pockets. He must buy her some. Diamonds? Sapphires? Anything to see her smile at him in her old way…

Damn it, what he wanted most had nothing to do with clothes or jewels! He wanted to hold her close, to have her respond to him as she had done such a short time ago. To have her love and tenderness wash away the feelings of sadness and betrayal roused by his visit to Henry Seymour that afternoon. But that was not possible.

'I hope you found the visit to your friend enjoyable,' she said.

'It was…depressing, rather than enjoyable,' he replied. 'But interesting. How was your day? Did you find what you wanted? You look excited.'

'I am! But not about dresses. Lady Wroxford has invited us again to dinner tonight. And she has managed to persuade Stephen Hargreaves to come too!'

'Stephen Hargreaves? Johnny's friend? Have you met him already?'

'Not yet, but I can hardly wait. He must be a very strong suspect. Red-headed, a friend of Johnny's, so he would know about Johnny's things, know what Johnny was doing… He *must* be the one you saw in the tavern!' She waited, then said impatiently, 'You don't seem very interested. Why not? It is perfectly clear to me that we might well have our answer this very evening! How shall we treat him?'

'Don't you think you're being over-hasty? You haven't even met the man yet.'

'No, but I feel it in my bones that he's the one. You'll see.'

Chapter Twelve

Dinner that evening was a lively affair. Lady Wroxford had invited a number of people, including Stephen Hargreaves and one or two more of Johnny's former companions. But after ten minutes of young Mr Hargreaves's company it was quite clear, even to Lexi, that he could not possibly be the mysterious man in the cape, red hair or not. He might be an amiable drinking companion, but no one as naïve would survive even five seconds in the devious and dangerous world of espionage.

After dinner Richard said quietly, 'Don't look so downcast, Alexandra. Hargreaves may not be our villain, but he can still be useful. Go and talk to him about your brother, while I have a word with the others.'

Lexi looked doubtful, but went to do as he said.

It took some time to turn the conversation towards Johnny. Mr Hargreaves was inclined to dwell at length on his own recent activities. But eventually she managed to persuade him to talk of her brother.

'I miss Johnny still,' he said mournfully. 'Very amusin' fella, old Johnny. Great fun.'

'I always thought so, too,' said Lexi. 'You saw a lot of him, I believe. Did you see him the day he died?'

Mr Hargreaves's brow wrinkled in thought. 'No, I didn't,' he said eventually. 'Odd thing that. But I saw him twice the day before. On the Wednesday. And that was even odder... It upset me rather.'

'I'm sorry to hear that. What was it?'

'You might think I was being too sensitive. M'mother says I am. But I liked Johnny, you see.'

'We all did. So...what was odd about him?'

'Odd?'

'Yes, you said there was something odd when you saw him on Wednesday?'

'Oh, that! Yes, well, I saw him twice, don't y'know. The first time he came round to my rooms. Damned early, too. Ate half my breakfast—Johnny was always hungry.'

'What had he come to see you about?'

'Told me he was going to be closeted with one of the bigwigs at the Horse Guards all day. Johnny worked there.'

'Yes, I did know that.'

'Of course you did! His sister, weren't you?'

'Exactly,' said Lexi, holding on to her patience. 'So...what was odd?'

'He said there was a big fuss about papers—I don't know what they were, I didn't pay much attention, as a matter of fact. But Johnny had to be there. He had expected to be free that day, and he wasn't too pleased, I can tell you. Nor was I. Well, I know there was a war and all that, but they shouldn't interfere with a chap's prior engagements, should they? I said he ought to tell them that—we'd arranged to go to Deptford, d'y'see? Or was it Dartford? No, it was Deptford. But Johnny wouldn't change his mind. He said he had to do his duty.'

'Deptford?'

'That's right.'

'What was happening at Deptford?'

Mr Hargreaves frowned and thought hard. 'There was a fair on. And we'd been told there was to be wrestling. You know the sort—anyone who wanted could have a go to see if they could floor the champion. Not my game at all—it's too rough for me. But Johnny was dead set on it—it was the sort of thing he enjoyed, don't y'know. The sideshows would have been amusin', I suppose, but I only said I'd go because of Johnny. Made all my arrangements—then, hang it, he said he couldn't come after all! No use goin' another day—it wouldn't be there!'

Richard had come over to join them. He said, 'I remember he mentioned the fair. You're right, he was raring to go. But he didn't?'

'No. That's why I was surprised when I saw him later that same day.'

'At Deptford?'

'No, no! There was no point in going alone. No fun at all, dammit. So I stayed in town and I went to see m'tailor—to tell the truth, I owed him a fair bit, and thought it was time to order something else to keep him quiet. I was afraid m'mother might hear if I didn't. And he's a damned good tailor, though not as good as Weston, of course. But Weston's a bit above my touch. That's a Weston coat, though, ain't it? You can always tell.'

'So where did you see Johnny?'

'Who? Oh, Johnny! Yes, I went to this fella, as I said, and afterwards I was walking along Piccadilly, and there was Johnny large as life, walking on the other side, if you please! I was pretty much annoyed, I can tell you.'

'What did he say?'

'Nothing. I couldn't cross at first, there was too much traffic on the road, so I waved to him. He looked straight at me, but he didn't stop. Then, when I did manage to get across, I couldn't catch up with him. From the way he was hurrying along you might have thought he didn't want to talk to me.'

'Why would he do that?' Lexi asked.

'I can't imagine. It wasn't Johnny's usual style at all. He must have been up to something he didn't want me to know about. Odd, wouldn't you say?'

Lexi looked apprehensively at Richard, who was frowning. This was hardly what either of them had hoped to hear. She said brightly, 'Perhaps he'd…he'd been sent on some errand by someone at the Horse Guards, and…and was in a hurry to get back?'

Mr Hargreaves stared at her, then broke into a beaming smile. 'That must have been it, Lady Deverell! I should have known! Johnny wouldn't cut a chap without good reason. I'm glad you thought of it. And all this time I've been thinkin' badly of the poor old fellow…'

They talked for a few minutes longer, but Mr Hargreaves had nothing of interest to add, and for the rest of the evening Richard and Lexi mixed with the rest of the company, talking, laughing, and being entertained by the performances on the harp or at the piano of the younger ladies of the company. Any private conversation would have to wait. At last the evening was over and they returned to Brook Street.

* * *

'If you are not too tired, Alexandra, I should like to have a discussion about what we've learned so far,' said Richard as they came in.

'I agree. Will you...would you like to hold it in my room? I think we should be more comfortable there. I asked the housekeeper to make sure the fire was well stacked.' Lexi didn't feel like saying that this was in case she had another sleepless night. 'I expect she has left a tray as well.'

'She usually does. Very well. I'll come to your room for a minute or two, but I won't stay long.'

At first there was an inevitable air of constraint between them, but they sat down in armchairs on either side of the fire to discuss the day. Richard spoke first. He had learned nothing, from his conversations with the others at Lady Wroxford's. No one had found anything unusual about Johnny's behaviour either in the last days, or earlier. As Richard had said, he was looking forward to going to the races the following week. No one had ever seen him engaged in conversation with strangers. They all said he had been drinking quite a lot, but hadn't found anything unusual in that. There had been nothing of real interest in any of it.

Then they came to discussing what Stephen Hargreaves had had to say. Richard said with a dry smile,

'By the way...I said you knew nothing of Johnny's world, Alexandra, and I was right. The idea that a serving officer would be sent ''on some errand'' by anyone at the Horse Guards when you can't move in the place for messengers employed for that very purpose is so ridiculous that only a fool like Hargreaves would believe it for one second. He clearly has as little experience of the Army as you have. Don't try it on anyone else, will you?'

Lexi bridled and said, 'I only wanted to divert suspicion from Johnny. And you might at least give me some credit for persevering with Mr Hargreaves!'

'Don't say you still suspect he was the villain? Now that would really surprise me!'

Lexi sighed. 'You know I don't. I was wrong about him. I had such hopes of him, too. But all we seem to have established is that on the day before he died Johnny was up to something he didn't want his friends to know about.'

'Don't sound so discouraged,' Richard said abruptly. 'Tonight may not have done much for us, but I do have something else to tell you. I have found out that, whatever else Johnny did, he wasn't the traitor we were looking for all those months at the Horse Guards. That was someone else altogether.' Then, as she looked at him in dawning hope, he shook his head. 'No, Alexandra. It isn't as encouraging as that, I'm afraid. It doesn't clear Johnny of what you might call our affair. The traitor wasn't even in London that night. Nor does he resemble Johnny in the slightest.'

Lexi looked down. 'Another disappointment!' she said bitterly. 'First that stupid Hargreaves man and now this… For a moment I thought…I hoped…'

Richard's voice was bracing rather than sympathetic. 'I'm sorry, Alexandra. But you mustn't despair like this. There are still people to see, enquiries to be made. We haven't finished yet.'

Lexi's voice was muffled as she said, 'I know. But for one wonderful second I thought it was over.' She looked up. 'If we had found enough to convince you, we could soon have gone back to Channings. Perhaps started again. Perhaps found that world we had there for such a short, short time.'

Richard got up and stood with his back towards her, gazing down at the fire. 'Did you?' he said sombrely. 'I'm not sure that's possible. I'm not even sure it was real.'

'It felt real enough.'

'Perhaps it did at the time. But it turned out to be a chimera, a dream. The first breath of doubt blew it away. What sort of reality is that? No, my dear, it's best forgotten.' He spoke in such a cool, almost impersonal tone that Lexi felt chilled. She got up and put a hand on his arm.

'Richard, don't! Don't sound so…so remote,' she pleaded. 'You said you loved me. Was that a lie?'

He turned to face her and she realised just how much control he had been exercising. For a moment there was such a blaze of anger in his eyes that she took a step back. 'No, dammit, it was not!' he said fiercely. 'Why do you have to ask? Why else am I here in London, when I want to be in my own home in Somerset? Why am I opening old wounds, stirring up old scandals, when for years I've been looking forward to a time of forgetting, healing, a time to build a new life at Channings? But you've asked for my help, and, whether Johnny was innocent or not, I am giving it to you *because* I love you! I tell you, I am tired of your doubts.'

He stopped for breath, and after a moment started to move towards the door. 'And now,' he said wearily, 'if you don't mind—or even if you do—I am going to my own room, to my own bed. And tomorrow, to please you, I shall carry on poking into matters that in my opinion would have been better left undisturbed. Goodnight, Alexandra.'

She suddenly didn't want to see him go. 'Richard!' she said softly, 'You could…could share my room tonight if you wished.'

He stood in the doorway, so tall that the top of his head almost touched the lintel. 'Why? As a reward? For working well, finding part of an answer, even if it isn't the one we want? Perhaps you regard it as a form of consolation—for having to witness today the miserable wreck of a man I once counted among my friends?' He came back into the room and stood very close. 'Or, Alexandra,' he said softly, 'is it perhaps because *you* feel the need for company? Is that it?' He shook his head and moved away again. 'Whatever it is, my reply is the same. Thank you, but I'm afraid I must refuse. Ask me again when you are free of those doubts of yours, and I might have a different answer for you. But until then I'll sleep alone.'

She had been a fool to make the offer. 'Very well,' she said stonily. 'I have no idea how long that will be, of course. A lot will depend on the effort you make to convince me. But perhaps you would begin by letting me accompany you on some of these excursions of yours. At the moment I feel that my mind might be more ready than yours to find evidence in Johnny's favour.'

After a moment during which he seemed to be weighing her up he said, 'Very well. You shall come with me tomorrow. I plan to make two calls. I hadn't thought I would take you to the first, but perhaps it wouldn't do any harm for you to see the misery in which some others live. Be downstairs before ten o'clock. And wear something discreet—something shabby, if you have such a garment.'

* * *

They had breakfast together the next morning, and afterwards he looked her over, advised her to remove the earrings and bracelet she was wearing and then produced a dull brown pelisse and a neat but shabby bonnet. 'Put these on.'

'Why? Where did you get them?'

'I borrowed them from one of the maids—she looked your size. Don't worry. They aren't her best.'

'But why do I have to wear a maid's coat and bonnet?'

'Because where I'm taking you the residents don't look kindly on the rich. You'll be safer dressed like that. Hide that hair of yours under the bonnet, and don't do anything rash such as leaving my side, or talking to anyone. They'll probably stare at you, but don't stare back. They don't like it. Stay between Coles and myself if you can.'

'Goodness, Deverell, you are sounding mysterious!'

'It isn't a joke, Alexandra.' For a moment he looked doubtful. 'Perhaps this isn't such a good idea, after all…'

'No, please! Please let me come! I promise to do as you say.'

'Very well.'

They left the carriage at an inn on the edge of the City, then walked just a few hundred yards further east. A few hundred yards, thought Lexi, shuddering, but it might have been a different country. Here the stench was almost overpowering. The streets ran with dirty water, and at the sides they were piled high with rubbish of every description. Ragged children ran barefoot, shouting at them in raucous voices, shoving filthy hands into their faces. Lexi tried not to look, but it was almost impossible to avoid doing so. Richard grasped his stick in one hand and held her with the other.

'Do you wish to turn back?' he asked.

'No. But where are we going?'

'To call on a former sergeant of mine. He was wounded at Waterloo, and I'm afraid he's fallen on hard times since peace was declared. One of the things I planned to do when I came to London was to find out where he lives and see how he is faring. From the sound of it, that isn't too well. I'll see if I can do anything for him.' They reached a house that was slightly apart from the rest, and, if possible, more tumbledown than the others. Large parts of its roof were missing, and the walls on one side leaned dangerously outwards. 'This is it.'

Leaving Coles on guard at the door, they picked their way over a pile of stones and went into the one room that was complete. The light inside was dim, but Lexi could see a sort of cot in one corner. It was neatly made up with a pillow at one end and what looked like a woollen cape spread over the rest. In the middle of the room was a table with a bench on either side. The table was rickety, but it looked clean. A man was sitting on one of the benches. He was wearing an old uniform, which looked as if its wearer had lost a great deal of weight since it had been new. Though it was shabby and torn, it had been brushed and the tears in it carefully mended. The man's moustache and beard were trim, but there were lines of pain on his pale face. He was clearly a sick man, but he had an air of stoic endurance that brought a lump to Lexi's throat.

'Sergeant Chalmers?'

The man peered at Richard, then struggled to get up,

holding himself stiffly upright with the aid of a stick. 'Captain Deverell! Sir!'

Richard moved forward and clapped the man on the shoulder. 'Sit down, sit down, man. What the devil are you doing in a place like this?'

The sergeant sat down again. 'Nowhere else to go, sir. Can't do no work, y'see. No money for anything better.'

Richard looked round. Except for the cot and the table and benches the place was bare of any comfort. 'But have you no one else to stay with? No family?'

'None left, sir.'

'What about the homes for ex-soldiers? One of them would surely be a better place for you than this?'

'Beggin' your pardon, captain, there ain't that many, and they ain't not for me, they ain't. I don't fit in. Shirkers and shifters, that's what's in them homes. I don't want charity, sir.'

'I see... But how do you manage? Is there someone to look after you?'

'Folks is good. They give me what they can, but they haven't much. Not that it matters—I don't have much of an appetite. I carve bits of wood for the children sometimes, and they bring me things. But, no, there's no one special.'

'Well, I'm glad I found you. You can't stay here, and I've a use for a man just like you down in Somerset.' When Chalmers looked doubtful, Richard said firmly, 'It won't be charity. You were always one of the best menders and makers I ever came across. We could do with someone like you at Channings. Don't worry, you'll earn your keep, sergeant. Say you'll come.'

'Aye, captain, I will. Gladly. And thank 'ee.'

'Don't thank me. I should have taken the trouble to

find you months ago, but…I've had a lot to do. Good. Now, I dare say you're wondering about the lady with me here.'

'I don't see no lady, sir,' said Chalmers. 'Leastways not a proper lady—just a pretty young maid.' He smiled at Lexi.

'Be careful, sergeant! She's a very proper lady. My wife, in fact!'

'Your wife, sir!' The sergeant struggled up once again. He gave a curious little bow. 'I'm sorry, ma'am. Honoured to meet you.'

Lexi nodded and smiled. 'Sergeant.'

Richard helped Lexi to sit down opposite the sergeant, then sat beside her. He said quietly, 'My wife wants to talk to you about Captain Rawdon. He was her brother.'

A frown appeared on the soldier's face. 'Captain Rawdon?' he said cautiously.

'It's all right,' said Lexi. 'I've been told what is supposed to have happened the night my brother died.'

'Supposed to have happened?'

'My wife doesn't believe her brother was guilty.'

The sergeant nodded sympathetically. 'That's only natural.'

'And she intends to prove it.'

'Well, now, I'm not sure I would be of much use, ma'am,' the soldier said, scratching his ear. 'I don't see as how I could help. The captain knows—we did all we could at the time.' He glanced at Richard.

'Tell me why you were so sure it was my brother in the tavern,' said Lexi.

'The hat, ma'am,' said Chalmers. 'Very fond of that hat the Captain was. He was never without it in Spain. We all knew it.'

'How did you know it wasn't some other hat like it?'

'There wasn't another like it in the whole of England. I'm sorry, ma'am, but it was unmistakable. There was even a hole in its side made by a French musket ball at Vittoria. I saw it that night.'

'So you recognised the hat. Nothing else?'

'I suppose his hair, ma'am. It was red.'

'But you never actually saw his face?'

'No, I can't say I did.'

'What about the day before, Sergeant?' asked Richard. 'On Wednesday. Sergeant Kettle and I were looking for Bénuat, but you were left behind. Did you…did you see Captain Rawdon at all? In the afternoon?'

Lexi gave him a startled look. Richard already knew the answer to that. Mr Hargreaves had told them that Johnny had been walking down Piccadilly.

'No,' said Sergeant Chalmers slowly. 'No, I didn't. Not in the afternoon. But that wasn't surprising, was it? He was in with Lord what's-'is-name.'

There was a little silence. 'Did you see him at all?'

'I heard him talking, though I didn't see him. I was on duty at the Horse Guards that day. Outside the door. And I saw him when he came out. That was well on in the evening—six or seven o'clock.'

Richard leaned forward. 'Did he come out of that room at all during the afternoon?'

'Not while I was there. And I was on duty from midday till the time they finished.'

'Let me get this quite clear, sergeant. You saw Captain Rawdon at the Horse Guards the day before he died. You're sure it was that day? Wednesday.'

'Oh, yes, sir! The meeting was about those papers. Captain Rawdon was there because they'd been given to him to look after. I wouldn't forget a thing like that, sir. Not after—'

'Quite. So…on Wednesday, the day before he died, Captain Rawdon was with Lord Bathurst, at the Horse Guards, the whole time between midday and six or seven o'clock.'

'That's right, sir.'

'But I don't understand—' began Lexi. A look from Richard silenced her.

'Thank you, Sergeant Chalmers,' he said, getting up. 'No, don't stand up. I'm glad you've decided to join us at Channings. It might take a day or so, but someone will come to fetch you. They'll see you safely on your way to Dorchester, and one of my people will meet you there. Will that suit?'

'Very well, sir.' He looked at Lexi. 'I wish I could've been more help, ma'am. A very popular officer, Captain Rawdon. As brave and true as you'd meet. I don't understand what happened, that I don't. But…we did the best we could for him and his family.'

Lexi took his hand. 'And I thank you for it,' she said warmly. 'We shall see one another again at Channings, sergeant.'

Richard turned to go, then stopped. 'One other thing. Did you ever talk to anyone else about what happened that night in the tavern?'

Sergeant Chalmers looked shocked. 'No, never, sir! After all the pains we'd taken to keep it quiet, why would I do a thing like that? Not a word have I ever said to anyone, I promise you.'

'Of course you wouldn't. Thank you. Alexandra?'

When Lexi turned back at the doorway, the sergeant was sitting at his table again, but he looked a different person, someone with hope.

'That poor man. He doesn't look at all well,' she said as they picked their way back to where the carriage was waiting and got in.

'He looks terrible. I blame myself. I should have rescued him from that hell-hole before now.' Richard sounded angry.

'I don't see how you could, Richard. You had other things to think of. Will you send Coles to look after him on the stage?'

'No. One of the other servants can go with Chalmers. I need Coles for myself. I...I may go out of London for a day or two.'

This was a shock. 'Out of London? Where to?'

'I think I'd rather not tell you. Not until I'm sure.'

'Is it to see your other sergeant?'

'No, that's where we shall go this afternoon.'

'I hope he's in better circumstances than poor Sergeant Chalmers! How can the country treat its soldiers like this, after all they have done for us?'

'You'd better ask the War Office, my dear. Except that they probably wouldn't know what you were talking about, and if they knew they wouldn't care. That's why it's up to me to look after Sergeant Chalmers now that I've found him. But you needn't worry about Sergeant Kettle. According to my informant he was lucky enough to meet and marry a cosy little widow. They're now living happily together in her house in Kensal Green. I must admit I'm interested to see what she's like. Kettle was a bit of a rogue.'

As they drew up in Brook Street Lexi said, 'You said before that we were going out of London, but then refused to tell me any of the details! That's not very reasonable, Richard. You must tell me something of your plans. I need to think of what I shall take with me. When are we leaving?'

'I'm sorry,' Richard said. 'But nothing is fixed at the moment. Except that I don't intend to take you with me. I don't expect to be away long.'

Lexi bit her lip. 'Pray don't hurry back on my account,' she said, angry again. 'Take as long as you like.'

'Don't waste your time quarrelling with me, Alexandra,' he said calmly. 'You'd do better to put on your proper clothes again. Kensal Green is quite a respectable place. You mustn't let me down in front of Mrs Kettle.'

Lexi gave him a searing look, then marched up the stairs, calling for Cissie.

The drive out to Kensal Green did something to restore Lexi's temper. The day was cold but bright, and the air outside the centre of London was fresher. By the time they reached their goal she was able to talk to him again at least with the appearance of civility.

Mrs Kettle's house was a small cottage set back from the road, with a garden that would be very attractive in summer. To the side of the house was a large vegetable patch, and here they found Sergeant Kettle busy at work. He stopped and rested on his spade when he saw their carriage draw up.

'Well, I never did!' he said. 'It's the Captain!' He came over to them, rubbing his hands on his trousers. Turning towards the house, he shouted, 'Minnie! Minnie! Come out here, quick!'

When Mrs Kettle appeared Lexi had a hard job not to smile. The sergeant was over six feet tall, his wife not much over four and a half. They made a comic couple. 'Well, what is it, what is it? And how many times have I told you not to wipe your hands on those breeches, Joe Kettle?'

The sergeant looked briefly penitent, then gave her a huge grin and said, 'We've got visitors, Minnie. You mustn't let them think I've married a shrew, now!' He gave Richard an impressive salute. 'Captain Deverell, sir.'

'Sergeant.' Richard turned and helped Lexi out of the chaise. After a number of introductions, followed by apologies, which were entirely unnecessary, for the state of the house, the party went inside. Mrs Kettle busied herself in the kitchen while Richard and Lexi were taken into the parlour. After some minutes' talk Richard looked round.

'You've found yourself a snug billet here, sergeant,' he said.

'None better, sir!'

'I expect you're wondering what the reason for this call is.'

'I'm sure you'll tell me, sir!'

'It's about Captain Rawdon.' Sergeant Kettle shot an anxious look at Lexi. 'Lady Deverell knows about Captain Rawdon. He was her brother.'

'I can see you're worried you might upset me, sergeant,' said Lexi. 'But you needn't be. You see, I don't believe Captain Rawdon was guilty.'

'But, ma'am—' The sergeant stopped and said, 'Excuse me a minute.' He went out to the kitchen, where he could be heard talking to his wife. Then he came back and carefully shut the door.

'My lady, I wish I could say different. Captain Rawdon was one of the best officers I ever served under. A bit lively, mind. And apt to take risks. But straight as a die. I couldn't believe my eyes when I saw him that night.'

'I don't suppose you saw his face, though.'

'Not clearly. But I'll take my oath it was the Captain.' He gave her an apologetic look.

'You were with me off and on for a good bit of that day,' said Richard. 'Did you see the Captain at all?'

'No, sir. Not till the evening.'

'Do you remember anything strange about him in the days preceding that meeting? Or did you hear anything about him—about his behaviour or his looks, or what he said, anything?'

'I don't think so… Well…there was the question of the message…'

'What message was that?'

'Mind you, it's hearsay. I had it from Banks, Major Aubrey's man. You remember Major Aubrey, sir? Killed at Waterloo afterwards?'

'Of course I do! Get on with it, man.'

'Banks said that Captain Rawdon had asked the Major why he hadn't turned up at Jackson's on that Thursday morning, as they'd arranged. Major Aubrey was surprised. He said he'd sent a note crying off. But Captain Rawdon swore he hadn't had any such note…' Sergeant Kettle paused.

'Well?'

'Well, Banks told me that he knew for a fact that he *had*. That he—Banks, that is, sir—had handed Major Aubrey's note to Captain Rawdon himself.'

Richard looked interested. 'He was quite certain it was Captain Rawdon?'

'Oh, yes, sir. Banks knew him quite well.'

'Hmm. Was this in Captain Rawdon's rooms?'

'No, Banks had met the Captain outside his rooms in

St James's Square, and passed the note to him personally. But Captain Rawdon didn't remember him doing
anything of the kind. Now, that was odd, don't you
think?'

'Odd,' said Richard thoughtfully. 'That word "odd"
again.'

Lexi shook her head. 'Perhaps Johnny was sick,' she
said.

'I don't think so.' Richard sounded very sure.

'But he must have been! He was behaving so
strangely.'

'I think Sergeant Kettle has told us as much as he
can, my dear. Shall we let Mrs Kettle in again?'

'Oh! Oh, yes, I'm sorry! Of course!'

They travelled back to Brook Street almost in silence.
Richard was deep in thought, though from time to time
he looked at Lexi almost as if he was sorry for her. Lexi
was convinced it was because they had met with such
little success in their visits, and she made no effort to
get him to talk to her. She didn't want to have it pointed
out that nothing they had heard that day had helped to
absolve Johnny from suspicion. On the contrary, what
the two sergeants had said only seemed to involve him
more deeply than ever.

But Lexi was wrong. What Richard had heard since
coming to London had *not* further convinced him of
Johnny's guilt. Quite the opposite. Richard was considering Hargreaves's report that he had seen Johnny in
Piccadilly at a time when he was quite definitely closeted in a room at the Horse Guards. He was also considering Sergeant Kettle's report that Johnny had denied
ever seeing a note that, significantly, had not been de-

livered to his rooms, but given to him in person in the open street. These events had both taken place on the same day—the day before Johnny's death. Adding all this together, he was coming to the conclusion that there must have been a second man in London that day, a man who resembled Johnny so closely that even people who knew him quite well had been deceived. Perhaps someone who had not only accepted Johnny's identity, but actually adopted it in the Cock Tavern for his own purposes.

And, if what he suspected proved to be correct, then Johnny was indeed innocent. But there would be little joy for Alexandra when they found out who the real criminal was.

Chapter Thirteen

The Deverells were engaged to go to a recital of poetry and music at Northumberland House that evening. Little though Lexi felt like it, she put on one of her new dresses, and allowed Cissie to dress her hair more elaborately than usual. Before the maid had finished, Richard came in and held out a case with Lexi's initials on it, which had evidently come from one of the foremost jewellers in London.

'I thought you might like to wear these tonight,' he said briefly.

Lexi gazed at him in surprise. A present from Richard—and from Rundell, Bridge and Rundell—was the last thing she had expected. He moved to go.

'Won't you wait,' she asked, 'till I see what it is?' He hesitated, then moved over to the fire, where he sat down in one of the armchairs and watched her. She opened it. Lying on a bed of velvet inside was a parure of diamonds—necklace, earrings and a delicate aigrette. Lexi was filled with wonder and delight. She hardly heard Cissie's gasp of admiration as she picked up the necklace. It glittered and flashed, slipping through her fingers like a waterfall of light. It was a beautiful piece—the diamonds in it were of the first water, and the workmanship was superb.

She turned to Richard. He was no longer looking her way, but was leaning back with his legs stretched out negligently in front of him. He looked as if, having handed the diamonds over, he was taking no further interest. Why had he given her the jewellery? Whatever his reason, it deserved her thanks. She got up.

'Richard! What a magnificent present!'

He rose and said coolly, 'You have very little jewellery. I thought you should have more. Will you wear them tonight?'

His continued indifference took away some of her pleasure in the gift. She discarded any notion of asking him to help her to put them on, and gave the aigrette to her maid. 'Of course,' she said, trying to speak equally calmly. 'This is just what I need to finish off my coiffure.' She sat down again at her dressing table and watched Cissie fix it in her hair. Cissie's eyes were full of awe as she next picked up the necklace and clasped it reverently round Lexi's neck. But as Lexi leaned forward to put on her own earrings she dimly saw Richard's reflection in her mirror. It was only a fleeting glimpse, but the expression on his face was not at all indifferent. He looked like a man dying of starvation. She turned round swiftly, but the expression had vanished and she wondered if it had simply been a trick of her imagination, a distortion of the glass.

As soon as she dismissed Cissie, he too started to go.

'No, wait!' she said on an impulse. 'Just a moment, Richard. I haven't yet thanked you properly for these lovely things.' She came over to kiss Richard on the cheek. But as she was about to kiss him he turned his head and their lips met. The slightest touch was enough.

With a muffled groan he put his arms round her, and suddenly they were lost, engulfed in an explosion of feeling. The kiss changed. Deep and long, it was so intense that, though they hardly moved, they seemed to melt into one another, transmute once again into one being, one life.

But just when Lexi felt she could hardly bear another moment of such sweetness, Richard broke away and went to stand in front of the fire. Neither was able to speak. They stood in silence, breathing rapidly, until Richard said unevenly, 'I'm sorry. I must have crushed your dress.'

'Richard—'

'No, Alexandra. No. You must tidy yourself. We'll be late. I'll send Cissie in again, then wait for you downstairs.' And he was gone.

Lexi gazed after him in despair. How could he simply walk away? It was clear he was not half, not a tenth as affected as she had been by what had just happened. Did he realise how cruel he had been to give her another glimpse of the world he said didn't exist any more, only to snatch it away again? He couldn't have. If he had any idea of what a tumult of emotion had been roused by that kiss, he wouldn't now calmly expect her to tidy her dress and join him downstairs, to go with him to meet the polite world at Northumberland House, to make suitable conversation, to listen with civilised interest to an evening of poetry and music! But if she had any pride at all she must do all of that.

She walked over to the mirror and gazed into it. In her mind's eye she saw Richard's face again. Had she imagined his expression? She must have. Her own eyes were feverishly bright, as bright as these damned diamonds! Why had he given her such a costly present from the most expensive jeweller in London? For a moment she had thought he had wanted to show her how much she meant to him, but that had been foolish. It now seemed more likely that Lord Deverell was anxious to see his wife as well dressed, as expensively bejewelled, as the rest of the ladies of society. Well, he ought to be satisfied tonight. The jewels were as beautiful as any she had seen, and her dress was the work of one of the foremost modistes in London. If that was what he wanted, Richard could be proud of her. Lexi submitted to Cissie's attentions and got ready to play her part.

And she played her part to such good effect that the people there that night declared that they had never seen Lexi Rawdon in such looks. They were impressed with her new husband's devotion, too. Not that one could see any change in his demeanour—one wouldn't expect it of Richard Deverell. He had never been one to reveal his thoughts—that was what made him such an excellent card player. But who would demand open demonstrations of affection from him when ample evidence of it was sparkling round his wife's neck? The new Lady Deverell was generally accounted to be a very lucky woman.

Among her admirers was Sir Charles Stainforth, who came over especially to talk to her in the interval.

'I dare say you don't remember me, Lady Deverell. When I met you last year you were always surrounded by your devoted admirers. A very successful Season, as I remember.'

'Of course I remember you, Sir Charles! Your wife is a good friend of my godmother's. We met at her house quite often. Is Lady Stainforth with you tonight?'

'Alas, no. Outside the Season Lady Stainforth prefers

to stay in our house in Surrey. I spend most of the week in town, but she usually expects me to be at home with her at the weekend. You'll find it so, Deverell. A man loses his freedom when he marries!'

'Ah, but they gain so much more, Sir Charles,' said Lexi, laughing at his glum face. 'I was about to ask you and Lady Stainforth to dine with us next week, but if you are at present on your own in town, would you like to join us tomorrow night if you are free? In fact, I have a favour to ask of you. Please say no, if you would rather not. I've been trying to find people who knew my brother, Johnny, and I think you had a great deal to do with his work at the Horse Guards. Could you possibly share some of your memories of him with me?'

'I'd be delighted to tell you anything I know—as long as it's suitable for a lady's ears, that is. Johnny was, after all, a lusty young man. I'm not sure his sister would like to hear everything he got up to, eh, Deverell?' Sir Charles grew serious. 'But I was very sorry to hear he had died. He is a loss to us all. Deverell tells me you were very close.'

'We were, but I saw very little of him during those last weeks. That's why I have asked you to tell me about him. Eight o'clock tomorrow? Good. Now, tell me what you think of our soprano tonight.'

The following evening Richard's manner as he welcomed Sir Charles was easy, even warmer than usual. No one would have suspected how tense he really was. A question was forming in his mind, and he was not sure whether he desired or feared the answer to it. He had even wondered whether it was better never to know the answer, but had decided in the end that he owed it to Johnny's memory to persevere. But the last thing he wanted to do tonight was to rouse the slightest suspicion that all had not been perfectly above board with Johnny Rawdon's death.

One fact was established quite soon. Sergeant Chalmers had been right. On the day before he died Johnny had indeed been with Lord Bathurst for all of the afternoon and part of the evening. A good dinner and more than a few glasses of wine had loosened Sir Charles's tongue, and even though Lexi was present he spoke quite freely about the confidential papers.

'Johnny wasn't taking part in any discussion, of course. He was there because Wellington's papers were strictly speakin' in his charge. Yours, too, but you were out a good part of that day, talking to various people about the Frenchman. Bénuat, wasn't it?'

Richard nodded and Sir Charles went on, 'We knew the French were after those papers. My goodness, what a lot of damage it would have done if they had got their hands on them! I was glad to see the back of the wretched things, I can tell you. It was like having the Crown Jewels in the place with no Tower of London and no proper guards! But Wellington refused to let any of us look after them—he didn't trust us!' Sir Charles gave a laugh. 'He may be the hero everyone thinks him, Lady Deverell, but he's not the easiest of men to do business with! At that time relations were so bad between the Iron Duke and the people at the Horse Guards that he wouldn't have trusted us with a bootlace, let alone papers as important as those!'

'You mustn't disillusion my wife, Sir Charles! She believes we were all under the impression that Bonaparte was the enemy! In any case, you were wrong about Wellington. He just thought serving officers were better qualified to explain things to the people who mattered.'

'Oh, I know that as long as you and Johnny Rawdon had them in your care they were safe enough. But, according to rumour, the French were offering a great deal of money to anyone who could steal them.'

'I don't suppose many people even knew they existed, did they?' asked Lexi.

'Impossible to guess. It was supposed to be a secret, but the Horse Guards is like a leaky sieve, everything comes through eventually. And if you'll forgive my saying so, Lady Deverell, I'm not sure your brother was always as discreet as he ought to have been. It was all a game to Johnny, poor fellow, though he was impressed at the amount the French thought the papers were worth. But tell me, Deverell. Why the interest in them now? There isn't any trouble, is there?'

'None at all as far as I know. I suppose Alexandra would want to know about anything that played such an important part in Johnny's life at the time he died.'

'Ah, yes. But you know, Lady Deverell, I'm not sure you should dwell so much on the past. Your brother was a brave and resourceful officer who has left behind an enviable reputation. He was young, of course, and was obviously bored in London. This might have led him into one or two…indiscretions, shall we say? But that would all have disappeared once he was in action. No, Johnny Rawdon is remembered with affection and respect by all of his army friends. You can be proud of him. And…' he gazed at her kindly '…let him rest.'

Lexi's eyes filled with tears. 'Thank you,' she said. 'You are very kind.'

After that they talked of other things until Lexi excused herself and left the gentlemen to their after-dinner port.

'That's a lovely girl,' said Sir Charles. 'And she has a heart, too. Of course, you and the two Rawdons were all children together, weren't you? You're a lucky man, Deverell. But I've said that already.' He regarded Richard quizzically. 'You have the look of a man who wants to ask me something. Fire away.'

'There's a small piece of unfinished business connected with Bénuat. It hardly matters now, I suppose, but I don't like leaving things unresolved.'

'What is it?'

'Bénuat disappeared, but he had an accomplice. I think, for reasons which I won't go into at the moment, that he lodged somewhere in the Seven Dials district.'

'And?'

'I'd like to find out a little more about him.'

'The war is over, Deverell. Forget that sort of thing and enjoy the company of that lovely wife of yours!'

Unmoved, Richard said, 'There's still a villain out there, whom I'd like to trace. Some of your people—I believe you call them, unofficially, your ''ferrets''—must be slightly underworked at the moment. I'd pay the expenses of one or two of them to sniff about in the Seven Dials area for Monsieur X. If he's there, they'll find him within a week or two. Your ferrets are very effective.'

Sir Charles shrugged his shoulders. 'I'll send someone round—tomorrow morning?'

'I'd prefer to come to your office, if I may.'

'Don't want your wife to know, eh? Very well. I still think you're being over-scrupulous, but you always were a stubborn devil.'

They rejoined Lexi in the saloon, but Sir Charles did not stay much longer, and the Deverells were left alone.

Lexi badly wanted to discuss the evening's revelations, but though Richard agreed with her that the details of Johnny's last two days were getting more and more mysterious, he was very disinclined to talk. She sensed that he was deeply troubled, but knew better than to ask what it was. In his present mood he would only put her off. In fact, thought Lexi sadly, Richard seemed to be getting more remote with each day that passed.

They separated soon afterwards, and went to their respective rooms.

The next morning after breakfast Richard invited her to come with him into the small parlour, and Lexi wondered what he was about to say to her. However, his first words, though slightly surprising, were ordinary enough.

'I have sent for Will Osborne. He should be here tomorrow.'

'I'm pleased to hear it, but why do we need him? I thought you planned to take Coles with you when you...when you go "out of London" to this mysterious destination of yours.'

'I *shall* take Coles. Osborne will stay here to look after you. I prefer to leave someone I can trust, and Osborne knows London quite well. I gather your father used him for a number of errands to the capital?'

'Yes, he did. Osborne was born here. His father brought him down to work at Rawdon when he was young, but he still remembers his way about the city. Papa used him a lot.'

'I'd like you not to go out without him. And I hope

you won't play any tricks on him as you did in Dorchester.'

'If you are so concerned for my welfare, Richard, why don't you take me with you?'

'I…can't. For one reason, I don't expect the journey to be comfortable—I shall be covering the ground as quickly as I can. I'm not even taking Phillips with me.'

'And the other reason is that you don't wish to have me with you. Don't worry,' said Lexi, coldly. 'I didn't really expect you would. And I shall find plenty of things to amuse me while you're away.'

Richard looked at her very seriously. 'I would like to forbid you to look for any further information about Johnny, Alexandra, but I know you too well. It wouldn't work! But may I beg you, most earnestly, to be patient. I have to go, but I won't be away for long. Could you leave it till I get back? I wouldn't ask if I didn't have very good reason for it.'

'But you can't tell me what that is?'

'No.' He added wryly, 'I hardly dare ask you to trust me.'

After a moment's thought, Lexi said, 'I do. In this. Very well, Richard. I shall behave like a typical young matron while you are away. I shall spend a lot of time with my godmother. I believe she wants to take me to a number of her favourite warehouses. I shall ask Sir Charles if he will accompany us to Lady Garmston's soirée, and take me to Somerset House to see the exhibition. I shall go for a drive in Hyde Park, accompanied, of course, by Osborne. And I shall perhaps ask Mr Hargreaves to accompany us on a visit to the theatre. Will that do?'

He smiled. She had forgotten what Richard's smile could do to her. Her resentment faded in its warmth.

'My dear girl,' he said. 'I shall be away for four days at the very most. You won't have time for such a schedule. You won't even have time to miss me.'

'Of course not,' she replied, wishing she could sound more convincing.

He hesitated, then said, 'I have an appointment this morning. But would you come out this afternoon with me? Just for pleasure?'

'Thank you,' she found herself saying. 'I'd like to.'

The day was dull and cold with a hint of rain. It was no weather for a drive and Lexi half-expected Richard to call the afternoon excursion off. But his intention was not to take her for any kind of drive, it appeared. Instead they drove down into Piccadilly, past Charing Cross, into the Strand and up Fleet Street to Ludgate Hill. Here the carriage drew up outside the premises of Rundell, Bridge and Rundell, and in a few moments Mr Philip Rundell, the senior partner, was receiving them with the sort of welcome only reserved for royalty or sources of a great deal of potential custom. Mr Rundell was far too discreet to ask Lexi whether the diamonds had pleased her, but when it became clear that Lord Deverell had in fact given them to his wife he waxed lyrical about their purity and size.

'And I flatter myself I have an equally lovely piece ready for your inspection, my lord,' said Mr Rundell, producing a velvet-covered tray on which was displayed a necklace. 'Sapphires, I think you said?'

Lexi gazed at the beautiful object, then looked in wonder at Richard. 'More jewels?' she asked.

Richard met her eyes. 'I want you to have them,' he said. 'I thought sapphires, for your eyes, but if you would prefer some other stone—emeralds, perhaps...?'

'If Lady Deverell would prefer emeralds,' said Mr Rundell smoothly, 'I happen to have some superb emeralds set in first-water diamonds—'

'No,' said Lexi, without taking her eyes off Richard. 'I should like sapphires.'

Mr Rundell gave a little cough to draw his customers' attention to the serious business in hand. They seemed to have forgotten he was there…

'Ah! Yes,' said Richard, recovering. 'Send the sapphires round as soon as the case is ready, Rundell. I dare say we shall see one another again. Are you ready, Alexandra?'

Assuring them of his best attention at all times, Mr Rundell escorted them personally to the door, and saw them out.

When they were back in the carriage Lexi said, 'You're being very generous. I…I'm not sure how to thank you.'

'Then don't try. But I hope you don't think I'm trying to buy anything with those jewels, Alexandra. They are yours, without strings attached. I wanted to give you pleasure before I leave.' The inside of the carriage was dark. Lexi couldn't see his face, but there was something in his voice that she couldn't quite understand.

'What is it?' she asked suddenly. 'I'm grateful for that beautiful sapphire necklace, very grateful. It is a wonderful gift. But why do I have the impression that there is more to them than that? What are you hiding, Richard?'

After a pause Richard said, 'You've had a great deal to bear recently. Perhaps I wanted to show my appreciation of your courage. Don't lose it. I think you might soon need even more, I'm afraid.'

'You mean you *still* think Johnny guilty? After all

we've discovered?' Lexi's voice revealed the depth of her disappointment.

'Ask me when I come back. I'll tell you then.'

He refused to say any more, and the journey ended in an uncomfortable silence. Lexi's excitement over the jewels had vanished. By the time they entered the house Lexi would have been tempted, if asked, to return the sapphire necklace to Rundell, Bridge and Rundell. What she wanted was her husband's confidence, not his gifts, however valuable.

They were out till late that evening and when they got back Richard made his excuses. He would not see her the next morning as he was setting off very early. He promised to be back as soon as he could, but there was nothing in his manner to indicate any regret at leaving her. On the contrary—he was more reserved than ever.

Accompanied only by his groom, Richard took the road north through Islington and Barnet; by demanding the best horses and pushing them hard, he reached Northampton by the evening. Here he established himself at the Angel, and after a hearty meal washed down with a pint or two of ale, he went to bed. He intended to be up and about in good time the next day.

This was not the first time he had been in Northampton. Earlier in the year he had come to seek out Mark Rawdon for Lexi's father. But on that occasion, he had been worried about the state of affairs in Somerset, and was anxious to get back as quickly as possible. And, as it turned out, his stay had been even shorter than he had hoped. Mark had needed very little time to clear up his affairs, and though Richard had offered to wait till the next day, they had in fact left Northampton that same day.

As a result, on that previous visit Richard had spoken to very few people in the town, and none of them had been connected with Mark. This time he intended to find out a little more about Alexandra's cousin.

The next morning he left Coles behind at the inn and set out to find the house where Rawdon had been living. It was deserted, and looked as if it had been empty ever since its occupier had left it three months before. When Richard saw an elderly man regarding him curiously from across the road, he asked where he might find the person who had lived there.

'What does tha' want to know fer?'

'I…might have some news for him. And if a man could direct me to him, or to any connections of his, there might be something in it for him, too.'

'Oh, aye? Londoner, are yer?'

Richard had no wish to confuse him with unnecessary detail. 'Yes.'

'Well, I might be able to help… But I'd want ter see tha' money fust.'

After carefully examining the coin Richard handed over, the old man pocketed it and said, 'You won't find that good-fer-nothin' in Northampton. He went off wi'out a word to anyone to pick up a fortune some-where else, and left Nancy Pelham to starve.'

'Who is Nancy Pelham?'

'You don't know much, do yer? She's the old woman who looked after 'em all. She'd been with 'em for years. But didn't make no difference to Mark Rawdon. Just up and left wi'out a word, 'e did. It's a good thing she 'ad a sister to go to. She'd ha' starved else.'

'Where is this Mrs Pelham now?'

'I just told you! Wi' 'er sister Aggie.'

Richard drew a breath. 'And where might that be?'

'Behind the baker's in Sheep Street. You can't miss it. Aggie Bell's the sister's name.'

After a minute's further talk Richard came to the conclusion that the old man had no more to tell him, and walked back to the centre of the town.

The cottage behind the baker's was small but well kept, and after presenting himself as Richard Deverell he was invited in. Inside, the cottage was painfully neat, but it was evident that the sisters lived on the edge of penury. Mrs Pelham was wrapped in shawls and sitting in a rocking chair by the fire. She was quite elderly, but far from the toothless old crone he had half-expected. Her faded eyes were alert, and she had retained the manners and speech of a well-trained servant. Her sister was younger and obviously very fond of her.

'I hope you won't upset Nancy, sir,' she whispered. 'Mr Mark didn't treat her very well. Has he perhaps thought better of it? Have you a message from him?'

'I'm afraid I haven't.'

'Oh? Well, I have to say I would have been astonished if you had!' she said acidly. 'Then why...?'

'Why am I here?' Richard smiled and said, 'Let me tell your sister, and if she agrees you can listen at the same time.'

This was settled on and Richard was invited to sit down next to Mrs Pelham.

'I remember you, sir,' she said when he got close. 'You came some time in the summer. About the end of August it was. You took Mr Mark away with you.'

'That's right,' said Richard. 'You were keeping house for him, I suppose. I didn't see you.'

'No, he kept me out of the way. Didn't want me to know what was going on.'

'He didn't want you talking to Mr Deverell, either, Nancy.'

'Oh? Why do you say that, Mrs Bell?'

'You might have heard the truth about him. Not that Nancy would have told you anything. Too soft for her own good, she is.'

Richard turned back to Mrs Pelham. 'I suppose you know that Mr Mark now owns a large estate in Somerset?'

'How should I know that? I haven't heard from him since he left. But I'm not surprised. He always said he would one day, and that he'd have a title, too.'

'Did he, indeed? I was under the impression he didn't know anything about it.'

'Did he tell you that?'

'Yes, he did. I'm sure he did.'

The old woman's face closed up. 'Well, it's not for me to say different, is it, sir? I must have misheard him.'

Mrs Bell intervened. 'Nancy! Don't be a fool!' When Mrs Pelham remained obstinately silent, she turned to Richard. 'There was never a woman more loyal than my sister, sir. She worked for the Rawdons all her working life, and if Mrs Rawdon was still alive I know I couldn't get her to say a word to anyone. Now the poor lady's dead, God rest her soul, and, though her son left my sister to starve, she still won't talk about him without good reason. What do you want? Are you a friend of Mark Rawdon's? You might not like what you hear, if you are.'

Richard said slowly, 'What I want is the truth. Whether I like it or not doesn't matter. I'm neither a friend nor an enemy of Mark Rawdon, but he's involved with someone…someone I have a duty to protect. I'd like to know the truth about him, good or bad.'

'You hear that, Nancy? Tell the gentleman.'

Mrs Pelham leaned slightly forward in order to see Richard's face, and what she saw there seemed to satisfy her. She said, 'Whatever he told you, sir, Mark Rawdon knew all about the family in Somerset. Mr Rawdon had a big Bible with the Rawdon family tree in it, and even when he was little Mark was always showing it to me. ''Look at that! After Papa I'm next but one in line, Pelly,'' he used to say. ''Just a boy called John between us and a big estate in the West of England!'' When I asked him about the girl called Alexandra, John's sister, he said there was no need for him to worry about her, that she couldn't inherit the title. Then years later—this was after Mr Rawdon had died—he saw in the paper that his cousin John had gone to be a soldier. You can't imagine how pleased he was. ''You wait and see, Pelly,'' he said. ''He'll be killed, and then when the old man dies I'll be a baronet. Sir Mark Rawdon!'' And then his cousin *was* killed.'

'But not fighting the French,' said Richard grimly.

'I didn't know that, sir.'

'Did you say you kept house for Mr Mark after his mother died?'

'That she did,' said Mrs Bell. 'And small thanks she got for it.'

'I suppose if you lived in, you would know if he ever went away for a day or two. To visit his relatives, perhaps?'

'I don't think he ever did that. But he went to London quite often. Two or three times this summer, before you came. Perhaps he met them there?'

'Perhaps he did,' said Richard, with an irony that was

lost on Mrs Pelham. 'I'll try not to take up much more of your time, Mrs Pelham.'

'I don't mind, sir. I wouldn't be doing anything else.'

'Could you remember exactly when he went?'

'Well, that's easy enough. It was my birthday. The seventeenth of May. He went to London the day before, and that meant I could spend the whole of the next day with Aggie. He was away that first time for a good bit, too—the Tuesday, the Wednesday and the Thursday nights.'

'Er...how did you know he was in London?'

'He stayed with Aggie's sister-in-law, Mrs Judkin. She keeps a lodging house in Brownlow Street. I don't know what part of London it's in, though.'

'Right. You said he went away again?'

'Twice, though those times he was only away for one night. Once in July, and once in August. You came to take him away not long after.' Mrs Pelham's brow puckered. 'Mr Mark's in trouble, isn't he? That's why you're asking all these questions.'

Richard took one of her hands in his. 'Mrs Pelham, will you believe me when I say that I hope more than I can tell you that he isn't.'

It was as if she had not heard him. 'He was always bad,' she said. 'His poor mother used to say he'd got it from his grandfather, along with the red hair and blue eyes. He didn't have any sense of right or wrong! If Mark Rawdon wanted something, he made sure he got it, one way or another. I suppose that would have been understandable. But sometimes he did wicked things just for the pleasure of it. He liked seeing people hurt or miserable. It seemed to make him happier. I thought sometimes the devil was in him, sir, and that's a fact.'

She turned to Richard with a look of bewilderment

in her old eyes. 'But the funny thing was, he had such a way with him, Mr Deverell! He'd do something terrible, then he'd laugh up at you with such a merry look in his eyes that you laughed with him, even though you knew you shouldn't. And clever! Oh, he was clever, that boy! He didn't often get caught, and when he was he could usually beguile his way out of it. But I was always sure he'd come to a bad end.'

Richard was silent. At last he said, 'You've been very patient. Thank you. Would you accept something from me? The Rawdon estate, of which I was a trustee, has a special fund quite separate from the rest of the estate for what it considers to be deserving causes. Sir Mark has neglected his duty towards you. I'd like you to accept a small grant of money from this fund.'

'Why, thank you, sir! But I'm not sure I should.'

'You take it, Nancy! You've earned it.'

Richard took out a small purse and passed it to Mrs Pelham. 'Take this for now. I'll see you get more.'

'Thank you, sir!' Mrs Pelham looked at the purse. She added suddenly, 'Why, that reminds me! Perhaps you'd be so good as to take a purse Mr Mark left behind him, sir? I don't like to keep it. Aggie will fetch it. It's in the box in the bedroom.'

With a sense of approaching doom Richard waited while Mrs Bell made her way up the stairs and down again. When she came back she had a purse in her hand. It was the purse he had last seen caught in the light in the Cock tavern, in the hand of the man he had thought was Johnny Rawdon.

Chapter Fourteen

Richard had always prided himself on keeping cool in the face of trouble or danger, but even he had difficulty in dealing with the conflicting emotions and ideas which passed through his mind during the sixty-odd miles back to London. His highest hopes, and his worst fears, had been confirmed. It had been proved beyond all possible doubt that Johnny, his friend, his comrade, his brother, was, after all, completely innocent. That purse had finally linked Mark to the man in the tavern and silenced all debate. Alexandra's belief in her brother had been vindicated, and one of the major bars to their happiness—his own inability to ignore the evidence—had been removed. The sense of relief was enormous.

Only now that the burden had been lifted did Richard realise how heavy it had been. The idea that Johnny could have behaved so dishonourably, so unlike everything he had believed his friend stood for, had shaken the very foundation of his world. After his father's rejection of him as a child the Rawdon family had represented the only security he had known. If Johnny Rawdon could be a traitor, then nothing was certain, nothing secure. For a short while he had managed to bury this uncertainty in the delight of loving Alexandra openly and fully, in a dream of perfect happiness at Channings. But the dream, built on such a shaky foundation, had been too fragile to last. The moment she had doubted him it had vanished, and he had decided he must make do with second-best.

But Johnny was innocent! The world had righted itself, the uncertainty was over, and Richard was now free, strong enough to fight for Alexandra's trust, to overcome all her doubts, to hope and build and enjoy everything that life with her could offer. He was in a state of such elation that he wanted to shout it aloud.

But after a while the euphoria faded and he began to assess the other side of the coin. Johnny Rawdon was innocent—but Mark Rawdon was guilty. There was no sense of personal betrayal in this knowledge, as there had been with his friend, but the implications were potentially catastrophic. Since Johnny had had no reason whatsoever to kill himself, it seemed quite likely that he had died at his cousin's hand that night. Not accidental death, as Richard had made it appear, nor suicide as he had feared, but *murder*. The more Richard considered it, the more convinced he was that that had been Mark Rawdon's main purpose in coming to London. His hopes of an easy way through to the title had been dashed. Johnny had survived all the fighting in Spain, and was now out of active service, working in the Army's headquarters. So…Mark Rawdon had decided to give Fate a helping hand.

As for the theft of the papers… Richard was willing to wager that that had been a touch of improvisation, a bonus. But it had been a brilliant stroke. It had presented anyone who was interested with a perfect reason for Johnny's ''suicide'', as well as providing Mark with a purse of traitor's gold. Exactly how Mark had learned of Bénuat and his desire for the papers was likely to remain forever a mystery. After Henry Seymour's defection, Bénuat must have been a desperate man. Richard could only assume that the Frenchman had decided to try a direct approach and had spoken to Mark, believing him to be Johnny. Mark had been clever enough and quick enough to seize the opportunity. But that could never be confirmed. Bénuat was dead, killed by Richard's own men, and Mark was most unlikely to confess.

The question now was—what would it do to Alexandra, who had already gone through so much, to learn that her sole surviving relative, the last of the Rawdon line, had probably killed her brother in order to succeed her father? She had been so passionately partisan in favour of her cousin, refusing to entertain any suggestion that his motives were not as pure as she thought. The truth was that she had *needed* to believe in him. Richard knew what it had done to him to discover, as he had thought, that Johnny was a traitor. He thought it might well be just as terrible a shock for Alexandra to discover that Mark was a murderer.

Dunstable, St Albans, Barnet, went by on the road, but Richard was hardly aware of them. His groom saw to the change of horses and the need for refreshment, but Richard was so deep in thought that he let it all happen without noticing. What was he to do about Mark Rawdon? To let him go free was unthinkable. Johnny's murderer must be punished. But how was he to achieve that without causing Alexandra so much more grief?

By the time he reached the streets of London he had decided, though not lightly, on his course of action. He would deal with Mark Rawdon in his own way without saying anything to Alexandra. He had even concocted a story that was close enough to the truth to satisfy her without revealing Mark's part in the affair. But she was so quick that she might well make the connection immediately if she got wind of this visit to Northampton. Coles must be told to keep his mouth shut. The decision made, Richard began to plan what to say to her about Johnny. He was eagerly anticipating the moment when he could assure her at last that he was wholeheartedly convinced of her brother's innocence.

Lexi had told herself Richard would be away for four days, so she had not been expecting him. On the evening he returned she had been out to the theatre with Lady Wroxford, Stephen Hargreaves and Sir Charles, and so came in late. Sir Charles Stainforth had escorted her back to Brook Street, but had refused her invitation to come in with her, for which she was grateful. His company was agreeable, and the farce that followed the play had been very funny, but her spirits were low, and she had the headache. As she went up the stairs she sighed. Still another day before Richard would return, and, though she had no reason to think there would be any change in their relationship, she missed him and wanted him back!

She was surprised to find that Cissie was nowhere to be seen when she entered her bedchamber. Where was she? It was most unlike her not to be waiting inside the door ready to take Lexi's wrap and any other outer garments before helping her to undress. She jumped as a long figure unrolled itself out of the armchair, stood up and said, 'Cissie isn't here. I sent her away. Will I do instead?'

'Richard!' cried Lexi in amazement. 'Oh, Richard!' She threw herself into his arms, headache and low spirits alike forgotten, and they kissed.

'I must go away more often,' said Richard shakily after a while.

'No, don't!' said Lexi, dropping her wrap and gloves on the floor. 'I missed you so much! Let me look at you.'

She put her hands on his shoulders and gazed up at him. After a moment she said slowly, 'There's something different about you... What is it?'

He took her back into his arms. 'Oh, my dear love,' he said, hugging her, his cheek against hers. 'I've come out of a long, dark tunnel into the daylight. I can't begin to tell you how that makes me feel.'

'What is it, Richard?'

'You were right and I was wrong,' he said, his lips at her ear. 'I am now absolutely sure, completely certain, that Johnny was innocent.'

Lexi pulled away from him in order to see him more clearly. 'What did you say?' she asked in a dazed voice.

'I'm now convinced that Johnny was innocent, the victim of a French plot.'

She looked at him with incredulity. 'I...I can't believe it,' she said. 'After all these weeks... But I think you mean it. Oh, oh, Richard!' Lexi threw herself back into his arms and burst into tears.

'Hey, hey, hey! I thought you'd be pleased.'

'I am! Oh, I am. I thought I should never hear you say that! Oh, Richard, it means so much. Thank God! Oh, thank God!'

He rocked her in his arms until she was calmer, then said with a laugh, 'I've so much to say to you. But all I can think of at this moment is that I can't hold you close enough. Your damned jewels are scratching me and your dress, though lovely, is in my way.'

'That's soon cured,' she said with a saucy, if slightly damp, look. 'Though it would have been sooner if you had left me my maid.' She sat down at the dressing table and started to take the aigrette out of her hair. Richard came over and stilled her hands with his. 'I'll do that,' he said. He carefully removed the aigrette, then took the pins out of her hair so that it fell down her back in a swathe of copper.

Lexi looked at his reflection. 'You've gone the wrong way about it,' she said breathlessly. 'How are you to find the clasp to undo the necklace?'

'Leave it to me,' he said, and lifted her hair to his face. Their eyes met in the mirror. 'When I was in Spain,' he said softly, 'I used to dream of doing this. It smells of you.' He buried his face in the mass of hair, then swept it to one side so that it fell forward over her bosom.

His fingers were busy at the back of her neck. The necklace was taken off and laid to one side, then one by one he undid the silver hooks at the back of her dress. The lacings underneath were loosened next and the sleeves of her dress gently pushed down. He paused and looked at her in the mirror. 'Alexandra,' he murmured, covering her neck and shoulders with tiny kisses. 'I think I have to ask you to stand up.'

Not taking her eyes off his, Lexi stood up and her dress slithered to the floor. He helped her to step out of it.

'Richard—' she said huskily.

'Hush, my love,' he said softly, pulling at ribbons and laces. 'Can't you see I'm doing Cissie's work?'

Lexi gave a choked laugh. 'Heaven forbid I should ever feel like this with Cissie,' she said.

His hands stilled at her bosom. 'Am I not doing it right?' he asked anxiously.

She put her hands on his. 'Stop teasing me, Richard. What do you want of me?'

'I would have said it was obvious,' he replied with a glinting smile.

Lexi removed his hands, and retied some of the ribbons. She turned round to face him. 'The last time I asked you to share my room for the night, you said you preferred to sleep alone. And the night you gave me the diamonds you kissed me so sweetly that I would have given you anything you wanted. But you didn't want anything at all. You apologised for crushing my dress, and said, quite calmly, that you would meet me downstairs. That is why I'm asking you now. What do you really want of me tonight?'

'I want *you*,' he said with a groan, pulling her to him. 'I've always wanted you. But now I want to show you how much I adore you, Alexandra. To make love to you so completely that you will never have another single doubt about what I feel for you. Yes, I want to protect you! Not because of any promises I made to your father or anyone else, but because I love you! I would give my life to protect you forever from hurt, danger, disappointment, anything that makes your life less than perfect.' He gazed at her, his grey eyes warm with love. 'You may believe me, Alexandra. Forever.'

Lexi smiled, a wide, joyous smile full of happiness. 'I do,' she said, 'I do, Richard. I'll never doubt you again.' She held out her arms, and he caught her up and took her over to the bed.

'My love,' he said shakily. 'My life!'

* * *

They made love that night with a depth and passion unlike any they had experienced, even in their closest days at Channings. Till now the spectre of Johnny's guilt had always hovered between them, a shadow with the hidden power to mar the perfect consummation of their love. But now that spectre had vanished and, released from its constraint, they were free to express their delight in each other, their desire to be one. Richard never even spared a thought for Mark. He represented a practical problem to be solved in the future, but, unlike Johnny, there was nothing about him to cast a shadow on this night's union between husband and wife, a total union of spirit, mind and body.

They lay late the next morning, still dazed with the glory of the night before, and filled with a delicious lethargy. But they gradually came down to earth and prepared to face a world that they thought would never seem the same again.

They were faced with this world as soon as they came downstairs. Lady Wroxford had sent a message to say that she would call that afternoon to take Lexi shopping again, and there was a sealed note for Richard from Sir Charles to say he had news from his "ferrets".

'My godmother thinks she is doing me a kindness in keeping me occupied this afternoon,' said Lexi ruefully. 'She probably guessed how much I was missing you, and she doesn't yet know you've come back a day early. It's late, but not too late to put her off. There's still half an hour before she comes.'

'No, don't,' said Richard. 'I have several business matters to attend to this afternoon. We can wait till this evening to be together. Did you miss me so much?'

Lexi came across and sat on his knee. 'I missed you

all the time,' she said softly. 'I missed you when you were away, and I missed you even more when you were here, but keeping me shut out. But you won't do that now, I think.'

Richard kissed her. 'I…I won't shut you out again, Alexandra. But I may have to ask you to trust me when I can't explain everything you wish to know.'

Her eyes searched his. 'Very well—as long as it doesn't happen too often,' she said with a smile. 'But do you have something specific in mind? Such as what lies behind the story of Johnny, for example?'

He shook his head ruefully. 'Quick as ever. You're right, of course, but I'll tell you as much as I can. Will that do? Tonight?'

'I look forward to it already. But don't let it take too long,' she said, looking at him under her lashes. 'Nowadays I quite long for my bed, even when it's still quite early in the evening. Why do you suppose that is?'

Richard laughed as he lifted her off his knee and got up. 'You're a shameless hussy! But since I love you, I'll forgive you and see what I can do. Er…may I take Osborne with me when I go out? You won't need him if you're with Lady Wroxford.'

'Of course.'

Richard waited till Lady Wroxford arrived, then excused himself and went round to the Horse Guards. Sir Charles looked at him with a puzzled frown. 'What have you been doing, Deverell? You look a different man. If you weren't already as rich as Croesus, I'd say you'd come into a fortune.'

'You might say I have,' said Richard. 'And you'll be pleased to hear that I'm about to take your advice.'

'Which advice was that?'

'To enjoy the company of my lovely wife and forget the war and all the rest of it.'

Sir Charles gave him a significant smile. 'Aha! Good!'

'But it would be churlish to ignore what your ferrets have been doing. I'd like to hear what they have for me.'

'An address. In Brownlow Street.'

'Really?' said Richard. 'How interesting.'

'How did you find out that Bénuat had an accomplice? Was he French?'

'It's a long story, and hardly worth telling. I'd just like to satisfy my own curiosity, and then, as you suggest, I'll leave it. Thank you.'

'Not at all. So, are you and Lady Deverell planning a honeymoon? I gather your wedding was a quiet affair.'

'I think we may. But I hope in due course you'll bring your wife to visit us down in Somerset. It's a beautiful county.'

'Thank you. We will. You'll take care in Brownlow Street, won't you? It's not the most savoury of places. One of my ferrets could come with you if you wish.'

'I have my groom—he knows his way about. My thanks once again.'

'I have the impression that there's a lot you're not telling me, Deverell. But I know I won't get anywhere by asking questions, so I won't! Goodbye and good luck to you!'

Richard collected Osborne and they walked together to Charing Cross, then up St Martin's Lane towards Seven Dials.

'I believe you know this area, Osborne,' said Richard.

'I was born not very far away, my lord. There've been changes, o'course, but not so many that I can't still find my way about.'

They chatted as they walked on up St Martin's Lane, but when they entered Brownlow Street Osborne suddenly fell silent. He watched as Richard inspected the houses, and stood to one side when they stopped in front of one that looked slightly more respectable than the rest.

'This is it, I think,' Richard said. He knocked, and when the door opened asked to speak to Mrs Judkin.

'That's me,' said the woman who had opened the door. 'What do you want?'

Osborne had turned to face the street, keeping their backs covered. Probably wisely, thought Richard. 'May I come in?' he asked.

It didn't take long. In a few minutes Richard was outside again, the poorer by a sovereign, but with the last piece of the puzzle in place. Mrs Judkin had an excellent memory—probably developed out of necessity in her line of business. Mark Rawdon had stayed with her on all the dates he had been absent from Northampton, including the three most important days in May.

They walked back along St Martin's Lane, and, under Osborne's guidance, turned off before Charing Cross through a small maze of streets into Piccadilly. The groom had become more than usually taciturn, affected perhaps by his return to the scenes of his childhood. When Richard thanked him he grunted and seemed keen to get away. Osborne, it appeared, considered himself Miss Lexi's servant, not his lordship's!

*   *   *

That evening Richard and Lexi sat at dinner, enjoying each other's company all over again. Lady Wroxford had complimented Lexi on her looks that day, and asked if she had won a fortune. On hearing this Richard burst into laughter and told his wife that he too had been asked almost the same question. 'We are obviously good for each other, my dear,' he said.

'I think so indeed, my lord,' said Lexi with a look. 'But first—'

'First? First before what, my love?' asked Richard with a familiar glint in his eye.

'Before we have a game of whist—what else?' asked Lexi wide-eyed. Then she became sober. 'We'll be serious for a moment and talk about Johnny. Are you going to tell me where you went?'

Richard was suddenly quite serious. 'That is something I can't tell you. But I can give you an idea of what I think happened. Can you be content with that?'

She gave him a slow, very sweet smile. 'I've promised never to doubt you again. That means I trust you to tell me everything you can. If, some time in the future, you find that you can tell me the rest, I'm sure you will.'

He came round the table to take her hands to his lips. 'When you finally give your trust you give it all, don't you, Alexandra? And I swear it isn't misplaced. Let's go through to the salon and sit together.'

They sat down in front of the fire in the other room and Richard began.

'I told you that there was a man in the Horse Guards, not Johnny, who was selling information to the French. But he had some remnant of honour—or perhaps it was a sense of shame. He told me that he never sold information that he thought was really important. When his agent, a man called Bénuat, wanted to buy something that would be a real threat to the British, he refused.'

'Are you talking of the papers Johnny had in his possession?'

'Yes. So Bénuat looked for someone who resembled Johnny to steal the papers and bring them to that tavern.'

'An Englishman?'

'Who can say? He could have been French. It was a very cunning plot. When this fellow got hold of the papers Bénuat had asked for, he took Johnny's hat and cape, too. And he came to the tavern that night deliberately dressed up to look like your brother.'

'But...but what happened to Johnny? He can't have killed himself. He had no reason to—he hadn't done anything.'

'No. He had perhaps been careless about those papers. If Bénuat had never heard about them, he wouldn't have wanted to steal them. Johnny wasn't the only one who could have talked, of course...'

'So what happened to Johnny?'

'I think he caught the thief in the act of stealing the papers, and was shot while defending them. The assassin then tried to make it look like suicide.'

Lexi put her face in her hands. 'Oh, Johnny!' she said. 'My poor brother.'

'If I hadn't interfered in the mistaken belief I was saving your family, Johnny might well have been given a posthumous medal.'

Lexi caught his hands and held them tight. 'I don't care about medals and nor would Johnny,' she said passionately. 'You were true to your friendship, and that's what counts. Oh, Richard, I was so wrong to threaten you as I did. I must have been mad. And you forgave me so easily—cared for me, were patient with me...'

'I loved you.'

She said impulsively, 'Richard, let's go back to Channings! Let's put it all behind us. I long to be there to start a new life with you, with no secrets, no shadows. Let's go back to Channings. Tomorrow!'

Richard was silent for a moment. He said at last, 'There are one or two matters I have to settle here in London. But we could go at the beginning of next week. Will that do? If the weather holds, we could take it slowly...'

'Perhaps we could stay at Basingstoke?' said Lexi innocently. 'The inn there always has plenty of rooms, I understand.'

'We shall take a suite, if that is your wish! But however many rooms there are, I must make one thing clear. You will share yours with me. Talking of which... Are you perhaps getting tired? I wouldn't want to keep you out of your bed.'

Lexi rose and put out her hands to draw him up beside her. She gave him a prodigious yawn. 'Please take me to bed, sir,' she said sleepily. 'I think I may fall asleep any moment. Do you know if the new maidservant is on duty tonight?'

He gave a delighted laugh. 'We'll be respectable tonight, my little minx. Phillips will be waiting for me, and Cissie will wonder what sort of a household she finds herself in if we don't preserve at least some of the conventions. But later...'

For the rest of the week they went about their normal business during the day. They saw their friends, went to concerts, visited the shops, preserving all the while a politely cool façade towards one another, in the mistaken belief that people who knew them, such as Lady Wroxford and Sir Charles, would not see how deeply, how happily, in love they were. But even during the day their feeling for one another ran like a tangible current between them, impossible to disguise, and their friends were not at all surprised when they heard that the couple were going back to Channings.

The weather was kind and their journey to Somerset was as pleasant as they could have hoped for at the time of year. The atmosphere in the carriage was completely different from that of the journey towards London such a short time before. They teased and laughed and made all sorts of suggestions for the future, some sensible, some absurd. No honeymoon journey could have been more light-hearted or so full of love. The subject of Mark was not so much avoided as forgotten—they had so much more to discuss and plan for. Christmas would soon be upon them, and they looked forward to celebrating it in the old traditional way, decorating the house with boughs of holly and garlands of ivy, and inviting all the able-bodied people on the estate to join them on the eve of Christmas for a feast in the huge kitchens. There would be visits to the sick and the elderly with boxes and baskets of food—everyone would share in their happiness. Channings, which had been silent and unwelcoming for so many years over the festival, would once again be full of comfort and good cheer.

But Mark had to be dealt with first. During their last week in London Richard had made his arrangements, and he was now ready to put them into effect. Just how urgent the matter was became apparent the day after they arrived.

He had spent the morning with Canon Harmond, and was on his way back from the Rectory. As he came in he realised that Alexandra had a visitor. He stopped to listen. Her voice, with its entirely characteristic deep, husky tones, still had the power to quicken his heart-beats, especially when, as now, she was excited.

But as he came along the passage to the blue parlour he realised that Alexandra was not simply excited. She was angry. Very angry.

'You have said enough!' she said. 'I will listen to no more of your insinuations, Mark. Richard and I now understand each other perfectly. I was wrong to listen to you in the past, and if you wish to remain my friend you will stop making remarks about my husband that only hurt and wound me. Why do you do it?'

Mark murmured something but Richard could only hear the name 'Johnny'.

'Be quiet! I am not distressed, I am angry! Richard no longer thinks Johnny guilty of anything! He is now absolutely certain that my brother was the victim of a French plot, and that his death was not accidental, but a case of murder.'

'Is that what he now says? How interesting!' Mark sounded casual, but Richard knew how very interesting Mark must find this piece of information. He was not surprised to hear Mark continue, 'Does he happen to have any proof of this claim?'

'I have no idea. I suspect he knows more than he is telling me, but I am happy to accept his word, fully and completely. I don't understand the game you've been playing, Mark, but it is over. You will not shake my belief in Richard ever again.'

This was a declaration worth hearing! For a moment Richard was filled with delight. But then he came down to earth. Alexandra had all unwittingly just revealed to Mark how close he, Richard, was to the truth. Suddenly it became perfectly clear to him, that if he wished to protect Alexandra, he would have to deal with Rawdon as soon as he could see the man alone. He smiled grimly as he opened the door. Mark Rawdon was in for a most unpleasant shock.

Chapter Fifteen

Lexi saw Richard come through the door and went over to take his arm. 'You're back!' she said contentedly. 'As you see, Mark came round. But he's just going.'

Richard nodded curtly, and Lexi wondered if he had heard anything of the discussion she had been having with her cousin. She hoped not. Though Mark had behaved badly, he was still all the family she had left, and she did not want a complete rift to develop. Now that she had made her position perfectly clear to him, he would probably not try anything again. But, if Richard had heard, it would prejudice him even more against her cousin. He might even refuse to have Mark in the house.

She held out her hand. 'Goodbye, Mark,' she said. 'I'm glad we had our chat. I meant what I said. Do think about it.'

Richard smiled at their guest, but his eyes were cold. 'May I call on you later?' he asked. 'I have a small business matter to discuss with you. In private.'

'Certainly. I should be delighted. Will you stay to dinner?'

'I think not.'

'What time then? Five, six o'clock?'

'Five.'

'I'll look forward to it.' Mark turned to Lexi, his blue eyes full of contrition. 'I'm sorry if I upset you. I didn't mean to. I'll take more care in the future, I promise.'

When Richard came back from seeing him to the door Lexi said, 'You heard him, didn't you? I thought you must have. You were quite right about Mark. He does try to make mischief, but, now that he knows he won't succeed, I don't think he'll try any more.'

'I'm quite sure he won't,' said Richard grimly.

Lexi put her hand on his sleeve and asked, 'Is that why you're going to see him this afternoon? You mustn't be too hard on him, Richard. Perhaps he's only jealous of our happiness.'

'It's just a last remnant of business. Nothing you need worry about. Forget him.'

Lexi smiled. 'Very well, I'll talk about other things. Sergeant Chalmers is looking better. I spent some time with him today, and he's a different man. He seems very happy here. He's made a lot of friends.'

'He's proving useful, too, though I doubt he'll ever be fit enough to ride again. He's only a shadow of the man he was.'

'He doesn't say much, but I think he's often in a lot of pain still.'

'I'll get Dr Loudon to have another look at him, but I don't think there's much he can do. I'm sure he enjoyed your company. What did you talk about?'

'Life in the Army in Spain and Portugal. What you and Johnny got up to. He's full of stories about "Captain Rawdon"—I think Johnny was his idol. Richard, is there anything to stop you telling Sergeant Chalmers that Johnny wasn't the man in the tavern that night? That he wasn't a traitor? It would make him very happy. The poor man is sometimes in the middle of telling me the things Johnny did, laughing about them, then he suddenly stops and looks so sad. I'm sure he's thinking of the last time he saw him. Can't you tell him the truth?'

Richard nodded. 'I will. And you're quite right— Johnny was always a favourite with him. I suspect Chalmers finished Bénuat off that night, so that the Frenchman couldn't talk. You're right, Alexandra. I'll tell the sergeant as soon as I can. He deserves to know.' But not the whole, he added mentally. Neither you nor he is to know how close to home Johnny's murderer is for the moment.

At five o'clock Richard presented himself at the door of Rawdon Hall, and was welcomed by the manservant and taken into the library. Mark was at the desk.

'Richard!' He gestured for Richard to take a chair nearby. They sat facing one another across the desk.

Richard waited till the manservant had left the room, then said coolly, 'I should prefer you to call me Deverell. I wish no kinship with you, Rawdon.'

Mark looked hurt. 'But, my dear fellow, we are kin. Lexi is my cousin.'

'From today that relationship will have no significance for any of us, especially not Alexandra.'

There was a short silence. Then Mark said, 'I take it you overheard my conversation with her earlier today. But isn't this a little draconian? I meant no real harm. You mustn't be petty, Deverell.'

'Your conversation today has nothing to do with it. And there is nothing at all petty about the matter I have come here to discuss. But you will not see Lady Deverell again.'

Mark leaned back in his chair. 'Oh, come! You can't mean that. Have you told Lexi? She likes me. She likes me a lot. In fact, if I hadn't been so…financially embarrassed, I might well have married her myself. I'm not sure she'd listen to you if you told her not to see me again.'

'But *you* will listen to me.'

'Oh? Why?'

Richard put his hand in his pocket, pulled out the purse and laid it between them on the desk. 'That is why.'

He watched with satisfaction as a flash of recognition was quickly veiled. For a moment Mark Rawdon looked worried. But he soon recovered. After regarding the purse in silence he said with amusement, 'What the devil has that to do with me? It's not mine.'

'It was in your possession. Mrs Pelham found it in your room after you'd left Northampton and asked me to pass it on to you.'

'So you've been talking to Pelly, have you?' said Mark, eyeing him speculatively. 'Sniffing around in Northampton? I wonder why. I hope you're not taking notice of anything Pelly said—she's past it.'

'I don't agree,' replied Richard. 'Mrs Pelham seemed remarkably lucid to me. She remembers dates very clearly. The eighteenth of May, for example. It was her birthday, and you weren't in Northampton. You were in London, staying with Mrs Judkin in Brownlow Street.' He paused, then said slowly and deliberately, 'That was the night you acquired that purse, Rawdon. Thursday, the eighteenth of May. I saw it myself that night. Bénuat handed it to you in the Cock Tavern.'

Mark lost a little of his composure. 'I don't think you can prove that,' he said, breathing a little faster.

Richard leaned back with a judicious air and said calmly, 'I think I can. In fact, I'm sure of it. You went to London intending to kill Johnny Rawdon, and you did. After killing him you stole some important papers he had in his possession and tried to sell them to a French agent. I'm quite curious to know how he came across you, by the way, but I don't suppose you'll tell me. You took Bénuat's money, which was in this purse, then you ran away. I connived in that, God help me. I let you escape because I thought, as everyone else did, that you were Johnny Rawdon.'

'And why would I do such a thing?'

'You took the money because you needed it. You killed Johnny because you intended to inherit the Rawdon title and estate.'

'This is nonsense. I didn't know anything about the damned title!'

'You don't remember your family Bible? You can't recall telling Mrs Pelham how rich and powerful you would be one day?'

For a moment Mark looked ugly. 'That old witch! She always hated me.'

'Is that why you left her to starve?'

Mark ignored this, his mind clearly busy with the rest of what Richard had said. Finally he smiled with a touch of mockery at Richard and taunted, 'Old women's gossip. Even supposing it's true, what can you do about it?'

'I've gathered together enough evidence to hang you twice over if the authorities saw it.' With a glance at the hand that was creeping towards the drawer in Mark Rawdon's desk, he went on, 'And in case you have any ideas about murdering *me*, I should tell you that my lawyers in London have the complete story, fully accounted for. It will remain there, under seal, as long as certain conditions are met, but in the event of my sudden death it will be opened and handed over to the right people immediately.'

'Really? Very good!' Mark was still smiling, though the smile was not quite as confident as it had been. 'You know, I could like you. You think of everything!'

'I could never like you, Rawdon.'

'Well, now, what happens next? Will you tell Lexi? I'm not sure how she will take the news that it was her beloved cousin, the last of the Rawdons, who killed her brother... And think of the public scandal there would be. It wouldn't do the precious Rawdon family name much good.'

'I don't propose to tell anyone if I can avoid it.'

Mark regarded him speculatively. Then his face cleared and he nodded and said, 'Quite right, too! Well, that's a relief! For a moment I thought we were all going to go down together...' His eyes sparkled with good humour and he laughed. 'Very well. You're a good fellow, Deverell. I'll do as you say and keep away from Lexi. I don't know how you're going to explain it to her, mind you, but you shouldn't have too much difficulty. I've always found her fairly gullible.' The touch of contempt in his voice enraged Richard, who said tightly, 'The only reason you could fool her was because you were her family and she trusted you. She won't make that mistake again.'

'Why? Are you going to warn her against me, tell her I've been a naughty boy, but give no details?' Mark's blue eyes twinkled engagingly at Richard, inviting him to share the joke. 'The situation has its piquancy, wouldn't you say? Aren't you afraid that Lexi will one day find out that her brother's murderer is living in her old home, where Johnny and she played together as children? How will you deal with that?'

'The situation won't arise. You won't be living anywhere near her old home.'

'What do you mean by that? Rawdon is mine!'

'You surely don't imagine I would tolerate a villain like you as a neighbour? Allow you to remain at Rawdon a moment longer than it takes to get rid of you? You must be mad.' The biting scorn in Richard's voice brought colour to Mark's cheeks and for a moment he looked murderous.

But he rallied and said confidently, 'Brave words. But what else can you do? You won't want to upset Lexi. No, I'm safe enough here. There is nothing you can do to get rid of me.'

'I've already done it.' Richard said calmly. 'I have arranged a passage in your name on the mail boat that leaves Falmouth in ten days for the West Indies. That's time enough to gather a few things together and sort out your affairs before you leave Rawdon, and England, for good. We shall see no more of you.'

Mark gazed at him in astonishment. 'The devil you won't! What makes you think I would dance to *your* tune?'

Richard rose to his feet. Till now Mark had been deceived by Richard's quiet manner into dismissing him as a dull country gentleman whose sole desire was to live at peace with his wife at Channings. In his overweening pride and conceit he had failed to see the strength that lay behind it, had ignored the years Richard had spent as a daring and resourceful fighter in Spain. Now, for the first time, Mark saw the ruthless determination behind the quiet façade, and realised that he was facing an enemy who would destroy him without hesitation if he thought it necessary.

'If you are *not* on that boat,' Richard said in a voice of steel, 'my lawyers have orders to pass the evidence against you to the justices. You'll be hanged.'

Frightened now, but unwilling to show it, Mark played the only card left to him—Richard's weak point. 'What about Lexi?' he asked.

Richard smiled contemptuously. 'You won't risk your neck, Rawdon,' he said. 'You'll go.'

After a moment Mark's eyes fell, and he said sulkily, 'I suppose a plantation in the West Indies might be better than this God-forsaken hole. What will you give me for Rawdon?'

'A small rent will be paid quarterly into the bank in Kingston. It should be enough to keep you alive, but not much more.'

'You're surely not serious! Rawdon should pay for a plantation at least!'

'The larger part of Rawdon will no longer be yours. You will keep only the entailed property, for which, as I said, I shall pay you a small rent. The rest will be returned to Alexandra.'

'Now, wait a moment...'

'The choice is yours, Rawdon,' said Richard implacably.

The two men faced each other, but it was Mark's gaze that fell first. 'Very well,' he said his eyes shifting. 'I suppose I'll have to do as you say.'

'In case you had any thought of absconding, or removing more than the minimum of possessions from the Hall, dismiss it. Sir Jeremy and his children have been well known and well liked in the district. There are plenty of people who will keep me informed of your movements, if the word is passed round. And if you *do* disappear to anywhere other than the West Indies… Or if you upset Alexandra in any kind of way…' Mark looked up at the sudden note of menace in Richard's voice '…I promise you, you will be hunted down wherever you are, then judged and hanged.'

Mark was beaten. He nodded and said petulantly, 'I understand. There's no need for such drama. Is that all? Because if so…'

Richard turned to go. At the door he stopped. 'Remember! Keep away from Alexandra!'

Richard rode back to Channings still wondering if he had done the right thing to let Johnny's killer go unpunished into exile. But, as Rawdon had pointed out, the alternative—the trial, the scandal—would be very hard on Johnny's sister, perhaps too hard. And what would be gained by it? As matters stood Johnny was dead, buried with honour in the churchyard at Rawdon, his name unblemished. To accuse his murderer would do nothing to help Johnny, and, in spite of what Richard had told Rawdon, the evidence against him was not completely watertight. Besides, it would open up all the business of those damned papers and the espionage, and create a huge scandal. To what purpose? To punish Mark Rawdon—and even that was by no means certain.

Yes, he had made the best of a bad job. Now he and Alexandra could live in peace. He started to plan how he could persuade her not to visit Mark again…

A week later Richard and Lexi had ridden to the village, but, just as they were about to return, Richard was held up. An icy wind was blowing and Lexi decided not to wait for him, but to ride on home without him, taking Osborne with her. Something she had heard in the village had disturbed her and she badly wanted to talk to Richard about it, but it wasn't a simple matter and would be better discussed in the warmth and peace of their own home.

But when they got back Osborne stopped Lexi as she was leaving the stables and asked if he could have a word. It sounded serious, so she took him into the library and invited him to sit down.

'Thank'ee, Miss Lexi, but I'll stand,' he said. He was quiet for so long after that, that Lexi asked him what was wrong.

'I don't rightly know what to do for the best.'

'Tell me.'

'The master…the old master, Sir Jeremy, asked me not to mention it to anyone, y'see. But I'm not sure that's the right thing to do any more.'

'Well, my father isn't here to tell you, Will. But you can trust me. It's clear it's worrying you, whatever it is.'

Lexi waited patiently while Osborne pondered over this for a minute or two. Eventually he made up his mind and started to speak.

'In the old days, at Rawdon, I used to do a number of errands for Sir Jeremy, especially when he didn't want it generally known. I usually went to Dorchester or Sherborne, but this summer he sent me twice to London.' He paused.

'Go on,' said Lexi.

'Each time he gave me a parcel to deliver to a certain address, and told me particularly not to mention it to anyone. He needn't have bothered. I never did talk to anyone else about the master's business.'

'What was in the parcels?'

'I dunno, Miss Lexi. But they were heavy for their size.'

'I see…' Lexi frowned. 'This happened in the summer, you say. Why does it worry you now?'

'Well, not so long ago his lordship went to the very same address.'

'You mean Lord Deverell? My husband?'

'That's right, ma'am. To the very same house.'

'Where was this?'

'Brownlow Street, Miss Lexi. Near Seven Dials.'

'What was his lordship doing there, do you know?'

'He didn't say. I went along with him to show him the way.'

'I remember—it was the day after he got back from his trip. But why didn't you mention it at the time?'

'I promised the master, the late master, that I wouldn't tell anyone.'

'But you've been worrying about it ever since?'

'Yes'm. I didn't think it could just be chance, d'you see?'

'I think you're right,' she said thoughtfully. 'And I think you should tell Lord Deverell what you've told me. It may be important.'

'Well, I will. If you think so, Miss Lexi.'

After Osborne had gone she sat and considered what he had said further. It sounded very much as if Will had been the means by which her father had paid the blackmailer. But what had Richard been doing at the same address? They had been so happy since their return to Channings that she felt some reluctance to ask him. Their sole disagreement had been about her cousin, and Richard's unreasonable request that she did not attempt to see him for a while. She had given in and agreed, but only after an argument. Lexi smiled as she remembered how the argument had ended... But though his kisses had convinced her at the time, she was still not sure he was right. The quarrel between Richard and Mark, if that was what it was, would surely be resolved more easily if they met. And if what she had heard in the village was true, he must agree it was high time they did.

As soon as Richard came in she said, 'They're saying that Mark is planning to go away. Do you know anything about it?'

'I had heard something of the kind,' he replied cautiously.

She could tell from his voice that he had known all about it. 'And you didn't think to tell me?' she asked indignantly. 'Why ever not? I *must* go to see him now, surely even you can see that?'

'Please, Alexandra. Mark has his reasons for keeping away. Let him do as he thinks fit.'

She frowned. 'Richard, what *is* going on? I finally agreed to stay away from Mark for the moment because I thought you and he would be more likely to sort out your differences without my interference. But there's something you're keeping from me, isn't there? I think this quarrel is more serious than you've said. Why won't you tell me the truth? I don't like mysteries. And there's something else you haven't told me. What were you doing in Brownlow Street? Had you found out something about Papa's blackmailer?'

'Brownlow Street?'

'Don't try to put me off! I know you went there. Osborne said he'd been there with you.'

Richard looked angry. 'Did he, indeed? I'll have a word with him—'

'No, Richard, don't get angry. He was worried. And I think he was right to be. Tell me why you went there.'

Richard paused. 'Charles Stainforth gave me the address,' he said eventually. 'He thought it was where the French agent had stayed.'

'The *French agent*? But I don't understand... Unless... You must have a word with Osborne straight away, Richard. He didn't tell you, but he had been there twice before on business for my father. He left a packet there each time.'

'*What?*'

'I might be wrong, but it sounds to me as if you could have found your blackmailer. The Frenchman you talked about.'

'By God, if I'd known that—' Richard stood as if turned to stone. 'The devil!' he said. 'The scheming, heartless, devil!' He looked at Lexi as if he had forgotten she was there. 'I must see Osborne. Where is he?'

'He was going over to Hansford Farm to fetch one of the horses. He should be back in about an hour.'

'I can't wait that long! I'll go to look for him.'

'But what about Mark?'

'Wait here. We'll talk about him when I get back.' And Richard strode out without another word to her.

Slightly annoyed at being left to herself again, Lexi fiddled about in the room for a while. But she soon got bored and wondered what to do next. She was still dressed for riding, and decided to go out again. The wind had dropped and the sun had come out. A pale, wintry sun, but all the same it brightened up the landscape quite surprisingly. Richard had told her to wait for him at home, but she would risk his anger and ride over to Rawdon to see Mark herself. If Mark was planning to go away, she must find out why as soon as possible.

Her decision taken, she didn't waste any time. She left a message for Richard with Kirby, and set off for the Hall.

She was relieved to find Mark in. When the servant admitted her he was sitting by the fire in the library, a decanter and a wine glass on the small table at his side. Her smile wavered at the sight. For a moment it could have been Johnny sitting there. He and her father had always used the same chairs, the same tables, one either side of the fire. Her father's hair had been grizzled, though it had earlier been just the same colour as his son's. Rawdon red. Like her own. Like Mark's.

'Lexi!' Mark exclaimed, getting up. 'Lexi, what are you here for? Does Richard know?'

'Not yet. He was out. I left a message for him.'

'You must go back. At once!'

Lexi came further into the room. 'Of course I mustn't. Don't send me away, Mark. This was once my home, too, you know.' She gave him a hesitant smile. 'I've heard you're planning to leave Rawdon. Is that true?'

'I'm afraid it is.'

'But why?'

'I have urgent business elsewhere.'

'But why did I have to hear of this in the village? Why didn't you come over to tell me yourself?'

'Er...the last time we met Richard made it clear that he wanted no more to do with me.'

'Well, you can hardly blame him for that. You weren't very nice about him, and he heard you. But that's no reason to go away. I would hate not ever to see you again—you're all the family I have. Papa loved you, and you were so kind to me when he died, even though—' She stopped and began again. 'I came over to see if I could do anything to help you and Richard settle your differences. And perhaps persuade you to stay after all.'

Mark shrugged his shoulders and sat down again. He finished his glass, poured himself another and drank it off. Then he turned to her and said with a charming smile, 'My dear Lexi, you have no idea what you're talking about! I'm leaving because Richard has said I must. He and I cannot stand the sight of each other. And after what he recently said to me, here in my own library, I have no intention of "settling our differences", as you so naïvely call it.'

Lexi looked at him, puzzled by the curious tone in his voice. 'Mark?' she said uncertainly.

Mark drank again, then looked up. His smile was no longer quite so charming. It had more than a touch of a sneer about it. 'Are you really as simple as you seem?' he asked.

Lexi was shocked, She stared at him as she asked, 'Mark, why are you talking like this? What's wrong?'

'Look at you! You really have no idea, have you? I called you gullible, and you are. Your brother was just the same. What a pitiably stupid lot you are, you Somerset Rawdons!'

'Mark!' said Lexi incredulously. 'Please, Mark! I know you're angry, but you mustn't say such things—'

'Is that a tear I can see in your eye, Lexi? Don't you like being spoken to like this? Of course you don't—

you belong to the superior branch of the Rawdon family, the refined Rawdons, the *rich* Rawdons.' He gave a little chuckle. 'You weren't so rich at the end, were you? I saw to that.'

Lexi went very still. 'What does that mean?' she said. 'What are you saying?'

But Mark did not appear to have heard her. He went on, 'Did you really think I was fond of any of you? Why should I be? You meant nothing to me, except what I could get out of you all. I didn't like you, I wanted you to hurt! It was fun to see you squirming away like a worm left out in the rain when you thought your precious Richard was a villain.' He looked at her, his bright blue eyes shining with malicious pleasure. 'Did you never wonder how you came across that page from your father's diary? Because I found it in the desk and put it inside the diary for you to discover, of course! And it worked! Oh, how it worked! It would have been even better if Deverell hadn't persuaded you not to shoot him. Such a disappointment! I wanted you to. I'd have enjoyed that.'

'You'd have *enjoyed* it?' For a few moments Lexi was too stunned to think, too full of hurt shock and disbelief. But then she began to recover her wits. She thought of the torture of those days before her marriage, how close she had come to shooting Richard, and started to get very angry indeed. The creature before her was no longer the cousin she had loved, but someone she had never known, and she was cool again, no longer affected by his efforts to hurt. Instead, her brain was working, busy with some of the things he had just said. After a moment she asked slowly, '*When* did you meet Johnny?'

'Did I say I had? I didn't mean to. Tut, tut, tut!' He shook his head. 'That was careless, wasn't it?'

She went on, 'When you arrived at Rawdon you said you had known nothing at all about us till you came down here. That was after Johnny had died. You never met Johnny. Unless…'

'What?'

'You met him in London!' Her eyes widened and she grew pale. 'Of course! Oh, I've been so blind! Why didn't I see the resemblance before? You were the one who looked so like him. *You* were the one in the tavern that night! You killed my brother!'

Mark waved a hand in her direction. 'Yes, I did. But it's all right, Lexi. There won't be a scandal. Richard— sorry! I forgot—Lord *Deverell* has seen to it all. The Rawdon name will remain unblemished.'

'I don't give a *damn* about the Rawdon name. *You killed my brother!*'

'Terrible, wasn't it? He was so pleased to see me, too, when I arrived. A long-lost cousin come to pay a visit! He even offered me a drink. As I said—gullible! Completely gullible.'

Lexi was shaking her head in disbelief. 'You're…a monster, an unnatural monster.'

Mark shook his head at her as he went over to the desk. 'How very rude of you! But you won't have to see me for much longer, if that's what's worrying you. I'll soon be away.'

'Away where? To hell? That's the only place you're going, Mark Rawdon.'

'I think not. Your husband has arranged for me to disappear. You'll never see me again. And now I want you to go. Immediately. If Deverell finds you here, he might do something we'd all regret.' Mark took a pistol

out of the drawer. 'I really don't want to use this, Lexi.
The risk of discovery would be too great. However, I
will if you don't leave. Now.'

'You may as well use it,' she said steadily. 'I'm not
going to let you escape without punishment. I was ready
to shoot the man I *loved* when I thought he had killed
Johnny. Now I know it was you, I won't rest till I have
destroyed you.'

'You're in no position at the moment to do anything
of the sort, my dear cousin. Surely even you can see
that I have the gun and you have none!'

'If you shoot me now, you will be hanged for it. You
won't be able to cover up this time by pretending to be
someone else. I brought Coles with me. He's waiting
for me outside. And your servants all know I'm here.'

'Oh, dear! I'm in a mess, aren't I?' Mark jeered. 'I've
nothing to lose, it appears. Well, Lexi, I think you'd
better change your mind. Either you agree to go along
with Deverell's plans for my future, or—' He raised the
gun.

After Richard had heard what Osborne had to tell
him, he was seized with fury. What sort of depraved
creature would kill a man's only son, then extort money
from the father by threatening to tell the world his son
was a traitor? No one who could possibly be allowed
to continue to live. One thing was perfectly certain. The
plans he had made for Mark Rawdon would be
scrapped. Alexandra herself would violently object to
any sort of compromise with such a man, and, whatever
the scandal, it could not be worse than knowing that
this creature still walked the earth. Mark Rawdon would
be given up to the law, and very probably hanged.

When he and Osborne rode into the stableyard at

Channings, Chalmers was sitting on a stool, working on one of the harnesses.

'Evening, captain!' he called cheerfully.

Richard nodded to him. He had told Chalmers about Johnny a few days before, though he had not told the sergeant the name of the man in the tavern. He wondered what Chalmers would say when he learned the truth.

'Mr Kirby was looking for you, sir. He has a message from her ladyship for you.'

'Right! Thank you.' Richard left his horse with Osborne and went in. But what he heard from Kirby brought him back to the stables in a very short time.

'Saddle fresh horses, straight away,' he snapped to Osborne. 'I have to go to Rawdon. Immediately.'

'Trouble, captain?' asked Chalmers.

'You could well call it that,' said Richard. 'I have to fetch Lady Deverell. There's something that tells me she could be in danger.'

'She can't come to much harm at Rawdon, my lord,' said Osborne. 'It's her old home.'

'You're wrong, Will,' said Richard, forgetting discretion in his anxiety for Alexandra. 'Lady Deverell is at the moment paying a call on her brother's murderer!'

'*Sir Mark?*' said Osborne, stopping to stare at him.

'Yes, man. Get on with it, for God's sake! I haven't time to tell you everything now. Rawdon killed your Master Johnny, and then blackmailed his father! Do you *still* think Lady Deverell is safe?'

They rode out of the yard, leaving Chalmers staring after them.

They arrived at Rawdon just as the sun was setting. The servant who opened the door told them that the master and Lady Deverell were in the library.

Richard turned to Osborne and said, 'Wait here for me.'

Osborne said in a low voice, 'I'll just go round the back, if you don't mind, my lord. I won't be happy till we've got Miss Lexi safe, and you just might need a helping hand. I know my way round this house, and servants use different doors from their masters.'

Richard said, 'We are quite possibly worrying over nothing, Osborne. Miss Lexi may be perfectly safe, chatting to Sir Mark. She doesn't know what we know—she still thinks he's a friend.'

'Better safe than sorry, my lord.'

Richard gave him a brief grin. 'You could be right. Very well. Good luck!' Osborne disappeared into the shadows.

Richard walked into the library. Alexandra was standing in the centre of the room facing her cousin, who had a pistol in his hand. It was aimed unwaveringly at Alexandra's heart. He heard Rawdon jeer,

'Oh, dear! I'm in a mess, aren't I? I've nothing to lose, it appears. Well, Lexi, I think you'd better change your mind. Either you agree to go along with Deverell's plans for my future, or—' Rawdon stopped short. His voice changed and he said without moving his eyes, 'Don't come any nearer, *Deverell*! I warn you. If you come a step closer, I shall shoot Lady *Deverell* straight away. And I won't miss.' He paused and added with a mocking smile, 'Dear me! How history repeats itself! Where have I heard those words before?'

'Rawdon,' said Richard urgently, 'don't be a fool. Killing Alexandra won't help you.'

'No, but I might enjoy it.'

'Wouldn't you enjoy killing me even more?'

'No!' cried Lexi. 'No, you mustn't!'

Still without taking his eyes off Alexandra, Mark said, 'To tell you the truth, I'd like to get rid of both of you, but, as you say, it wouldn't help me. Besides, I thought you'd already arranged something better for me.'

'Not since I learned that you also blackmailed Sir Jeremy to his ruin. You're done for, Rawdon.'

'Ah! So you know that now?'

Richard eyed Mark. The man was vain, and slightly the worse for wine. If he was kept talking, he might get distracted. Edging imperceptibly closer to him, he said scornfully, 'Wasn't that a little short-sighted of you, Rawdon? Ruining your own inheritance?'

'I wanted the cash! I was afraid I'd only get what was entailed, that the rest would go to my sweet cousin here, and I was right. It did, didn't it? So I took what I could, while I could. I didn't know the old fool kept all his capital in the land. It wasn't part of my plan to have him sell bits of the estate to pay me off! I thought there'd be plenty to spare! But I was never more disappointed in my life. Even with what you gave me, there still isn't enough to live the way I imagined I would. I tell you, Deverell, if I had known what I know now, I wouldn't have taken so much trouble to inherit this…this millstone.'

Lexi gave an involuntary cry of distress. 'Don't! I can't bear to hear you talk like this.'

'Can't you?' said Mark coldly. 'Then don't listen. And don't interrupt. As I was saying, Deverell… The situation has changed since this afternoon. Make a better financial offer, and I'll still disappear and leave you in peace. Otherwise we'll all go to perdition together. Your wife first.'

Richard's mind was busy. His hopes were with Osborne, but it would take some time for the groom to work his way round to the back—he must keep Rawdon talking. 'I should really like to know first how you managed it all, Rawdon. You called my wife gullible, but wasn't everyone else? You succeeded in deceiving everyone—including Bénuat, who was no one's fool. How did you do it?'

'Good Lord, it was child's play!' said Mark contemptuously. 'You might say they did it themselves.'

'How did you find Bénuat?'

'I didn't find him—he found me, the evening I arrived in London. I was having a drink at that tavern—the Cock. It's not far from Brownlow Street, and I wanted some company. He came up to me—' Mark started to laugh. 'He couldn't believe his eyes! The great Johnny Rawdon patronising a low tavern like the Cock! We got talking, though he did most of it. I didn't tell him who I was—I just kept my mouth shut and listened. He talked about those papers, and mentioned a sum of money that took my breath away, I can tell you. It would pay all my expenses in London and there'd still be something left to live on afterwards. Until I could come down here to "claim my inheritance".'

'What did you say to him?'

'I let him think I would get them for him and we arranged to meet the next night at the tavern. I wanted that money, though I wasn't really sure I could do it. How was I to know that my fool of a cousin would have the papers there ready for the taking?'

'So when you went to see Johnny you already knew about the papers.'

Rawdon nodded. 'It was all so easy! Wherever I went, people were falling over themselves to help me! The Frenchie told me about the papers and promised me all that money if I brought them along. And when I got to my cousin's rooms, the dear fellow welcomed me with open arms. I could see the papers laid out on his table, ready for me to help myself. So, after we'd had a drink together, I disposed of him, then put on the cape and the awful hat I found there, and went along to collect the gelt... It was all so easy till you came and interrupted us. And even then you let me escape.'

'You went back to Johnny's rooms.'

'I didn't want to. After I'd shot Johnny it had been a messy business, arranging it to look like suicide. But I had to, to get rid of the clothes.' He laughed again. 'You almost caught me there! So, that's how I did it.' His voice changed and he sounded more businesslike again. 'Now, what about it? What will you offer me?'

The servant's door behind Rawdon moved very slightly. Richard said quickly and loudly, 'You can have an annuity. Ten thousand a year.'

'Not enough!'

The door opened wider. 'It's a better offer than you're likely to get from the hangman,' said Richard, holding Rawdon's eyes with his own.

Mark's face grew dark. 'I'm not going to be hanged. And I want more than a paltry ten thousand a year.'

Osborne flung the door wide and came in at a run. Mark turned round with a curse and fired wildly. Richard threw himself at Lexi and pulled her down, covering her with his body. Osborne staggered and fell on to one knee, as Mark Rawdon pushed his way past him through the open door.

For a moment Mark was forgotten in the confusion.

Servants came running in, and Richard told them to see to his groom. He himself helped Lexi up and briefly held her in his arms in passionate relief. Then he went over to Osborne. Blood was welling up in a line along the side of the groom's head, but the wound was superficial. He was not seriously hurt.

Richard looked round. 'Where's Rawdon?' he asked. 'What's happened to him?'

But Mark, ever the opportunist, had escaped through the warren of passages that led out through the servants' quarters.

Mark came out at the side of the house and ran round to where Lexi's groom would be waiting with the horses. It was now almost dark outside and he looked round desperately through the gloom.

'Coles?' he called. 'Where are you?'

'Over here!' called a voice. 'Over here, sir!'

Mark breathed a sigh of relief and ran in the direction of the shrubbery that bordered the house. He'd take Coles's horse and then he'd be off.

The last thing he saw in his life was the flash of a gun. The last thing he felt was the gravel of the drive as his face hit the ground.

By the time Richard came out, followed closely by Osborne and Coles, Mark Rawdon was dead.

It was late before they returned to Channings, and they were still no wiser about who had killed Mark. He had apparently been shot by an unknown assailant, a stranger, who seemed to have dropped from the skies and then disappeared again. Everyone had heard the shot. Everyone in the household had been accounted for at the time.

When Lexi and Richard returned wearily to Channings in a carriage borrowed from the Hall, they were still mystified, but heartily glad that their problem had been so fortuitously solved.

'Perhaps Mark had enemies in Northampton who followed him here?' Lexi suggested.

'That is exactly what I said to the constable,' replied Richard.

Lexi peered at him in the dark. 'You know, don't you? I can tell. Who was it? Did you meet him in Northampton? Was I right?'

He leaned back and closed his eyes. 'It's a good thing you're not a magistrate.'

'Tell me!'

'Not yet. I need to confirm it. All I hope is that he hasn't killed himself, too.' He refused to say another word, even afterwards in the privacy of their bedchamber. When Lexi persisted he silenced her in the best way possible, by giving her something much more exciting to think about...

But Lexi found out for herself who had killed Mark.

The next day when she visited Sergeant Chalmers to tell him the news, she found him in bed, looking grey and exhausted. He was obviously in great pain, but when she said she would fetch Dr Loudon he roused himself.

'No, ma'am! No! Thank'ee kindly, but I don't need a doctor. He can't do any good now.'

Chalmers continued to refuse all offers of medical assistance, though he grew weaker with every day that passed. Lexi visited him as often as she could, and he always seemed happy to see her. He talked a lot about the old days on the Peninsula, and told her time and again of Johnny's exploits.

One day he seemed almost too tired to talk. After a long silence he said suddenly, 'I got it right in the end, didn't I?'

Lexi was puzzled but said quietly, 'I'm sure you did.'

'It was me that killed the Frenchie that night, just as Captain Deverell suspected. But it was the other one I should have got. And I did in the end.'

Lexi got up and bent over him. She smiled, then kissed him on the cheek. 'You got it very right, sergeant. Thank you.'

Chapter Sixteen

It was a warm spring day a few months later. Easter was less than four weeks away, and signs of new growth were everywhere. The birds were busy in the hedgerows, and small creatures newly emerging from their winter quarters scolded and scuttled away as Richard and Lexi took one of their favourite walks along the river bank near Rawdon. Nearly a year had passed since their conversation about Johnny on this same path, not long before he died. It had been a year of violence and death and much anguish, but the past three months had at last brought peace and healing, and a great deal of happiness to the Deverells.

The mystery of Mark Rawdon's death had never been solved by the authorities, but the rumours about what had really happened to Master Johnny had been sufficiently explicit for the local populace to see his cousin buried without regret. And the law had decided that, in the absence of any other male heirs, ownership of Rawdon Hall and its Home Farm should revert to Lexi, to be held in trust for her children.

As Lexi and Richard walked along the river they talked of their plans for the huge reception to celebrate their marriage, which was to be held at Channings on Easter Monday. Eventually they turned away from the river to retrace their steps along the path to the lane where they had left the gig. When they came to the stile at the end of the path Lexi stopped and waited on the step. Richard turned and would have helped her to jump down, but she put her hands on his shoulders and smiled at him. What she saw in his eyes then brought a flush to her cheeks. She asked softly, 'Do you…do you still want to kiss me, Richard?'

'Always,' he murmured. 'I never seem to tire of kissing you. When I'm dying I shall want to kiss you.'

He lifted her down and took her into his arms. The kiss was as exciting as that first time and as deeply passionate, and when it came to an end he refused to let her go, but kept her close, his arms wrapped round her. He looked down at her and said with a smile, 'Do you know what day it is today?'

'Tell me,' she said.

'It's six months since we were married.'

'I hadn't forgotten.'

'So what will it be, my beautiful wife?'

Lexi frowned. 'What will it be? What do you mean?'

'Last October you gave me six months to prove everything to your satisfaction. I promised you I would shoot myself at the end of them if I failed. So, what is it to be? Have I satisfied you?'

She pressed herself more closely against him. 'I should never have made such a bargain,' she said with a small shudder. 'I must have been mad. But I can say you have fulfilled the terms of it more than adequately.' They exchanged another kiss. Then Lexi shifted a little in his arms and looked up invitingly, 'I'm not *sure* you've *satisfied* me. But I'm willing to give you another chance. Several, if you wish.'

He laughed appreciatively. 'Would a lifetime be enough?'

'Perhaps. We'll see.'

They walked on a little. Then Richard said, 'This might be the moment to point out to you that I said that day that I would shoot myself but I never promised to *kill* myself. Indeed, I never intended to do so. A graze along the leg, a small wound in the foot was more the sort of thing I had in mind.'

'You cunning cheat!'

He laughed and caught her in his arms again. 'I was a soldier! And I didn't want to die. I wanted to *live*—with you.'

'I wouldn't have let you kill yourself anyway. Especially not now. Children need a father.'

He pushed her away in order to see her face. 'What did you say?' Then his eyes, normally so cool a grey, glowed now with love, and pride and purest happiness as she nodded. 'Alexandra! It's true then? I wondered, but when you didn't say anything... A child at Channings! Our child!' He held her as if she were something infinitely precious. 'My love, my heart's treasure, my delight!'

'I was waiting till today to tell you. And I want to say something else today. Though those vows we made six months ago meant nothing to me at the time, I cannot now imagine what life would be like without you. I do sincerely give you my troth, Richard. I do love and honour you, and I will even obey you. I shall cherish you and stay by you, for better or for worse, for richer for poorer, in sickness and in health. Till death us do part.'

'Alexandra…' Richard clasped her hands in his and held them to his lips for a long moment. Then he said softly, 'You always did mean them, my love. It just took a little time for you to recognise the fact.'

'Richard… My heart is so full of happiness. I'd like to visit the churchyard before we go back to Channings.'

She didn't have to tell him why. He knew.

The trees in the churchyard were showing a faint haze of green along their branches, and clumps of daffodils danced and fluttered in the light breeze. Johnny's headstone was weathering now, and Sir Jeremy's next to it was also looking less new. They stood by the two graves for a while, then moved on to one that was a little way away, though not too far from his Captain's memorial. This was a simple stone in memory of Sergeant Chalmers. At the end of a long list of military honours was a simple phrase: 'True to the last.'

Lexi put her hand in Richard's. 'That's not a bad thing for anyone to be, is it?' she said. 'True to the last.'

* * * * *

Introducing...

nocturne

a spine-tingling new line from Silhouette Books.

These paranormal romances will seduce you with dark, passionate tales that stretch the boundaries of conflict, desire, and life and death, weaving a tapestry of sensual thrills and chills!

Don't miss the first book...

UNFORGIVEN

by *USA TODAY* bestselling author

LINDSAY M^cKENNA

Launching October 2006,
wherever books are sold.

Silhouette® Desire®

**Introducing an exciting appearance
by legendary
New York Times bestselling author**

DIANA PALMER
HEARTBREAKER

He's the ultimate bachelor...
but he may have just met
the one woman to change his ways!

Join the drama in the story of a confirmed
bachelor, an amnesiac beauty and their
unexpected passionate romance.

"Diana Palmer is a mesmerizing storyteller
who captures the essence of what
a romance should be."—*Affaire de Coeur*

**Heartbreaker *is available from Silhouette Desire
in September 2006.***

If you enjoyed what you just read,
then we've got an offer you can't resist!

Take 2 bestselling
love stories FREE!
Plus get a FREE surprise gift!

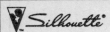